THE MAKINGS OF
EMILY JENSEN

THE MAKINGS OF EMILY JENSEN

Tales of birth, death and the weird stuff in between

Paul A Mendelson

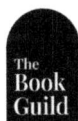

The
Book
Guild

First published in Great Britain in 2025 by
The Book Guild Ltd
Unit E2 Airfield Business Park,
Harrison Road, Market Harborough,
Leicestershire. LE16 7UL
Tel: 0116 2792299
www.bookguild.co.uk
Email: info@bookguild.co.uk
X: @bookguild

Typeset in 11pt Minion Pro

Printed and bound in Great Britain by 4edge Limited

ISBN 978 1835741 054

British Library Cataloguing in Publication Data.
A catalogue record for this book is available from the British Library.

To M

You are the makings of me

CONTENTS

THE MAKINGS OF
EMILY JENSEN

THE INCITING INCIDENT

When Francesca Jensen's waters broke during an arts programme interview on her local television station – an interview she was unfortunately in the process of conducting rather than simply watching from the discomfort of her own home – she reassured herself that life, which she had hitherto planned to the very last letter, could never again become more mortifying.

She really had no idea.

There was little need for Francesca to swiftly phone her best friend and birthing partner, the screenwriter Megan Peabody, when the incident happened. Megan had fortuitously been the programme's guest interviewee that same early Wednesday evening.

This was probably the only stroke of luck on so memorable a day. The originally invited subject, a well-known film director, had come down with a nasty and very public case of Me Too, so Megan, who by good fortune lived quite near Francesca on the Kent coast and hadn't harassed anyone recently, was hauled briskly in.

As Megan hadn't had a screenplay produced in the past few years and had frankly admitted to Francesca that she didn't currently have a thought in her head, having recently fallen in love with and married, for the first and blissfully unexpected time, an older and highly influential man with a love of travel,

Francesca decided to devote the entire segment to writer's block. She had thought this quite ingenious, and it was going rather swimmingly until, as her friend later referred the incident to all and sundry, '*le deluge*, after *moi*'. (In fact, it had also ironically provided this resting screenwriter with her first cinematic idea in some time, in which intriguingly each character, major or minor, has their own story to tell, in his or her own individual way. Which was, of course, quite exciting but rather defeated the object of this particular interview.)

Yet naturally, for so creative an endeavour, this screenwriter demanded far more details than Francesca, despite being Megan Peabody's absolutely best and most loyal friend since Cambridge, had rather selfishly been quite reluctant to impart. Details such as, first and foremost, *who the hell was the father?* If her BFF didn't enlighten her by the time the baby, a little girl called Emily Jane Jensen (Francesca has never cared for surprises) chose to enter the world, then she could forget about any future babysitting. And Francesca, despite being a resolutely single mum-to-be and a devout control freak, would still need all the help she could get.

*

"*Alright, Megan, I'll bloody tell you!*" shrieked Francesca Jensen from her prone position. "But can we get out of the sodding ambulance first?"

"Don't mind us, love," encouraged the kindly paramedic, "it's stories like these that make the job."

"I had the birth heavily pencilled for *next* week!" muttered the expectant passenger, which the men took to be just the usual ramblings of a mother-to-be in extremis but Megan knew to be utterly symptomatic of her friend's freakish obsession with planning (family and otherwise).

As it happens, Francesca had plenty of time in the maternity wing of her local hospital, if not exactly an unbounded inclination, to tell Megan Peabody everything the happily un-pregnant woman dearly yearned to know. And, of course, her old friend had all the time in the world. Megan had no children of her own to whom to attend but had recently, and happily, acquired two delightful stepchildren ('polysyllabic conversation and no stretchmarks').

It took a while for Francesca to get fully into her stride. Setting aside the pain, which she had been assured, by spasmodically attending professionals, would be of some duration, increased frequency and could only become worse, the disgruntled patient had been unnerved to discover one of her second year film studies students in the reception area, for reasons that weren't immediately apparent.

Of course, all her students, at the nearby university where she taught, knew that she was pregnant – film studies is a visual subject – but none were aware that there wasn't a resident father involved. Now Francesca suspected that the intrigued young person would logically assume the rather glamorous Megan to be partner in every sense of the word and was giddily speculating on the exact provenance and manufacturing process of the child in question. Well, so be it. It was probably a more intriguing story than the truth, which stories often are. Although Megan Peabody might soon choose to disagree.

Francesca suddenly wondered, with a markedly different spasm of discomfort, whether news of this evening's eventful and possibly unique television interview had already spread around the campus of the University of the Cinque Ports (formerly Dymchurch Tech) and, heaven forbid, way beyond. After all, as she would be the first to admit, Francesca Jensen was rather well known and not simply in academic circles. As 'the Popcorn Pundit', her film reviews of blockbuster movies reached that wide audience of the cinema-going public who didn't regard the notion of mainstream entertainment as something to be avoided like Ebola. The fact that she was an extremely attractive, flame-haired academic in her late thirties didn't exactly hinder her desirability as the go-to person whenever TV companies needed intelligent and intelligible commentary on some movie-related news. She also wondered briefly whether her long affair with a married professor in the history department had been quite as secret as she might have supposed.

"Well, it can't be Henry Montague, can it?" said Megan, just to get the conversational ball rolling, when the two of them were finally on their own and temporarily unbothered by nurses and midwives. "Everyone knows he's had the snip."

Francesca didn't bother to question her friend on exactly how the world would be so well-informed about a medieval history professor's reproductive potential, or lack of it, as she now recalled telling Megan that this was one of her reasons for concluding the relationship. In fact, the foremost one. At the age of thirty-nine, with her clock ticking like Big Ben on crack, Francesca Jensen had quite unexpectedly, yet utterly desperately, wanted a child. Not just intellectually, where her desires usually found their most fertile ground, but with every cell of her yearning body.

"No, of course it wasn't Henry. That was over some time ago. But good while it lasted. Well," she paused, before employing her own favoured reviewing system, "three tubs of popcorn... out of five."

Megan decided to keep her own counsel. She realised that her dear friend, despite the mounting unpleasantness, could well be on a roll. And now was certainly not the time to stem the (confessional) flow. Not if she wanted to hear every last juicy detail.

"I didn't want or need another relationship," continued the woman squirming on the bed. "It was all too raw after Henry and there was absolutely no one on the horizon, married or otherwise. As you well know. And, of course, time was running out. Or at least I felt it was. So I decided to immerse myself in a new and all-consuming project. With my usual meticulous attention to detail. No prizes for guessing."

Megan merely nodded her rigorously coiffured head in the direction of the massive bump. She wouldn't have been surprised if there was a whole troupe of Jensens lodging in there, although she had been reassured several times that it was a single occupancy.

The writer had, of course, known, or at least suspected, that her dear friend had been searching for some time for an A-list, cordon-bleu, Nobel-worthy sperm donor. A top seed in the high-stakes game of reproduction. Someone entirely of her own choosing, not selected from some vaguely untrustworthy computerised depository, with only a top-shelf magazine for encouragement. This had to be an intensely eligible male, with all the appropriate genes and qualifications and, of course, total obliviousness to the mental spreadsheet that had been constructed with Francesca's customary attention to detail. Someone preferably from well outside this green and pleasant land, whom Francesca would hopefully never meet again, but of whom she would be forever reminded in a fulfilling and biologically nourishing way.

"So," asked Megan, disapproval not entirely absent from her voice but hopefully overlaid with an overwhelming curiosity, "who *was* the lucky man? Did all your meticulous planning work out as planned? Knowing you, I can only assume that it did."

She looked into her friend's contorted face but couldn't quite decide whether it was contractions or recollection causing the oddly disturbing rictus.

"*Tell me quickly,*" she encouraged, "before you're in too much agony to do anything aside from scream."

Wondering once again whether Megan Peabody might not have been the most prudent choice of partner on this momentous journey, Francesca began her tale.

THE MOTHER'S STORY

O-kay. So, you may recall that some months ago – well, nine months ago obviously – there was the first ever Cambridge Spy Film Festival. I'm surprised they'd never done it before, considering this is where all the best spies came from. Not ours unfortunately but, of course, that just adds to the intrigue. It was a no-brainer that I'd attend. In fact, I'd been asked to introduce the Harry Palmer retrospective, commencing naturally with *The Ipcress File*. Actually, I'd been hoping they'd offer me *John le Carré Day*, but they got a real spy to do that gig, one of ours this time, so I couldn't really complain.

Naturally, everyone who was anyone in film studies and critical theory was there. And I had heard through the grapevine that they'd even invited Seymour Brodsky himself, from the California Institute of the Arts, to give his seminal lecture *Matt Helm vs Our Man Flint*. I'd met Seymour on Zoom a couple of times and approved of everything about him. Extremely tall, rather good-looking, Harvard-educated, funny, ferociously bright and single. What's not to like? So, I took one deep breath and decided to resume contact before the main event.

We seemed genuinely to click across the cyberverse – hate that word! – and I did believe he was being politely flirty. Nothing crude or lascivious but a definite spark in those intelligently cool, blue, East-Coast eyes. So when I heard that he was definitely flying over to Cambridge, I suggested I take him for dinner, as this was my sphere of operations, so to speak. England in general, I mean, not specifically fine-dining Cantab.

As hoped, my esteemed invitee very graciously jumped at the chance. Which I have to say I found promising. So, that was the first box ticked.

I took my esteemed guest on arrival to our old college, because, as you know, Emmanuel makes a big thing that John Harvard himself had studied there, and of course they had even preserved his old room, although God knows how they could have divined at that stage who little John was going to be or what he was going to found. Anyway, Seymour thought it rather charming.

The meal itself, at the University Arms Hotel, where we both fortuitously happened to be staying, was suitably delicious. As, even though I say it myself, was yours truly. And so indeed, after all this fervid anticipation, was the aforesaid Mr Brodsky. A paean to natural selection. I could almost feel my ovaries humming over the beautifully presented sea bass. *Oh don't make that face, Megan!*

So, that's when I plucked up all my courage – I wasn't quite as brazen as I might sound right now (despite these bloody contractions), and a bottle of fine red claret certainly helped. As the meal was drawing to its caffeinated conclusion, by which time I had almost exhausted my repertoire of meaningful looks, I finally offered up my carefully prepared and oft-rehearsed line.

"This may surprise you, Seymour," I began somewhat coyly, glancing slowly up at him across the candlelit table, "but I haven't been with a man – you know, like this – for some time."

He gave me the most appealing smile. "Oh, I have," he said.

Shit! I thought, feeling the 'optimum fertility' window slamming shut like an Old Bailey cell. How did I get the bloody signs so wrong? As you know, I'm feted in academic circles for my research.

So, anyway, I swiftly decided: sod this for a game of soldiers – if I scurry, I might just catch the late night champagne screening of *Modesty Blaise - the director's cut* at Trinity College. And that's exactly what I did, with very pricey sea bass and red wine and Irish coffee sloshing inside me all the way down King's Parade.

Which is how, serendipitously, I met little Emily's rather gorgeous, albeit home-grown, alpha-male, PhD dad.

Megan, does this baby seem to be taking a hell of a long time? ...No, I do *know* you're not a bloody midwife... I *am* getting to the good bit! Please don't rush me.

Okay. Cut to Trinity College. Same Day. Evening.

He was perched on a bar stool when I came out of the viewing room, halfway through the film. I was sneezing fit to bust, so I barely noticed him at first. It was only when he spoke to me that I fully turned to face him over my hankie.

As I said, he was rather good-looking, in a far more rugged, earthy sort of way than the poor guy I had just left back at the hotel. He was clad in a smart dinner jacket; you know, the way guys at Oxbridge seem to do on every conceivable occasion. Clearly he'd been to a far posher do than a *Modesty Blaise* retrospective.

"Don't be upset," he said, nodding his very slightly greying but reassuringly bushy head towards my streaming eyes. "It's only a film."

"Eh? It's not the film, for pity's sake," I told him. "It's your bloody weather!"

That's when I segued into more sneezing, which isn't my most attractive function, but you know me and my allergies.

"*Every time I come here!* I swear there's a fen or something with my name on it."

He picked up an open bottle of rather good red wine from the table beside him and found a couple of glasses behind the unmanned bar.

"On behalf of the whole of irritating East Anglia," he smiled as he poured the wine, "I apologise."

I couldn't make out his accent. It was English, but not posh English. So he had clearly arrived here on merit, which was promising. As you know, I'm not a snob... I'm *not*, Megan!

He offered me a rather full glass. "Here, have something to warm you up," he said, quite charmingly.

He clinked the glasses and our eyes fully met for the first time. And for maybe a fraction of a second too long. He had soft brown eyes you could get quite lost in. And a wide, crinkly smile that animated his whole face. He really was quite attractive.

"So why aren't *you* in there?" I asked, nodding towards the little makeshift cinema.

"Because the booze is out here." He nodded towards the pretty decent Cabernet. "*Wet work.* That's a CIA—"

"I *know* what it is!" I looked back towards the cinema. "I suppose I should go back in."

"What the hell for?"

"It's my job."

"Watching crap old movies? Any vacancies?"

"I'm a senior lecturer in film and communications studies," I explained. "I've been referencing this film for three years. It was directed in 1966 by the great Joseph Losey. Pinter co-wrote the screenplay. And I've never actually managed to see it through to the end. It's quite seminal."

He just laughed at this. Rather a lot. I could have taken offence, but I actually found myself laughing with him. That's when he sat down quite close to me.

"Not a course we do here in Cambridge, is it?" he said. "Y'know, Film—"

"Well, that's where you don't quite cut it, isn't it?" I said, a bit sharply. "I'm at the University of the Cinque Ports."

"Oh yeah. Dymchurch Tech. I had a friend who moved down that way."

"Uh huh," I opined. "And I suppose you're a rocket scientist."

"Me?" He smiled again with that smile he probably keeps on file for such occasions. Then he put on a pair of thick-rimmed glasses, as if he wanted to look more – I dunno – *donnish*. "No. Micro-bacteriological research. In layman's terms, the common cold." He grabbed my hankie – I still had it crumpled in my hand. "Can I have that when you've finished with it?"

"I never exchange bodily fluids on the first date."

He had the courtesy to laugh, as it was rather a bon mot, and poured us some more wine. And it was then that he said something so intuitive that I wondered for just a moment if he had sussed out my true motivation for this trip to the flatlands of the East.

"Happy in your work, are you? In your life. Fulfilled?"

"Yes, I am. Of course I am," I said, perhaps rather too speedily.

"Good. Well… that's good. I mean, just think of all those grateful students who, if it weren't for you, wouldn't know how to… er… go to the pictures."

"Listen, you condescending academic elitist, what I do at UCP is not some Mickey Mouse course… although we do have an animation option in year three."

"I bet you're a great teacher."

Where did that come from? I wondered. It was rather a nice compliment. And quite perceptive. So I thought it was only fair to return the gesture.

"And I bet you're an excellent—"

"Don," he finished for me.

"Yes, don. I think I'd better be on my—"

"Hey, hang on!" he said, gently touching my sleeve. "They'll all be out soon. You can finally find out how this one ends."

"Oh, I can guess how it ends: 'the apparently tough female

stereotype falls suddenly and helplessly into the arms of the strong and handsome male archetype'."

"The sixties! Thank God we've moved on since then. And talking of moving on…"

"Thanks," I said, "but I really do have to go."

My Cambridge don threw me that look again. "What have you got to go to?"

"Er… fair point." I certainly didn't wish to bump into sweet but unreliable Mr Brodsky. "I just don't want to see any more students *or* academics."

"Well," he said, getting up from his seat, "I happen to know a bar that's so scuzzy even students won't go there."

"No such place exits," I said. "I was a student here."

But there was. And we went. And then he very graciously saw me back to my hotel room and quietly slipped away very early the following morning. Without a word, a note or a backward glance. I didn't even catch his name! Which I suppose, in retrospect, was all to the good, although I must admit to being just a tad miffed at the time.

And – well – here I am now, carrying a potential microbacteriologist. Daughter of a seriously good-looking and very personable Cambridge don. Although, of course, he will never know it.

That's all there is, Megan. Mission accomplished. Not something I would include with excessive pride in my autobiography – or indeed tell Emily, when she's old enough. Well, not in every exact and far from wholly unpleasant detail – but, hey ho, what's done is done. And rather well done.

Now, despite that signature look of disapproval, I *know* you're already thinking of this as a film script. Well, just *don't* – okay? Could you please hold my hand, Meg. Tight please. *Really* tight. I think it's going to be a rather long night.

THE FATHER'S STORY

What gets me is that I probably would never have known about it if I hadn't seen those students staring at their phones and laughing. Although, between you and me, I already had the strangest feeling that today was not going to be an ordinary day. I get like this sometimes. Spiritual. I can feel things, like they say, in my water. Or my beer. Or my Cabernet Sauvignon.

I was behind the bar at the time, same college but not in my DJ. That's only for special do's – you know, the posh ones. When they pay you a bit extra and want to impress the world. Because they're Cambridge, where everything has a different name. Like where the river goes behind the colleges is called 'the backs' and the poor women who clean up after the students, 'cos the little lambs can't make their own beds, are 'bedders'. And May Balls are in bloody June. I make a lot of dosh behind the bars those weeks.

Don't get me wrong. I like students. I'm not jealous or anything. Well, maybe I am just a bit. But I've made my own bed – unlike them – so I just have to lie on it. Although occasionally...

"So, what are you lot laughing at?" I finally asked them, because there's nothing worse than hearing folk laugh and not knowing what the bloody joke is.

"Play it back," says one of them. "Play it for Don."

And that's when I see her. The redhead from whenever it was. In some poncy TV studio, in the middle of what looks like an interview with another posh woman in fancy dress, talking about some block where writers live, probably local to that area down in Kent. And right in the middle of the whole thing, my one stops and, I swear to God, she says out loud, in that throaty, hoity-toity, but actually not unsexy voice of hers, "Oh shit, Meg, I think my waters just broke!"

Francesca!

That was her name. I can remember names – it's a sort of a gift and pretty useful in my line of work. And elsewhere.

So I figured it out – it was that wanky film festival! Yes! She was quite a looker, as I recall. Bit of fun too. And nice with it. Cut above my usual… *It was almost nine months ago to the day when she and I…!* Well, when she and I, it would seem, made a sodding baby.

Unless, of course, she was putting it out a bit around the same time. But you know what, although I didn't know her that well – hardly at all, actually – I truly don't think she was the type. You get a sense, don't you? Well, I do. What we had, it wasn't just a one-night stand.

Okay, it *was* just a one-night stand, obviously.

But if things had been different, you know; timings, circumstances and me really being a microbacteriologist and not just a freelance barman. (I mean she wasn't going to spend the night with a barman, was she? Not someone all classy and educated like her. Unless she went for a bit of rough. As they sometimes do. But not our Francesca. Not her.)

Actually, I'm *more* than just a barman. I'm one of Cambridge's finest. You just ask around about Don Sanderson. It's quite an art, you know. There's a lot more to it than just sloshing booze into a glass. There's – well, there's lots of things. Cocktails for a kick-off. And, you know, people skills.

Anyway, that's not all I do. Not by a long chalk. I've got my own business. I make adult garden gnomes. I don't mean the gnomes are adult – they probably all are, when you think about it – it's more the things they get up to. The lady gnomes and the gentlemen gnomes. And sometimes just two ladies together or two gents. Or, by special request, a sort of gnomic orgy. It's how they fit together so perfectly, that's the skill. My dad was a carpenter, but I don't think he truly appreciates what I do. Wonder if Jesus's dad felt that way.

Anyway, the moment I saw that video clip, something deep inside of me burst, just like that Francesca's waters on the telly. She was having a baby – *my* baby most likely – and she didn't even have the courtesy to bloody tell me!

You don't think that's what she, y'know, intended all along? No, surely not. Who would *do* something like that?

So, know what I did? Straight away, without even thinking about it, I just left those students and the bar and the college and the viral video or whatever it was, and I got on the blower to my best mate here. *"Cliffy, I need you!"* is what I think I said.

Cliff was a minicab driver – still is, bless his heart – and he owed me big time. Well, okay, he didn't even owe me little time but he's a very old mate and this is what mates do for each other, especially when one of them's lost their licence.

Isn't it?

THE MINICAB-DRIVING
FRIEND'S STORY

*Y*ou ask me how long I've known Donnie Sanderson? *Jesus!* – I'd have to say forever. Or longer. Our mums were pregnant together, we went through all the local schools together, from nursery right up to GCSEs. The boy and I even had chickenpox together! (We also got chucked out of the same comprehensive together, but I won't go into that.)

Don was best man at my wedding to Jools – of course he was – and that wasn't yesterday. *Moreover*, he's been godfather to at least four of my kids. Naturally, I was best man at his do. But sadly he and Lucy weren't quite so – what's the word? – compatible. And now she's about as far away from here – and from him – as it's possible to get, without being six feet under.

In fact, that was one of the first things he said to me when I picked him up outside the college bar he was working at that evening. (I'm still asking myself why I agreed – my Jools hasn't stopped asking me – but it's what you do for mates, isn't it? Drive them one hundred and twenty miles in the darkness to the arse-end of nowhere to check out if a child that's about to be born, a little person some posh woman truly didn't want you ever to know about, *genuinely* is the one you made by pure bloody accident on a drunken one-nighter... Yeah, alright.)

"I *can't* lose another kid, Cliffy!" is what he actually said to me, as he slipped into the back of my cab. I know he's a mate and not a fare, but after so many years behind the wheel I find it a lot easier to talk to folk in the mirror rather than turning my head. Pisses Jools off no end.

Now, Don didn't lose a kid as in the kid's not around or breathing any more, heaven forbid. But with Lucy in New Zealand with the bloke who came to fix their double-glazing, the little lad is hardly in cuddling distance. Not so little now – must be ten at least. I think Don does the odd Zoom call to the boy, often as he can really, but he might as well be a stranger.

I had to get real with my pal. I think I was entitled, considering I was doing all this bloody driving, and I could whistle for the petrol money. Not that I'd ever ask for it and not that Don would ever offer.

"So, you're just going to barge in on a woman who doesn't want you anywhere near her or the kid she probably hasn't even had yet. A lady who didn't tell you about it for an entire bloody pregnancy. How's that going to work out for you?"

"Maybe she *tried* to find me, Cliff, but she couldn't."

"Oh come on – you wouldn't be that hard to find," I said. "She knew where you worked and what you did."

I can see why they say in books that the silence is deafening. The only thing I could hear in my ears was the sound of my own voice saying, "Oh shit!" over and over again.

"You did your Cambridge don thing, didn't you?"

His worried face in my driving mirror looked even more sheepish, lit up as it was by the motorway lights and the odd passing car.

"Yeah. Okay, sort of," he admitted. "A bit. Well, come on Cliffy, a cool bird like her wasn't ever going to take up with a jobbing college barman, was she? A bloke who only got a woodwork A-level."

"You didn't actually..."

"No. Okay. But I could've."

I could see from his face that he had just talked himself out of any good reason why 'a bird like her' would exactly light up to see him now, in the maternity ward of her local hospital. Or anywhere else for that matter. Unless...

"You're not going to, y'know, carry on with this act?" I could tell that he hadn't junked the idea entirely. "'Cos if you are, I'm turning this bloody cab around now!"

"*Cliff!*"

"I'm serious, pal. I am *not* being part of yet another great big Donald Sanderson whopper! Not when this poor woman is probably even now having her contractions. If only from embarrassment at what just went down on the telly."

"This 'poor woman' *used* me, Cliffy. She used me as – as a sodding sperm donor."

"And how off the mark was she in that?"

"Well, I dunno. My boys had a pretty good strike rate. Bullseye first time, so far as I can see."

"Yeah, but Cambridge barman sperm. Not...?"

"Microbacteriologist."

"*Jesus!* Is there even such a thing?"

"How the fuck would I know? I'm a Cambridge barman."

The conversation went on like this pretty well all the way to the hospital. We weren't even sure if it would be the right place, although it was only a smallish town, so there probably wouldn't have been a lot of choice.

But, thinking back, I do recall him saying he had this weird spooky feeling when he woke up that morning. You're probably thinking 'yeah, right' but, as I say, I've known Donnie forever and sometimes he can go a bit funny like this. I mean sort of new-agey. He knew my Jools was pregnant before I did. (And no – don't even go there!)

We had a much better idea that we were 'on site' when we rocked up outside the main hospital entrance and I saw that there was a whole load of camera crews and reporters all waiting outside.

"Oh Christ," I said, because I didn't think Don had noticed yet. In fact, I reckon he was starting to doze off. This is always something that amazes me about the guy – his ability to sleep absolutely bloody anywhere. Especially classrooms, as I recall.

"Don, we're here… Donnie, wake up, pal!"

"Eh? Oh, sorry, Cliffy. I get sleepy when I'm in shock. And when I'm really angry."

"Yeah. They're the triggers. Have you noticed we're not alone?"

That's when he spotted all the folk huddling by the hospital entrance. People who, I had to assume, were wanting to know a whole lot more about the famous baby that started life's exciting journey on early evening TV.

"Oh God. *Parasites!*" he moaned. "Well, at least this must be the place. Can't be two news stories in a dump like this. But I'll never get in there now, will I?" he moaned.

I could see now that I had to be the voice of sanity for my oldest, best and way most irresponsible friend, even though the whole malarkey was totally insane and bound to end in tears. With possible arrests thrown in.

"'Course you will. You're the bloody father. Possibly."

"*Definitely.* I'd even take a paternity test."

"It'd be the first exam you'd ever passed in your life." A bit snide, I know, but it was late and I'd just driven one hundred and twenty sodding miles. For free!

And that's how we got through the hospital security. It must have been put together bloody quickly behind those electronic doors. I was surprised that some enterprising reporter hadn't already thought of the 'I'm the dad' excuse. No initiative these days.

It was a different matter at reception. Even when my pal tried his hardest to wipe that look of desperation from off his sweaty face and put on his best and most charming, father-to-be smile.

"Hi," he said to the middle-aged Asian lady, who was already looking suspicious. "Archna," he read. "Lovely name. My – er – my wife's having a baby. It was on the news."

"It was on the news," repeated the unsmiling receptionist. "What is she, royalty?"

"Er, no," he explained, "although she'll always be a princess in my eyes."

I don't think I said 'Christ!' out loud but I could see the much younger receptionist next to old Archna smiling.

"I think it must be the poor lady all these people outside are here about," she said to her bemused colleague. "The one who started having it on the telly."

The older woman nodded indifferently. "Name?"

"Oh," said Don, "we haven't decided yet. If it's a little boy—"

"Name of the patient!"

"Oh. 'Course. Francesca. Yes. It was definitely Francesca. So just point me—"

"Anything else you can add?" she said with a sigh.

"Please?" suggested Don.

The woman sighed again.

I don't know whether he was stressed, tired or just plain thick but there was only one thing I could do. I scooted back to the electronic doors and collared the first reporter I could find.

"Who are you waiting for?" I asked.

"Francesca Jensen – duh – obviously."

I went back inside and whispered the magic word to Don.

"JENSEN!" he shouted at the shocked lady a tiny bit late but with a bucketload of uncalled-for enthusiasm. "Er – yes. Francesca Jensen. Like the car."

The lady clicked a lot of times on her computer. "Maternity. First floor. Room 14A." She waved us in the right direction. Hopefully.

"Good luck," said the younger girl, smiling at Don and crossing her fingers.

I had a feeling we'd be needing a lot more than that.

"Anybody going to Cambridge?" I said hopefully, under my breath. But I knew in my gut there would just be my one very non-paying passenger.

*

RANDOM SCENES FOR 'UNDER THE MOON' (WORKING TITLE) BY MEGAN PEABODY

INT. HOSPITAL DELIVERY ROOM. NIGHT.

The room is spare and clinical. Peeling pale green walls. Monitors in action. On the bed is FLAMINIA JACKSON (39). (*Note to self: name sufficiently different?*)

She has been given an epidural, so the pain is almost manageable. She utters a more than occasional and long drawn-out 'ooooff!'.

It is clear from the attention being given by those around her that the birth of her first child is fairly imminent. As she is 'of a certain age', they appear to be taking extra care.

Her best friend MORGAN, smartly dressed and looking very attractive, despite the lateness of the day, is by her side, holding her hand and trying to mask her totally understandable discomfort and nausea.

The SENIOR MIDWIFE, a large jolly Nigerian lady, is very encouraging. A young NURSE is assisting her.

MIDWIFE

That's it. Just push. You're doing really well, Flaminia.

FLAMINIA

Oh, please don't patronise me. I'm a doctor myself.
How long is all this going to take? It's been hours!

MIDWIFE
Well, we've never known one to stay in, have
we, Nurse? Nobody told me you were a doctor.

MORGAN
Her doctoral thesis was the definitive work on
the films of Jackie Chan.

MIDWIFE
O-kay.

FLAMINIA
I don't think this epidural is working.

MIDWIFE
Just imagine you're Jackie Chan. Now push.

There is a sharp knock on the door.

MORGAN
Come in!

Morgan looks at the stern midwife and SHRUGS
apologetically.

DON enters the delivery room. He holds a huge bunch of
flowers. (NB: *We have to keep Don's first name same as in real
life. Check legal situation.*)

DON
Hi, Flaminia! Remember me?

He smiles pointedly at her. She looks at him, blankly at first, then with awful, gut-churning recognition. *SHIT!* If she wasn't *in extremis* before…

FLAMINIA

Aaagghh! OH NO! Oh, Jesus Christ! Who let you in? Doesn't this bloody hospital have *any* security? Oofff!

MIDWIFE

Sir, I'm afraid you will have to leave. Just stand with the other reporters outside the front doors.

FLAMINIA

Reporters?!

DON

Your little interview went viral. Everyone's seen it. You made quite a splash.
(to Morgan)
Saw you too, love.

MORGAN

(quite pleased)
Oh. Did you?… Sorry, who exactly *are* you?

FLAMINIA

He's nobody! NOBODY!

The midwife and the nurse are MOVING sternly towards him. More serious 'ooffs'.

DON

I'm not bloody nobody! *I'm the baby's father!*

The women PAUSE. And stare.

MORGAN
(excitedly)
You're the don! The microbacteriologist! From Cambridge!

MIDWIFE
(to Don)
Is this true?

Don looks torn. Then sheepish.

DON
Well, sort of. I am a Don – Don Sutherland.
And I *am* from Cambridge. I'm – at the bar.

We hear a sudden SCREAM from Flaminia. Contraction – or
deep shock?

FLAMINIA
Aaagghh!! WHAT?! NO! WHATTT? Get him out of here! NOW!

The nurses ease Don out. Morgan is fascinated.

MORGAN
Do you mind if I step out too, Flam? Feeling
a wee bit wobbly.

FLAMINIA
No! Yes, *yes*. Go! Pay him off. Kill him off!
He's a sodding BARMAN! Baby'll probably pop
out pulling a pint! Oooooofffff!

Morgan leaves the delivery room. We hear '*almost there*'
sounds. She winces.

INT. WAITING ROOM. CONTINUOUS.

CHRIS (Don's pal and driver) is already in the waiting room. Don ignores him. So does Morgan.

> DON
>
> Call this a maternity ward! What about *paternity*?!
> What about *fathers'* rights? She brings some strange
> woman off the bloody telly to be with her!

> MORGAN
>
> I'm actually her oldest friend. Morgan Prescott. Hi, Don.

> DON
>
> Oh. Sorry. Hello, Morgan.

> CHRIS
>
> I'm Chris.

> MORGAN
>
> That's nice. Sorry – this is a private conversation.

> DON
>
> He's my best friend. And driver.

> MORGAN
>
> Oh. Right. All getting very complicated, isn't it?

> DON
>
> Not really. Your bestie in there used me as a
> sperm donor. That's pretty simple.

> MORGAN
>
> And you used her as...?

CHRIS
A one-night stand.

DON
Chris!! Well, yeah, okay. But that's my future
son or daughter about to happen in there!

MORGAN
Daughter actually. Emma Jane Jackson. (*NB: Too
close?*) Our Flaminia isn't one for surprises.

CHRIS
Bet she got one just now. Sorry… sorry. Lips sealed.

DON
(excitedly)
A daughter? A little girl? Well, okay!

MORGAN
Glad you approve.
(taking the bouquet)
Lovely flowers.
(reading the card on them)
'*Mazeltov on the triplets. Aunty Rose and Uncle Jack.*'

DON
Ahh. Triplets. What's 'mazel…'?

MORGAN
She's not going to want to see you here. Donald.
Y'know, after…

DON
Kids need their dads, Morgan. Especially daughters.
And sons.

CHRIS
And anything in between. Just saying.

MORGAN
Well, Flaminia has everything worked out. Maternity
leave – Zooming from home. Even a new book deal. So…

Morgan shrugs and gazes at Don empathically. We can tell
what a genuinely nice person she is.

DON
I am *not* letting that child out of my sight. Even if—

The young nurse ENTERS. They all turn to her.

NURSE
We're nearly there. She wants you back in.

DON
On my way.

NURSE
Er, no. Sorry. *Her.*

MORGAN
(squeamishly)
Me? Oh – er – I'm really not… wouldn't she
rather have the… you know – daddy?

NURSE
No. She says she wants him to leave the hospital.
Well, she said planet but – come on. *Now!?*

With an apologetic shrug to Don, Morgan FOLLOWS the nurse out. Don looks at them hopelessly, then at Chris.

CHRIS
Maybe we should go.

Close in on Don's lost and disappointed face.

Cut to Morgan, outside the delivery room, steeling herself for her major supporting role. Whilst still looking rather attractive.

(Note to self: should the next totally unexpected, life-or-death, dramatic scene be from the struggling baby's POV? Too tricksy? Too yucchh?)

*

Excerpt from the first draft of *I'VE NEVER KNOWN ONE TO STAY IN!* – the Memoirs of Blossom Danjuma, an African midwife in Kent.

I had thought that when we got rid of the tall, good-looking man who kept saying he was the baby's father that all of our troubles were over. Especially when the mother-to-be said she never wanted to see him again (which was a bit sad actually, as the poor man seemed really upset).

Maybe I am a very old-fashioned lady, but in my opinion babies need fathers. My own babies certainly did. Perhaps not the one they got, but this is another story. (See Chapter Six.)

Yet, as every midwife knows, in this profession you have to expect the unexpected. And be ready for it with both sterilised hands. And this is exactly what happened that early morning when the mummy (*note to me: call her Francesca for now but remember to change it later*) was just about to give birth. The very well-turned-out lady who came in with her – her best friend, I think – was standing by the bedside looking awfully pale, even for a white lady, and like she was going to be sick any minute. I needed this, as they say here, like a hole in my skull.

But I could not allow myself to be distracted. And I suddenly noticed something going on down there that wasn't quite right – possibly a long, long way from being alright. So, without worrying the mother, who had plenty enough to be thinking about, I very quietly asked the young nurse standing beside me to go and quickly fetch the doctor.

To my surprise, Francesca suddenly grabbed my arm really tight. Despite all of her exertions and the epidural and the bossing people around like there was no tomorrow – and, of course, the pain – she seemed to be very aware of what was going on.

"Where's she gone – where's that little nurse gone?"

I was about to tell her not to worry when the door opened, and my nurse came scuttling back in with a young doctor. They were both looking very serious.

"Who the hell are you?" asked my patient.

The doctor did not answer her. He was too busy checking the monitors and looking at the baby's head.

"Is everything alright?" said the mummy's friend, who was looking even paler. I have seen a dead catfish with more colour.

Then suddenly the door opened once more, and the father was back in again! It was like Piccadilly Circus! I had thought the guy had left the hospital by now. Some people just cannot take the hint.

"What's going on?" he asked, looking very concerned. I have to say, I felt a bit sorry for the man. He had a nice kindly face and lovely hair. "I saw the doctor rush in. Is Emily okay?"

The doctor didn't look up. He just said, in a very firm voice, "I want everybody out, please. *Now!"*

I tell you, the best friend couldn't get out of there quick

enough. Even in her high heels. She actually bumped the father out the way and nearly knocked the guy over.

"What's wrong, please?" said Francesca, this time in a tiny, worried voice.

"Don't worry, Francesca," I said very calmly. "This sometimes happens."

"WHAT sometimes happens?" called the father from the doorway, as the best friend rushed full speed out into the corridor. I just threw a look to my nurse, who nodded and gently escorted the very troubled man out of the room. I could still hear him shouting, *"What is it? What's going on?"*

"Oooogggghhhhh!" screamed Francesca.

"You're doing very well, darling" I said, which is what I always say. We all need a bit of encouragement. But I truly hoped she wouldn't be picking up the mounting concern in my voice.

"I'm going to have to suction the nose and mouth," said the doctor. *"Nurse!"*

My nurse, who is the sweetest little Filipino girl – *well, they're all little next to me!* – handed the young doctor – *okay, they all seem young to me!* – the relevant equipment. You'd be amazed how much stuff we have on hand, ready for any emergency. Which this certainly was, although not one that I had never seen before in my working life. Trust me, I have seen most things.

As you can imagine, Francesca was looking quite terrified, while the young doctor hurried to stick a tiny tube into her not-yet-quite-born baby's mouth.

"Now just don't you worry, Francesca," I said, in my most reassuring voice. "You just do your job and carry on with all the yelling and the pushing—"

"DON'T WORRY," she screamed. "Don't fucking worry?" *(Note to myself: do I keep the bad language in? You hear a lot of it in my work.)* "He's sticking a fucking tube into my fucking unborn baby!"

31

I have to hand it to the doctor. Even though he was really busy, he had the good sense to explain to Francesca what was going on – because he didn't want her to just give up and stop the pushing.

"It's called MAS," he explained very calmly, as he carried on with the job. "Meconium Aspiration Syndrome."

"What the hell is that – in English? Oooofffff!"

"Well basically, it means your baby has inhaled its first faeces."

"Oh shit!" cried Francesca, but I don't think she really knew what she was saying, as her poor little one was just about to make her way, coughing and spluttering like crazy, into this tricky old world.

"Here she comes, Francesca," I encouraged her. "That's it. Just one more great big push. You can do it. That's my girl. *Puuuuusssshhhh!* Just one more. Now another great big one. Good mummy. One more for luck. And here comes baby."

"*EMILYYYYYYYYYYYYY*," screamed Mummy, with a final agonised push. And a tiny but beautiful baby girl emerged, all scrunched up and crumpled, giving a very weak, choked-up and coughy little cry. A sorry cry of distress, as well as of pure surprise at just being born.

Well, wouldn't you be crying and coughing and spluttering fit to bust if you'd just swallowed your first ever poo?

I had to say that the poor wee thing was looking far from well. I didn't say this, of course, but I certainly worried to myself a bit.

You may think that someone who has delivered so many babies just takes everything that happens as part of their job. In the stride, as they say. But each time it's a new little human, isn't it? A very special, brand-new person the world has never met before but who, you never know, might just change it. For better or for worse.

I don't know if you people out there who are reading this

are religious, but to me it is a miracle. The Lord's miracle. One of His best. No question.

The doctor was examining baby Emily's breathing, and I could tell that he was a bit concerned. Maybe more than a bit. (*Note: make sure the reader gets the full drama of this. Diagrams? Medical photos? No – they don't want to see a newborn with poop in its mouth.*)

"She needs to go to ICU now! *Incubator!*" ordered the doctor.

So, as soon as the cord was cut, the poor little one was bundled inside the brilliant and totally sterile contraption that was right there on hand and then wheeled smartly off by my nurse, with the young doctor close behind.

"We'll take good care of her," said the doctor very sweetly to Francesca, as he left. "Please don't worry."

Poor Francesca. I hate it when mummies can't hold their babies. You know, when the tiny newborns have to go straight bloody quick into intensive care. It feels too wrong, doesn't it? The lady was so weak and so very scared. So... depleted. This pretty woman, who I guessed was extremely confident as a general rule – I think someone said she was a professor or something grand at the university here – looked completely spent and empty.

"This wasn't supposed to happen," she said very quietly.

Mummies who have just given birth say a lot of silly things. You always think you've heard them all, then another one comes along and smacks you in the head. And even though the words are coming out of their mouths when the new mummies aren't quite themselves, they do reveal things about their characters that maybe they try to hide a bit better when they're not under such pressure. And I think what this particular lady was telling me is that she likes to control absolutely every last thing.

"Mummy," I told her, in what I hope was the kindest of ways, "somebody once said, 'if you want to make God start laughing, just tell him about your plans'." I have no idea where I first heard about this. It isn't in the Bible because I know my Bible, but it must have been someone spiritual who thought of it.

"Well, I bet God's up there wetting himself now," she said, starting to cry. "Can you please send in—"

"The daddy?"

"*Christ no!* No way! He's not even who he said he was. Bastard's probably in the pub by now anyway. My friend, please. If she isn't in the loo, throwing up."

I left Francesca with the nurse and went into the corridor. To my surprise, there were three people waiting just outside. Hovering, you might say. The mummy's best friend, the gentleman who said he was the father, and another man about the father's age. They all looked very worried. Obviously they had watched the little one being wheeled out at some speed.

"She's okay," I said.

"The baby?" said the father.

"I hope so. I think so. But I meant Francesca."

"What happened? *Tell me!*" demanded the dad, looking frantic.

"She ate her own poo."

"*Francesca?!*" said the best friend and we all threw her a look, until she understood. Then she gave this disgusted face. "Oh, please!"

"The mother wants you to go back in," I said, looking at the friend. But then the father made for the door. "*Not you – her!*" This was all getting very confusing.

"But I'm the dad!" protested the father, turning to the well-dressed woman. "She's – nobody!"

"You obviously never saw *House of Lies*," said the friend, which made no sense to me at all. Or to the men. But before they could ask her to explain, the woman was striding off towards the delivery room. "Two BAFTA nominations and a Golden Globe!" she called back, which made even less sense.

34

I followed her in but not before I heard a huge shout from behind me.

"I'm bloody well staying here! For as long as it takes!"

And do you know something – he did! Even though our Francesca wouldn't have anything to do with him, and avoided him like the plague, the man who said he was the father just waited around day after day, night after night, sleeping on those uncomfortable waiting-room chairs and living on sandwiches from the café. All for just one glimpse of his new little baby girl.

I do think that our team felt really sorry for him. So, although we knew Mum didn't want him anywhere near her child – *their* child, possibly – we tried to keep him updated whenever we could on Emily's progress. Which I have to say, thank God, was encouraging.

Her little lungs were clearing slowly, and it looked like, the fingers crossed, she was going to be just fine. I try to keep track of all my babies, at least until they leave the hospital. And the mummies too, because we've gone through something special together. I'm only human – I like to think that when my ladies look back on this magical, life-changing day, they remember old Blossom just a little bit too.

I recall now that the father did keep muttering something about not wanting to lose another child, but it wasn't our business to question him about that and we really didn't want to upset the poor gentleman even more than he already was. I suppose that we could have asked his friend, you know, just casually, but the man had gone back home in his minicab after that first dramatic night. To Cambridge, I think it was, as he apparently had a house-load of children of his own, God bless him.

There was also something about Cambridge, I recall, that Francesca kept going on about. Putting two and two together without making six, I believe that she had assumed the father was someone very big and important at the university, but he turned out to be a barman there. You don't have to tell me how many babies are made when there's too much drink involved.

We aren't the busiest maternity ward in the country – at least, we weren't that particular week (nine months after Christmas is our all-systems-go time!) – so Francesca, who was in quite a state, let me tell you, mentally and physically, was able to stay in for a few days just to heal, body and soul, to express her milk and to regularly visit her baby in the ICU. (*Without* the father in tow, I hasten to add. We did our very best to make sure their paths didn't cross.)

(*Note: do I mention the reporters and TV people still waiting outside or is it not very nice to identify who the the mum really is? And can I be sued? It's hardly medical anyway – although it did all start with waters breaking on the telly!*)

Francesca dearly wanted to express her milk for Emily, but I did hear that she was finding this pretty hard going. I think our mummy was someone who expected everything in life to run and flow just like clockwork. But unlike for most of us – who know that life just isn't like this, don't we – it came as something of a shock.

I did notice the best friend popping in now and then, each time in a different, always smart and clearly expensive outfit, but I can't imagine that she was the most supportive person on the planet, if her behaviour in the delivery room was anything to go by. But then who am I to judge?

And then Grandmother turned up!

Which I only heard about much later. I don't know the details, so I can't tell you them, because of course I had more lovely new babies coming, and my life had to move on.

I suppose I'll never discover what happened to poor bossy Francesca or my brave little Emily or the persistent barman called Don with the twinkly brown eyes. They didn't exactly behave like a match made in heaven, I can tell you that much.

You don't ever hear the full story in my job. But if you're any sort of a human being, you can't help wondering how people's lives turn out, can you?

I do hope things worked out alright. Especially for the little one.

Now for the incredible tale of the Romney triplets...

*

RANDOM JOTTINGS FOR UNDER THE MOON (WORKING TITLE) BY MEGAN PEABODY

(Note to self: this may be too close to the facts. But go with it for now.)

INT. HOSPITAL. SPECIAL CARE INTENSIVE
BABY UNIT – DAY

Flaminia is watching baby Emma in her incubator. The woman looks even more exhausted than before. No make-up, her hair unkempt.

Morgan stands behind her, in a hospital gown. Despite the drably unfashionable garb, she still looks radiant and amazingly youthful for her age.

FLAMINIA
I so wish I could just hold her. Don't you
think she's beautiful, Morg?

MORGAN
(good-humouredly)
Please don't call me Morg. Not here.
And I'm sure she's beautiful to you.

FLAMINIA
They all say she's doing fine. Some poor mites

37

get it so much worse. And they promised I'll be
able to hold her soon. Oh Morg – an, I can't bear
not to hold her!

MORGAN
Flammy, one word – about the future –
then I'll be quiet forever.

FLAMINIA
Crèche? Nanny?

MORGAN
Adoption.

FLAMINIA
I've asked Medea to be godmother!
(on Morgan's shrug)
Morgan, I can *do* this. Okay, we've had our drama,
and I know how you revel in drama, but after this –
well, anything's got to be plain sailing… hasn't it?

MORGAN
(doubtfully)
Flammy, I'm not Penelope Leach but.. *you* –
and an infant? Let's just say, I'm surprised
you didn't call her Alexa.

FLAMINIA
I'm not that anal, am I? Can't you see – this
is what I've been waiting my whole life for!

MORGAN
A fatherless child?

FLAMINIA

Morgan, I teach students to look at 3,000 feet of
celluloid and find the emotional truth. Well, this is
my emotional truth. Something to shake me up.
Make me whole.
(smiles)
Something to give me a *reason* to be home. Or at
least to come back home after work.

MORGAN
(shrugging)
Well, that's all crystal clear then. But what
about Cambridge Don?

FLAMINIA

What about him? And please don't call
him that.

MORGAN
He hasn't gone away, poor guy.

FLAMINIA
No? Well he has to me.

CUT TO:

INT. WAITING ROOM. SAME

Don is sitting there, eating a sandwich. Same clothes. A three-day
growth on his weary face. Looking worn-out but determined.
Checking his phone.

We hear a voice from off-screen...

SYLVIA (O.S.)
Flaminia! What a vile hospital!

CUT BACK TO:
INT. HOSPITAL. SPECIAL CARE INTENSIVE BABY UNIT.
DAY.

We are one side of the glass screen. Incubators on the other. Flaminia can't hide the HORROR on her face as she registers her mother's shrill voice. She gasps at Morgan, who winces.

They turn to see her mother SYLVIA (imposing, early sixties and a bit scary) and her father DEREK (mid sixties, kindly, tolerant but not weak).

FLAMINIA
Mum! Dad! You didn't have to…

SYLVIA
Yes, of course we did. Don't be ridiculous, dear.
We'd have come sooner, if you'd told us in good
time.
(looking around)
Doesn't that Poly of yours even give you private
healthcare?
(to Morgan)
Do you work here? Is there a beverage service?

DEREK
(apologetically)
Hello, Morgan.

MORGAN
Hi, Derek.

Derek goes to kiss Flaminia.

DEREK

Hi, darling. Sylvia, you've met Morgan every time we've
come down to see Flammy.
(to Morgan)
I reckon she must wheel you in for protection!

Ignoring Morgan, Sylvia pushes Derek away and bustles over to
Flaminia, giving her a rather brittle kiss on the cheek.

SYLVIA

Well, your prayers have been answered.
Mother's here.

Derek and Sylvia stare down through the incubator at Emma.
The baby is crying in a husky, spluttery way.

SYLVIA (CONTD)

Coo-ee, love!

DEREK

It's only Granny and Grandad.

SYLVIA

She must call me Sylvia. I'm far too young to
be a Granny.
(to Morgan)
That's what I tell her younger sister's three. She
married a hugely successful actuary. They have
a delightful home in Sunningdale. With a pool.

Flaminia, clearly uncomfortable, stands with her parents.
Derek puts an arm round her. Emma is crying.

DEREK
(hugging Flaminia)
Good set of lungs on her. She's going to be fine,
sweetheart.

FLAMINIA
Hope so. The doctors do say she's over the worst.
A couple more days and we could be home. But I'll
have to keep a really close eye on her.

SYLVIA
Poor little thing. Imagine coming into the world
and first thing you know, you're in the tabloids!

MORGAN
(changing subject fast)
So – how was your journey down?

FLAMINIA
TABLOIDS! Morg, did you know about this?

MORGAN
Who reads the tabloids!

FLAMINIA
Er – most people! This is all I sodding need!

SYLVIA
Language*! The Sun*, Flaminia! And they're all still
out there, hovering! Waiting for a photo.
(as Flaminia moans)

Your sister made do with a discreet
announcement in the *Telegraph*.

FLAMINIA

Brilliant! You've managed to compare me
unfavourably to Clarissa within two minutes
of walking into the room. A personal best!

SYLVIA

At least Clarissa—

FLAMINIA

Married the one actuary even other actuaries
find tedious!

DEREK

Are you sure you're okay, love – all on your
own here? You look so exhausted. Have you
had… any other visitors?

SYLVIA

He means the father. *You mean the father!*
We thought that once she was born, he might
at least have crawled out of his… laboratory or
whatever to take a peek. But I suppose you're still
not going to tell us who?

FLAMINIA

(wearily)

We have been through this! The father is
wedded to his research. He's not going
to be involved. Not if he wants to get his Nobel
next year.

Morgan can't stop herself coughing. Sylvia shifts away.

                        SYLVIA
            Shouldn't you be wearing a mask?
                (to another incubated baby)
            Is she even sure *who* the father is,
            I wonder?

                        MORGAN
                        (quietly)
            Oh, she's sure.

Flaminia throws her an angry look.

                        SYLVIA
                    (looking round)
            There must be *somewhere* round here one
            can get decent soya decaf cappuccino!

THE MOTHER'S STORY (RESUMED)

I warned Megan sodding Peabody before she left the hospital that if she turns this sorry drama into one of her movie scripts, I shall personally de-nipple her with her own clapperboard. (And no, she can't just change the names!)

Furthermore, if the woman speaks to the press, who apparently are still loitering out there in hopes of a heartwarming baby-snap, all bets are off.

She did reluctantly show me a recent copy of the *Daily Mail*, featuring a screen-capture picture from the television. You probably recall the one – yours truly bent almost double in that TV studio, under the headline 'BREAKING NEWS: TV BABY NOW ON LIFE SUPPORT'. So somebody must have spilled the medical beans. (If it was Father of the Year, I'll clapper him where it hurts too!)

Of course my BFF left me to sit on my own in the hospital canteen with my parents. Cowardly cow.

When people in there began to stare, I thought maybe my blouse had fallen open. But I soon realised that they recognised me from TV. But sadly not as the Popcorn Pundit. More as Our Lady of the Maternal Lake.

"Have you noticed how NHS doctors and nurses all look sicker than the patients?" observed my mother a bit too loudly, as she glared around the busy canteen.

"So," I said, wanting to change the subject to the only

one of any importance, "what do you think of your new granddaughter?"

"Oh she's very bonnie, darling," gushed my dad sweetly. "And she's a little fighter, that's for sure. Well done, love."

"Mm," semi-agreed my mum, "but what with your sister having the three girls, I was rather hoping for a boy."

Jesus!

"Can't do anything bloody right, can I?" I snapped. "I wish I'd kept the receipt."

"You really must try to calm down, you know," said the over-coiffured woman, conscious that people were still staring. "It's so bad for the feeding. You are going to feed?"

"Of course I am!" I protested, although to be honest, I wasn't entirely certain. Even expressing was a nightmare. "Look, you didn't have to come all the way down here, you know. I'd have brought Emily to see you. Eventually."

"Oh, we couldn't not come," said my dad, gently tapping my hand.

"We *are* poor Emily's grandparents!" added Mum. "The only ones she's got, apparently. Anyway, we've got a little bit of news for you."

It was either my sister was popping out another one or, against all odds and reason, my mum had been made chairwoman of their local Ladies Rotary. I knew I had better prepare my 'delighted' face.

"We're getting a divorce," said my dad.

"*Oh that's wonderful!,*" I said, before his words had fully bedded in. "Say again?"

"Your father and I had a good long chat the other day," explained my mum, quietly, "and we realised that after forty-one years of marriage, we basically despise each other."

What do you say in these circumstances?

"So… it's amicable, then?"

Possibly not that.

"Oh yes," said my dad, reassuringly. "But we're not going to rush into things. It's a once-in-a-lifetime event. We want to do it just right."

"I-I'm gobsmacked," I told them, wondering if there might not have been a less febrile time to share such momentous, albeit not wholly unexpected, news. "Of course – I knew you two had problems. The whole neighbourhood did. But if it's been so awful, why didn't you do this ages ago?"

"We were waiting until you settled down," explained my dad a bit limply.

"But as that's obviously never going to happen," his soon to be ex-wife sighed. I admit I winced at this. "So, anyway, we've just got to sort out the details."

"Your mother's demanding eternal life," explained my father.

*

You read the expression in old novels – she 'took to her bed'. That's what I found myself doing.

Yet truly the shock of my parents' news was nothing compared to the worry I still had, and no doubt always would have, about Emily and her health. And, of course, the bone-rattling fear everyone had drummed into me regarding how many apocalyptic and unstoppable changes in my life were on their way, courtesy of parenthood.

Plus – *big* plus – there was that unspeakable East Anglian imposter still apparently loitering in the waiting room.

My stalker.

Well, not even mine.

Emily must have been the youngest person in history to have an obsessive human being monitoring her every move. Didn't the bloody man have a pint to pull or a cocktail to mix, if indeed he had even graduated to this latter formidable skill?

I found myself gazing concernedly at that poor, vulnerable tot in her incubator and seeing if I could detect any aberrant, uneducated, essence-of-peasant traits, which of course was total snobbery and my way of beating myself up for the all too obvious fact that I couldn't distinguish a cocky barman on the make from a serious world-class microbacteriologist on – well – the make.

*

The last time I actually saw Emily in the ICU was the day following my parents' momentous surprise visit and just after I had been informed that my newborn daughter was definitely going to be okay.

I discovered our lovely, kind midwife already there, taking a justifiably satisfied look. Blossom, I think her name was, which summed her up, although she was definitely more of a sturdy tree than a fragrant flower.

"Hi, Mummy," she beamed. Understandably my name had probably faded in her memory by now. "How's she doing?"

"Her poor little lungs. I wish I could do the breathing for her."

"The machine's been doing that perfectly well. You should be sleeping, my lovely. She's going to need your milk."

"Could you sleep – with all this going on?"

"Not a wink. But I hope they're giving you something to help you."

"I had it all mapped out, you know, Blossom. We were going to manage fine, Emily and me. I'd done everything just right. You should have seen my spreadsheet – couldn't move for red ticks! The exercises, the breathing, the nappy gear. Oh – and of course her sweet little bedroom (no pink, can't abide pink). If this hadn't happened…"

"Something else might have. Remember what I told you about God and your plans? I could write a book about mummies and their expectations. Ha – you know, maybe I will.

48

Sweetheart, there's a lot of people out there who are rooting for that little baby."

"Yes, I've seen the flaming *Daily Mail*," I said. "And I bet they're still outside, wanting their million-dollar photo. But when the circus leaves town, it'll be just Emily and me, won't it? Oh, but we'll be great. Perfect. You'll see."

Without thinking, I leant my head on Blossom's ample shoulder. She didn't say anything but just stood there with me for a while.

When I returned to the ICU the next day, Emily's incubator was *empty!*

*

Sorry!

It's the film-structure maven within me. (Never underestimate the potency to an audience of the visual surprise.)

Nothing terrible had happened.

Emily had simply been moved to the crib next to my bed, prior to baby and me hopefully taking our leave of this hospital. I had just come back today to say a heartfelt thank you to all concerned and to collect something.

But here came another big surprise. This time for an audience of one.

Donald Sanderson, dishonourable member of the Cambridge bar, had turned up just before me. I recognised him even from behind. (Which means nothing!)

Who let HIM back in?

This was all I needed. I would have thought he'd be back home and on to pastures new by now. Pulling fresh pints and gullible women.

Even with his back to me, I could hear him whimper. Now, this I wasn't expecting. *Should I just turn and go*, I wondered, *before he even notices me?*

"*Oh my God!*" he said to himself, but I still heard it. "Oh no – oh Jesus! No! *Nurse!*"

"She's fine," I heard myself saying. Well, what else could I do – I'm not a complete sadist.

"*W-WHAT?*" he said, spinning round.

It was the first time that I had seen him since the whole delivery room nightmare. In fact, as I grimly recalled, he was a leading cast member in that fateful scenario.

I had no idea whether he had been secretly visiting Emily in the meantime or simply that the nurses had been sneakily passing on bulletins to him. Staring at the man now, I wondered if he had even been home over the past few days, wherever home was. The guy looked wrecked. Good. Perhaps that was at least some penance for what he did. For what he was *still* doing.

It's not as if he had *wanted* a child. Or even had the slightest intention of *making* one. All he really seemed after was a casual shag and he was fully prepared to big himself up (in more ways than one, as I recall) to attain it.

Alright, perhaps the more judgmental amongst you might deem that I myself wasn't behaving entirely with honour that particular evening. But I had absolutely no intention of further involving him in any way. His job ended quite satisfactorily at around 12.45 that morning. So he could congratulate himself on a task well done and take the rest of his and Emily Jane Jensen's happy life off.

"She's doing great," I reassured him. "Her little lungs are working on their own now. Good as new. The doctor just told me I could take her home!"

"Where's home?" he said, but this was one question I most certainly wasn't going to answer.

"I just came here to get her name tag," I explained. "That one there on the incubator. I'm going to make a scrapbook for her."

A nurse recognised me. With a gentle smile, she lifted the 'Baby Jensen' tag from the glorious, life-saving apparatus in question and handed it to the parent closest to her. He in turn delivered it to me.

"Thank you," I said politely. No need for more hostility. "And goodbye - Don." I wondered if he would once again notice my wince at this short but mendacious name. I had just turned to go, when his wearily plaintive voice stopped me.

"Can I see her, Francesca? Baby Jensen. Just once."

"*No!* No, of course you can't," I countered immediately. "She's mine. Why?"

"Why do you think?" He stared at me through tired and admittedly sad brown eyes. "Only... a quick hello. And a goodbye. One tiny look? Please... Francesca?"

I gave a huge sigh that was intended to convey both frustration and magnanimity. I do a consummate sigh.

"Oh, I suppose. Now you're here. But give me the camera."

"What?"

"The camera. On your phone or wherever you've got it stashed. Give it to me."

The man looked horrified. "I can't have a photo of my own daughter?"

"To sell to the newspaper guys outside?"

He looked suddenly guilty, so I knew that I had pushed the right button. *Jesus!* Once a cad...

"Tell you what, I'll send you one. Sometime."

"You know what? *Forget it!* I'm only the father of your child, but if you can't bloody trust me—"

"Oh, now why wouldn't I trust you? No - don't tell me. Got it! You're a congenital sodding liar!"

"And you're a manipulative, stuck-up, control-freaky, conniving - *woman!* That poor baby is doomed! God help her if she takes after you."

"Well, she's already tried taking after you!"

He looked confused by this.

"She was full of shit!"

I couldn't beat that rejoinder – especially not with the tears forming in my eyes, tears that had never been far away for days. And neither, of course, could he. So I simply turned on my slippered heels and walked swiftly back to my new little daughter, who I really did think I could hear crying for me.

With a bit of luck I would never see him again. But, of course, as I had already discovered, that fickle old lady doesn't always stick to her brief.

*

Later on that same fateful day, I was sitting on the less-than-comfy chair by my bed and trying without much success to feed poor little Emily. I soon realised, from my body's noticeable shivers, that I must have been feeling more rattled than I thought, after my unscripted encounter with the phantom pint-puller of the Fens.

I was so involved in these thoughts that I didn't immediately see my visitor as she drew back the tatty curtain. Nor, of course, did I hear her above Emily's frustrated and famished cries.

"Hey, look who's back!" said the newcomer elatedly.

Closing the curtain with a teeth-jangling clang, Blossom stomped excitedly over to admire one of her recent and possibly most problematic births.

"You gave your mummy and me a very big fright, young lady," she told Emily, with a huge beam of satisfaction on her kindly face. She nodded towards the bobbing head of my still whimpering child. "How are you doing, Francesca?"

"Still not great, Blossom, but thank you for asking. See that girl in the bed over there – eighteen years old, just had twins – she's going at it like United Dairies!"

The midwife just shook her large head. "Look what you've

been through, my darling. You're stressed out. *And* you're facing this all on your own."

I pointed towards the window. "Except for half the national press. What sort of world are we in, Blossom, when a single, heavily pregnant woman can't be allowed to let her waters break in the privacy of an on-air TV station!"

"Shameful. Hey, what happened to the daddy, by the way? I got the impression that gentleman isn't high on your Christmas list."

"Oh, I gave Don from Cambridge short shrift, don't you worry. He's one guy we won't be seeing again, Blossom."

As we talked, the curtains opened slightly, and I watched the massive head of a huge and over-plush toy giraffe start to insinuate itself slowly into the room.

By this time I had truly had it!

"Oh for crying out loud!" I shrieked, shocking my ravenous child. "*Why don't you stick that fucking giraffe right up your lying East Anglian arse?*"

The poor midwife looked stunned. But no more so than my mother, as she followed the massive furry animal into the makeshift room.

"And she wonders why she can't get a man," grumbled my mother to a confused and giraffe-threatened Blossom.

"Daddy couldn't make it today," continued my mother, dumping said animal on the bed. Despite the high-pitched clamour, she barely acknowledged her fourth and newest granddaughter. "He's pranged the Mercedes. Oh, don't look so worried. He's fine. He did it to spite me. Half of that car's mine, you know." She turned to Blossom. "You couldn't make us a nice pot of tea, could you, dear? Earl Grey. Skimmed milk."

"How about some scones and clotted cream?" said Blossom, with her sweetest smile. "See you later, Francesca. Good luck!"

As my one-time saviour diplomatically withdrew, my mum

simply shrugged and yanked the curtain back around the bed with unnecessary vigour.

"Don't want every Tom, Dick and Harriet knowing our business."

I thought I had better address the elephant in the room. Anything was better than the flaming giraffe.

"So how is the... you know?"

"You *can* say 'divorce', you know. It's not like saying the c-word."

I wasn't aware she even knew the c-word until I realised she meant cancer. She actually seemed the jolliest I had seen her for some time.

"Do you know, I believe I'm more excited than I was for the wedding. Anyway..." She took her first real look at the still struggling Emily and shook her head. "Tsk, look how tiny she is. And how the hungry child's bawling! She'd be so much better off with a bottle, Francesca. I had magnificent feeding breasts. Probably still do. Anyway, I've just been talking to my solicitor about you."

"*What?*"

"Well, about your stingy bastard of a father actually. But I had to pay the lawyer for a full hour, so he's come up with a plan."

"Mum, I'm so not interested. Emily and I will be home in a day or two and then I'm just going to get on with my life. Our lives. We'll be fine. In due course I'll find a crèche or get a reputable day-nanny, go straight back to work and—"

"*Work?* With a newborn baby! You didn't catch me working after."

"Or before."

"Still. None of my business. But don't expect me to be shooting all the way down here every five minutes to bail you out!" She took another glance at Emily. "She does look a bit peaky."

"Yes, it's that special look children of single, working mothers get. There's been a lot of research."

"Oh Francesca, what kind of man gets a woman your age pregnant and then just disappears?"

She was making me feel so unwell, banging on yet again about this. I began to wonder how far a giraffe's neck could go down a mottled throat.

"He did NOT disappear! We had an – arrangement. He's on a research fellowship – at Harvard. Yes. On cold... sores."

My mother dipped into her bulging handbag and thrust a business card at me.

"Well, Mr Owen-Jones of Ramsay McNaughtan thinks you've got a very good case. So I *insist* that you give me the man's full name and we slap a bloody great writ on him. He'll be earning a good deal more than you are at your place. Especially if he's teaching a proper subject."

"Not necessarily!" I protested, rather feebly. "Mother, do you need subtitles? He is *out* of this. He is *out* of Emily's life. He is actually *out* of the country."

Of course, with the way my life was going, it was almost predictable that Don Anderson or Sanderson or whatever his bloody name was would select this very moment to pop his stupid (but granted not *totally* unattractive) head around the curtain.

"Hello again!" he said, with breathtaking originality.

"*Bugger off!*" I responded equally wittily.

Now the miscreant had the bare-faced audacity to shrug charmingly to my mother.

"*Hormones!*" he adjudged. "And just listen to that poor little tot screaming for her tea. Sorry, who are you?"

"I'm Emily's grandmother," she announced proudly. "And you are...?"

"Well, I'm glad you asked," he said, throwing me a swift but not exactly friendly smile. "If you must know, I'm Donald Sanderson. I'm Emily's f—" He suddenly stopped.

He must have noticed my clenched eyes, teeth and hair and whatever colour I still had after the past few days swiftly draining from my mortified face.

"*Physician?*" he hazarded. "Gynaecologist, if you want to get all technical." He saw my head slowly shaking, as I mouthed the correct word. "And... obstet – rician. Yeah. Double whammy! Doctor – doctor!"

I almost fainted with relief. Alongside an unwelcome emotion I could only regard as gratitude. Both were still lingering, even as I watched the man produce those shameless spectacles from his pocket – the ones I suspected had no optical qualities whatsoever – and 'don' them with a flourish.

My mother appeared instantly impressed, yet perturbingly still a tad sceptical. She put out a faux elegant hand.

"Sheila Jensen," she announced, before eyeing his casual yet weary unkemptness. "You don't look like a doctor."

"And *you* don't look like a grandmother," he replied, taking her hand.

"Four times!" she gushed.

"*Never!*"

She nodded four times.

"Oh, and do please excuse my appearance, Sheila – I was just on my way home after a particularly rough and gruelling twenty-four hours."

My mum looked unnecessarily intrigued.

"Yeah. Tricky rectal delivery. They're the worst."

I just moaned yet my mother appeared utterly smitten.

"But I just had to pop in on my journey," he continued gently, "to check on my favourite patient." He turned to me. "The baby – not you."

Okay. Enough was enough.

"Well, we're all peachy, thank you, Doctor," I reassured him. "Appreciate your dropping by."

"I'll be the judge of that," responded 'Doctor' Don. And with a mumbled 'excuse me', the cheeky sod moved briskly towards me and hoisted my screaming baby up and away.

I quickly covered myself, but the man was certainly not ogling me this time. Every fibre of his rather tall body was concentrated on the minute creature now suddenly enveloped in his sizeable arms. A child who, to my intense relief but also massive chagrin, had instantly ceased her bawling.

Not a peep. Not even a hungry whimper. Talk about ingratitude.

Yet as I watched them together, man (okay, father) and daughter, as I noticed his brown eyes soften and moisten, whilst his breathing appeared to stop altogether, I went through a maelstrom of emotions, most of them, but disturbingly not all, unpleasant, that sent me both drained and reeling.

The weirdest thing was not, however, the way this Don person was gazing at the child he had quite unintentionally helped to make. It was how this same child was calmly looking up at him. Gazing up. Surely they can't do this, can they? Not at this age. My logic had clearly left me, along with my placenta.

"Doctor? *DOCTOR!*" I interrupted.

The dolt eventually looked up, but not until a few more uncalled-for yet intense bonding moments had passed.

"Can I have a private consult – *please*? And my child back."

"Shall I step out for a second?" suggested my mother, with unusual sensitivity.

"*YES!*" we both chimed as one.

"*Now give me my bloody baby back!*" I hissed with vituperative alliteration when my mother had disappeared.

Of course, the moment Emily Jane was back on me again, my mercurial child resumed her high-pitched bawling. Loyalty was clearly not one of her major qualities. (A deficiency clearly inherited from her father.) I glared furiously at this Donald Sanderson person.

"*You bastard!* You think it's not bad enough having Mother Superior out there happily turning up to bully, humiliate and generally disapprove of me, as she has done my entire bloody life? Now you have to breezily swan in with more of your lies and impostures. *Gynaecologist*? You probably couldn't even spell it! What do you *want* from me?"

"To see my kid," he said softly. "I just wanted, y'know, to see my little girl. Emily. Emily Jane. Of course, if you prefer, I could pull back the curtain and reveal to glamorous Grannie out there who I really am. One-Night-Sanderson, the horny barman from the windy—"

"NO!" I shrieked, rather too loudly. My mum was back in a flash. "No... that won't be necessary, Doctor," I continued, in a calmer voice.

"Everything alright?" she asked of my 'physician'.

"Absolutely, Sheila. Your daughter is in tip-top condition, considering her advanced years." Before I could protest, he was back on his roll. "Francesca was just going off to find us a nice cup of tea."

"*WHAT?!*"

"Oh, what a good idea," agreed my mum. "The machine will do fine, darling. Earl Grey, no sugar. I'm trying to get back into shape, Doctor, now that I'm on the market again." The brazen OAP even flashed her eyes at him!

"Oh. Right," said the man. "Well, I'd say you're perfect just the way you are... Sheila."

With a backwards grin at me, the interloper blithely picked up Emily once more. And, of course, the crying immediately ceased. Just like that! Muttering darkly, I stomped up the corridor towards the nurses' station.

"Can you call security?" I asked the first nurse I could find.

"What's happened?" she asked.

"Nothing. Yet. I just want you to throw out my baby's father."

"He's worse than your mother?" asked another nurse, who had obviously already encountered Sheila Jensen. "I'll see what we can do."

When I returned to the room, Donald and my mother were staring at Emily, who was now in her grandmother's arms and, to my relief, loudly whimpering.

"No. I'd say she has her father's eyes," said the man somewhat bafflingly. Before Sheila Jensen could interrogate him on his source for this information, I was back in the room and a bawling baby was in my inadequate arms once again.

"Sorry. All out of tea. NHS cuts. Mother – time to go."

"Aren't you going to try feeding Emily again?" she asked above the plaintive and now somewhat relentless wails. "She looks so undernourished."

"She's just come out a sodding incubator!" I protested. "And I am *not* going to feed my newborn daughter in front of *him!*"

My mother just shook her rigid-haired head. "Darling, it's just your boob, for pity's sake. I'm sure it's nothing he hasn't seen before."

"Oh, you're so right there, Sheila," said the awful man, predictably. "On you go, Mizz Jensen. Fire away."

Instead of the justifiable anger you might have expected, I suddenly found myself feeling uncomfortable for all the wrong reasons.

"Actually," I admitted, a bit sheepishly, "I... can't. I'm having a bit of trouble producing milk. At the moment." I stared at them. "They say it might be because of stress."

Of course this went way over my mother's head, but the Sanderson person did appear to take it onboard, or as much as his most probably alcohol-addled brain might have allowed.

"Well, you wanted to go it alone, dear," ranted my mother, with a series of dramatic sighs. "I mean, men are bastards, granted – but they're better than nothing." She turned to fake-doctor with a final sigh that lasted the entire length of her next sentence. "Now, I know it's not your place to judge, Doctor…"

"Oh, I wouldn't say that," said the man.

"But do you truly honestly think it's healthy for a baby to be brought up by a practically forty-year-old single mother without proper job security?"

I tried to interrupt but I might as well have attempted to send the rolling waves that were happily sloshing away not far from here right back to where they came from.

"Especially one who goes out and gets herself – well, in the family way. By some gigolo she barely even knows!"

The bugger actually went and smiled! Donald, I mean – my mum was too demonstrably shocked and appalled to allow mirth into the equation. I felt myself tumbling even further into a hell predominantly of my own making.

"Well, funny you should say that, Mrs Jensen…"

Oh God, I thought, *here it comes. The big third act reveal. Gasps all round.*

"Because I really think that's Francesca's business. Don't you?"

I heard a very loud '*EH?*' then I realised that it was coming from me. My mother was rather more restrained.

"Well, yes, Doctor. But I'm her mother."

"The likeness is unmistakable. But I'm her gynaecologist."

"Obstetrician," I reminded him.

"*And* obstetrician. So it's my job to see that Mizz Jensen and the nipper… kid… infant are, y'know…" He glanced swiftly at me.

"Thriving," I suggested.

"Yes, thriving. And there's nothing sadder and worse for society than a child who has never throved. Thriven."

My mother managed to utter a still semi-defiant, "Well, yes, but…"

Donald went and sat down next to her on the bed. He gently took her be-ringed hand and she made no move to withdraw it.

"You see… Sheila," he said in his best bedside manner (and the man was, of course, no stranger to bedsides), "if a nursing mother is made to feel nervous, and tense and anxious, well – medically speaking – it's like the milkman's had a blow-out on the A258 and his best customer can't get their gold top."

"Medically speaking?"

"Yeah. And what we've got here is… a clapped-out old milk-float. I mean, look at her."

"Yes, okay, Doctor," I said. "Point taken."

"You can't be suggesting it's me," protested my mother. "I only just got here."

My 'obstetrician' shook his bushy head. "Oh it's not *just* you, Sheila, it's all that awful publicity as well. After she quite literally burst onto our TV screens."

I started to moan.

"And then there's her attitude problem."

Of course, my mum nodded vigorously to *that*.

"So, I think the best thing we can do for your bonnie new granddaughter is to leave poor old Francesca here alone. You know, just 'til little Emily gets settled."

He began very gently to usher my befuddled mum out of her chair and towards the curtain.

"Alright," said Mother, more docile than I believe I had ever seen her. "If it's your medical opinion?"

Donald nodded and I confessed I almost smiled in what could easily be taken as some modicum of gratitude. Until the woman looked up into the man's beaming face.

"And you'll send me a copy of those photos?"

"Photos?" I said.

"Oops! Is that my pager?" said the guilty party. "Or are you just pleased not to see me? Bye, Emily, sweetheart."

And with that he was gone.

"*WHAT PHOTOS?*" I asked. Well, yelled.

"Oh." My mum smiled, picking up her handbag. "The lovely

doctor wanted me to take a photo on his phone of him with Emily. Isn't that nice? To remember his little patient by. She was so calm in his arms. I took at least three. He's going to email me the best one."

"No need," I groaned helplessly. "Just buy tomorrow's *Sun*."

*

RANDOM JOTTINGS FOR 'UNDER THE MOON' (WORKING TITLE) BY MEGAN PEABODY

They avoid photographers by leaving the hospital via a side entrance.

(Or maybe better – there's a dramatic chase and Morgan's incredibly adept driving round the town's dingy back streets totally saves the day.)

EXT. FLAMINIA'S BLOCK OF FLATS. DAY

Morgan's nippy but stylish sports car pulls up outside the modern seafront block. She tentatively but lovingly helps Flaminia and Emma in with their luggage. Then winces.

MORGAN
Er, what's that smell?

Flaminia stands in her outer doorway, *daunted* but resolute. A shiver runs through her.

FLAMINIA
What do you bloody think it is? Looks like we
managed to avoid the photographers. That's
something. Although, of course, there's still…

                              MORGAN

Cambridge Don! Well, he did get your ghastly mother
off your back. Oh and at least his baby snaps haven't
been printed yet. My guess – he's saving it for the Sundays.
They probably pay more.
                    (on Flaminia's sigh)
Do you want me to come in, lovey?

                             FLAMINIA

Yes. But no. It'll only be so much worse
when you have to leave. I resolved to do this
on my own, Morg. My own is now.

                              MORGAN
        You don't have to be a martyr, you know.

                             FLAMINIA

What *are* you on about? Single mums do this
all the time.

            INT. FLAMINIA'S FLAT. MOMENTS LATER.

The door opens, pushing back a load of junk mail. Flaminia
comes through the door, carrying Emma. She stops.
    We pull back to show the eerily quiet, pristine minimalism
of Flaminia's world. The occasional movie poster – a colour-
coded assortment of books.

                             FLAMINIA
        Well, Emma. Here we are. Home at last, eh?
        So, what do you think?

Emma starts to bawl. Flaminia just stands there. Alone. Then
moves on.

                                63

INT. FLAMINIA'S FLAT. EMMA'S ROOM – MOMENTS LATER

Flam brings Emma into her new room – freshly decorated with Postman Pat wallpaper. Yet still somehow a tad soulless.

> FLAMINIA
> And this is *your* room, Emma! Yes, it is.
> Look – it's Postman Pat!
> (sings)
> *Postman Pat, Postman Pat…*
> (floundering)
> *With his little… hat… cat… something.*

Emma bawls even louder. Flaminia looks like she might be about to follow suit. But she takes a deep breath – chin up, Flam.

DISSOLVE TO:

EXT. FLAMINIA'S FLAT. THE EARLY HOURS.

A single light is left on in the flat. From inside, we hear Emma crying.

INT. FLAMINIA'S FLAT – THAT MOMENT

Flaminia is desperately trying to feed Emma.

> FLAMINIA
> Oh come on, please love.
> (sigh)
> What was that about God and plans?
> (concernedly)
> And you're not the only thing Mummy's got to

worry about now, are you? No, you're not. Thanks to your bell-end of a father. Who no doubt is already happily back in Cambridge, pissing away whatever blood money the Sundays just paid the feckless bastard. I only hope that you have more – feck.

INT. FLAMINIA'S FLAT. MORNING.

A new day.

The doorbell rings. Flaminia appears. She's wearing a dressing-gown flecked with baby sick and she looks like death. She opens the door to a beaming, radiant Morgan, holding a large plastic bag.

MORGAN
Morning, munchkin! Sleep well?

Flaminia scowls at her. Morgan recoils from her pal, and from the nappy-basket that her pal is holding.

FLAMINIA
What?!
(checks dressing-gown)
Oh, yeah. Like it? Fresh from the Stella McCartney 'vomit' collection.
(As Morgan stares at her)
It's the first day, Morgan! Did you get them?

Morgan holds up the plastic bag – filled with newspapers.

MORGAN
I haven't checked them yet. Exciting, isn't it?

Flaminia just SNATCHES the papers. And hands Morgan the nappy-basket. Yuchh!

65

DISSOLVE TO:

INT. FLAMINIA'S FLAT – MOMENTS LATER

Flam and Morgan have the tabloids spread on the table in front of them. They're PORING over them. Flaminia frantically. Emma is with her, grizzling as usual.

FLAMINIA
(flicking through papers)
Where is it? It's not here… or here. *Must be somewhere!* Morg, will you *stop* reading them and start *checking* them!

MORGAN
It's not in *The Sun. Express* neither. Or the *Mail. Sunday People*? No – nothing.
(holding up *Daily Star Sunday*)
But ooh – Elvis has been found in Tibet.

A look from her friend silences her. Flaminia stares at the ravaged papers – confused.

Emma starts to BAWL.

MORGAN
Is she going to do this all the time?

*

A TELEPHONE CALL FROM DONALD SANDERSON TO SAMARITANS.

A volunteer in one of the centres picks up the phone.

ALICE: Hello, Samaritans. Can I help you?

DON: Oh hi. Is that Samaritans – oh, right, you said it was. Okay if I talk to you? Sorry, I'm not – y'know, suicidal. Or anything.

ALICE: It's okay. Don't be sorry. I'm Alice.

DON: Don. My name's Don. You don't need second names, do you – Alice? Nice name.

ALICE: Thank you. Don't even need first names. This is your call. (*silence*) Is there something you'd like to talk about, Don?

DON: Oh, yeah. I've never phoned you before. Or anyone like you. Not even when my ex-wife pissed off to New Zealand with our kid. Bloody double-glazing!

ALICE: Oh. I'm sorry... double...?

DON: Doesn't matter. But I've bored my best mate Cliff senseless. Can't bother him anymore, can I? Not if we want to stay... think he's pretty glad I moved down here. Ha.

ALICE: So – where's 'down here'?

DON: Oh, aren't you local? To the Kent Coast, I mean?

ALICE: No. It's a national service. I'm actually in Gloucester. So—

DON: Ever get down this way at all?

ALICE: This call isn't really about me, is it, Don? Where did you move down from?

DON: Cambridge. I'm a Cambridge Don.

ALICE: Uh huh... oh, right. Ha – I get it. And is it the move that you're finding difficult? Sometimes it can be. New place, new people.

DON: No. Not really. The people are very friendly. The sea's – cool. Well, bloody freezing actually. Ha! I'm doing my bar work, like I did back home. And making my adult interconnecting gnomes.

ALICE: Your...? Okay. So what's really troubling you, Don?

DON: Well Alice, this is going to sound a bit weird.

ALICE: I'm okay with weird. This is a safe place.

DON: I'm not talking kinky weird, love. Don't worry. But do you remember about six months ago there was this woman who nearly had her baby on a local TV arts programme? Well, local to here. Where I am now. While she was doing a sort of interview with her posh pal.

ALICE: Oh, yes, do you know, Don, I think I do. Her waters broke on air, poor lamb. The clip went viral, didn't it? And all the papers picked it up. I felt so sorry for her. They were on about it for days. I hope everything was alright.

DON: A few hiccups but yes, the baby's fine. I think. I hope. The mum's a bit tricky, but hey – you can't pick your parents.

ALICE: Indeed. Sorry, Don, what's this got to do—

DON: With our chat? This *is* confidential, Alice?

ALICE: Yes, Don, it is. You can talk as freely as you wish. And no one is going to judge you.

DON: Well, I'm the father. (*silence*). Hello – Alice?

ALICE: …You're the father – of that baby who nearly got born on TV?

DON: Yeah. Not on purpose, you know. The fathering I mean. The mum – well, she used me to get herself pregnant. Can you believe that? I only found out 'cos of that telly business. I did get to hold her once, Alice. The baby, that is. Little Emily. Just the once. (*A sigh then silence.*)

ALICE: Don? Are you still there?

DON: Mm? Oh, sorry. Yeah. And now – well, now she doesn't want nothing to do with me. The mum, I mean. The kid too, I suppose.

ALICE: Oh. Oh dear. And tell me, Don, is this why you moved down? To Kent.

DON: You're very good. Did you know that, Alice? A good Samaritan – ha!

ALICE: Thank you. So…?

DON: Yeah. This is why I – like you said. Moved here. To be nearer my kid. Emily Jane. 'Course, it's not like I was consulted on the name, but could've been worse. Y'know, like Clarissa. Or Bethany. Alice would've been nice.

ALICE: Okay. And how's that working out for you? The moving down, I mean.

DON: It sort of isn't, Alice. Not really. See, the woman made it clear at the hospital that she doesn't want me in her life. In *their* lives. I think I just make her nervous. Like I'm a stalker or something. Or maybe she's scared I'll blurt it all out, y'know, to the press – and embarrass her folks and her friends. And the people she works with. Students and professors and that.

ALICE: And that's not something—

DON: Sorry, Alice, love, I've just got to talk. Ta. See, I reckon she's basically shit-scared I'll tell the world she pulled a boozy one-nighter with a bit of Cambridge rough and got herself up the – you know. Well, I mean, that's no good for her daughter, is it? *Our* daughter. Having a stressed-out, angry mum. An *even more* than usually stressed-out, angry mum. That ain't gonna help with the feeding and the bonding. And the – what do you call it? – the thriving. So I've made sure I've kept well out of her way. *Their* way.

ALICE: It's lovely that you're putting your daughter's interests – *and* her mum's – so far ahead of your own. You sound like a good dad. But Don, can I ask you something?

DON: 'course – Alice?

ALICE: If you're not trying to see your little daughter, why did you bother to move all the way down there?

DON: Well, it's obvious, isn't it?

ALICE: Er…?

DON: In case my daughter, Emily, wants to get in touch with me.
ALICE: Uh huh. How old is Emily again?

DON: Six months, two days and four hours. I think I'd better go now. Evening shift coming up. Thanks for listening, Alice.

ALICE: You're, er, welcome, Don. We're here.

The caller ended the call.

EMILY JANE JENSEN'S STORY

*B*et you didn't think you'd hear from me in this tale. Even though I'm definitely the most important person in it.

But I'm still not very old.

So, don't expect some of the flowery stuff like you've just been reading. Especially not like Aunty Megan's silly film script. *Flaminia! Morgan! Emma!* (If that ever gets made, I'm sure not going to see it and I hope none of my friends will either. And Aunty M will be dead by that time, because my mum will have killed her.)

Yet I am old enough to understand things that I'm not really supposed to hear. And sharp enough to work out stuff I wouldn't be expected to put together. Because, even though I say so myself, and I'm only repeating what my mum tells me now and then, "Emily Jane Jensen, you are a bright little button. Too bright for your own good, sometimes."

But it's not brightness I'm talking about right now. It's something far weirder. Spookier even. And if you asked someone a whole lot older (and maybe even brighter) than me to try to explain it, I'd bet you a whole month's pocket money and my new ninety-six-piece junior make-up set that they couldn't.

Not for one single moment.

They say you can't remember things that happened to you before you were about two years old. Well, maybe that's true. So perhaps I'm just remembering what I've been told since.

(Although I'm pretty certain that somewhere in your body you store up your most important feelings and memories, even if you can't yet put them into English. Or whatever language you speak.)

So, just tell me – since you're probably quite a lot older than I am – *how on earth do you bloody explain this?* Pardon my French, as my grannie says. (She's a story all on her own, my grannie. Grandpa is fun though, and so is his new wife, who's a whole lot younger and prettier than his last one.)

What happened was, one blowy and fairly drizzly Sunday afternoon, when I was still quite little and had not long been shifted up from my pram to my pushchair, my mum decided to take me for a walk.

Nothing unusual in this. She took me on a lot of walks. 'Promenades', she called them. Especially by the sea. Sometimes she took me for a promenade in the middle of the night, which wasn't the most fun. I think the movement of the pram helped to stop me crying. Apparently, I was a pretty grizzly baby. Although, if you ask me, I'd say at times she was a pretty grizzly mum.

I can't say I blame her. Not really. She was all on her own, in her forties, trying to do a really tricky job as best she could from home. A few tricky jobs, including parenting me. Of course, she was on what they call maternity leave but she still had to write her articles and do her film reviews, didn't she? To make ends meet. Especially as she was now supporting two people. Even if one of them was pretty tiny.

This maternity leave thing doesn't last forever, although maternity apparently does. So she had to think pretty fast of something to do with me, like a nice crèche or a good daytime nanny or something.

She did try out a few nannies – well, more than a few – but first of all, they are expensive. I mean *really* expensive. Second of all, none of them met Mummy's standards or expectations, which are pretty high. Like the moon or something. And thirdly and maybe most importantly of all, these ladies really didn't take to my mum. They simply couldn't stand her. (She is quite a tricky person. Kindly, but to be honest, a bit of a control freak and awfully fussy. They say it can come from being on your own too long, but what do I know?)

Now that I think about it, there was also a fourthly.

Fourthly – each time one of these possible nannies picked me up, I would start to cry like there was no tomorrow. Bawled my little head off – screamed and screamed until I was practically blue and breathless. I think that bit brought back bad memories for Mum of what happened to me in that hospital, you know, when I swallowed my very first poo. I don't really want to talk about that. I mean, would you? But I clearly wasn't happy in someone else's arms. (Not that I was one hundred per cent full of the joys of spring in the arms of the woman who gave birth to me! I was a very teary tot.)

So, Mummy was getting just a wee bit desperate when we went for that particular damp Sunday promenade.

I do think she was looking forward to being back at the university, with persons her own age, who she could talk to about films and life and nipple rash and stuff. And spending quality time with young people who didn't wet themselves. (Or at least not too often.) She really is, from all I've heard, a pretty good teacher. Although I'm not sure how great that has been for me growing up. While other kids were watching *Teletubbies* or *Thomas the Tank Engine*, I was having to sit through *Citizen Kane* and *Rashomon*. With running commentary.

I'm still not sure why on that particular miserable Sunday afternoon she decided to veer away from our usual route. Perhaps she felt that it was too breezy for me to be beside the sea, what with the rain just starting to get serious. Or maybe she just fancied a change.

I can't say that I minded much, because I could tell somehow, even through the blurry rain cover, that this was a different part of town. Mum knew that I could sense this because, as she told me later, my little head was whizzing around in all directions, like something out of a film called *The Exorcist*, which thankfully I haven't caught yet, although it could be nearly time. It was as if I was almost totally overwhelmed by all the new things I could see.

To be fair, at that age, a different type of dog poo on the ground or a used cigar butt could be the most fascinating things in the world, so I was hardly seeking out material for an updated tourist guide to Kent's most beautiful coastal towns.

But then the rain got so bad that I began to scream. At least, this is why my mum firmly believed I was screaming. But here's the spooky bit. I really don't think it was the rain at all, nasty and noisy as it was. I truly believe I was screaming because I wanted to go to the pub.

The pub?!

"Do you want to go into the pub, Em?" said my mum, with a tickled little laugh, as if this was the very last thing a wee girl in her pushchair would even be contemplating.

But I simply kept on crying, the gush of my tears almost matching the force of the rain that was by now tipping down on us.

"Well, alright," continued my mum, "but if I hear someone shout, '*Hello again, Em, a pint of your usual?*' there will be words, young lady."

Parents do this a lot. Say things to their children the kids can't possibly understand but it gives the grown-ups a big laugh. You just have to accept it.

All I knew, at that rainy moment, was for some weird, unexplainable reason I needed quite desperately to pop inside this quite ordinary-looking pub, in a fairly run-down part of town. I can still remember that feeling, somewhere. I'm sure I can. And I was going to yell my tiny tonsils out and fog up my rain cover until we did so.

"It's pretty miserable out here and it looks so cosy in there, doesn't it?" agreed my weary mother. "And Mummy could do with a little drink and getting off her feet."

And so she manoeuvred us both through the small doorway into the embracing warmth and chatter.

I immediately stopped crying.

All at once.

Instantly.

Instantaneously.

(I read quite a lot now. I know a lot of words.)

I could tell that my mummy was quite surprised by this sudden, unexpected silence from me, but also, of course, very much relieved. She hadn't really wished to spoil all the other customers' peaceful afternoon with a screaming, red-faced infant in a rain-soaked pushchair.

Of course, she simply assumed my 'drying-up' was all because we had escaped that awful rain and were now in a really cozy and comforting, beer-scented room. It even had a roaring fire behind a heavy metal grill.

So she happily parked me beside a tiny table and went to the bar to buy herself a drink. (I don't think she's what people would call a heavy drinker, but I did see her quite often, when she was really tired and feeling just a bit sad and alone, reaching for the white wine. Of course, I just assumed all grown-ups did this and it was simply their variety of milk.)

It was when the barman turned round from taking a gold coloured drink off the wrong-way-up bottles on the back wall that I heard my mummy scream.

It wasn't the loudest scream, as screams go, but babies always recognise their own mum's cry and whilst this one had a slightly higher pitch than normal, it was definitely her.

Of course, I didn't pick up their conversation then – I was just basking in this new but incredibly nurturing feeling that I couldn't quite understand – but I can piece it all together now that I'm into double figures and apparently more precocious.

"*What are YOU doing here?!*" yelped my mum.

"Hello, Francesca," said my dad, who didn't seem quite as surprised by the meeting as Mum was. But then, of course, he already knew that he had moved all the way down here. And to be honest, he had that – well – special frame of mind.

"*Are you STALKING me?*" she said.

"You mean by walking into the pub where you work? Oh no, sorry, that was you."

"*I don't believe this!*" she said, shaking her head. She has lovely red hair which it doesn't look I'm going to inherit any time soon. Mind you, my dad has a really nice healthy clump of brunette that seems to have been passed directly down the line, without as yet the little silvery bits.

Mum was clearly about to say a whole lot more when she noticed that my dad's eyes weren't on her furious face any longer but staring right over her head. And directly down onto my pushchair.

"Is that…?" he said softly, his face lighting up and his eyes glistening, almost as if he'd seen Baby Jesus himself gurgling happily beneath the collection of horse brasses and old farming implements.

"No, I just had to pop out another one because the first birth was such fun," snarled my mother.

But when she followed the direction of his big, brown, teary eyes and caught me gazing straight back at the huge man with my little blue ones, staring at him in a way she had never noticed me looking at anyone in my short life, perhaps not even her, she found herself lost for words.

And when I began to smile, a big drooly kind of adorable smile, all she could do was just watch this silent but meaningful exchange with her own slightly dryer mouth wide open.

"Can I – can I just go over there and say hello to her?" my dad asked, very meekly. "*Please*, Francesca?"

My mum, of course, was all for wheeling me well away from

the lovely fire and straight out into the pissy rain (pardon my French!) once more. But then she saw them, pinned up behind the bar.

The *photos* of baby me with my dad. You know, the ones my grannie took back at the hospital.

The ones that had never been anywhere near a daily or a Sunday newspaper.

"Oh, I *suppose* so." She sighed, softening just a tiny fraction. "And then maybe you can tell me why the hell you're down here in Kent. In *my* town."

"I can tell you now," said my dad, moving out from behind the bar. "I'm here for this."

My mum just shook her head. "*This*?" She raised her voice, as she backed away from the bar towards me once more. "What the *fuck* is THIS?"

I started to cry. Not just cry. I bellowed. Not just bellowed. I bawled. I blasted. I boomed. Even when my mummy picked me up out of my pushchair, the ear-splitting cries didn't stop.

That was when my dad held out his arms.

Mum couldn't decide whether she wanted to offload me onto this 'peasant' (as she had called him) or hold onto me even tighter. Not that she could hold me that much tighter, at least not without cutting off my breath entirely.

By now, the whole pub was staring. They all seemed to know my dad and had possibly even been told about the pictures behind the bar.

Finally, with yet another of her long and meaningful sighs, Mum set me gently down into my father's massive (well, massive to me), pint-pulling, gnome-carving arms. As he held me so close to his chest, and that special feeling came shooting back into me – you know, the one my little body must have stored-up most of my life-so-far as the most magical of memories – the crying immediately stopped.

Yet the silence, blissful as it must have been for all concerned, only lasted a moment, as it was followed very swiftly by applause from what seemed like the entire pub.

"Oh, for pity's sake!" groaned my mum.

I knew she was seriously rattled. Bothered that what had happened months earlier in the hospital, when my dad first held me, seemed to happening all over again. *In a pub of all places!*

You're right – I couldn't, of course, have remembered the details of when my father picked me up for the very first time. Hey, I was only a few days old. But don't try to tell me my tiny little body didn't recall the feeling – and the comfort – and that familiar, wonderful smell. Of somebody who was such a big part of me, and I was a whole load of them.

But just then I must have realised, felt it somewhere way down deep inside, that from this moment on it was all up to me.

My entire future.

"Okay," said my mum, a bit sharply, "you've had your little cuddle—"

"Still having," said my dad, nuzzling.

"Okay, well, when you've *had* your little cuddle, you can pop happily and speedily back to Cambridge or Beirut or the seventh circle of Hell, in the full and certain knowledge that Emily Jane *Jensen* is all well and bonnie and thriving and your highly questionable genes are being offset by some truly excellent nurture."

"So," asked my dad, totally ignoring what my mum had said, "are you going back to work, Francesca?"

"Not that it's any business of yours," my mum sighed, "but I *have* been working. From home. Very hard, actually. I'll go back to my teaching—"

"Movies and stuff."

"*Film Studies* – just as soon as I can sort out…" She paused for a moment. Too much information. "Anyway, it's all in hand. Going swimmingly. Now, can I have my child back please?"

With a total lack of enthusiasm, like someone handing over a ransom or an overdue library book, my dad slowly started to pass me back to Mummy.

Okay – now or never.

My very last chance.

All or nothing.

I began to *scream.*

And scream. And scream.

No warning. No starter sobs. No wimpy whimpers. The full thing.

I didn't even wait until the handover was complete. I just shrieked and howled until my little face turned blue all over again.

I had already begun what I think is called hyperventilating when I was still in mid-air!

Without thinking, in a sort of reflex she really would prefer she didn't have, my mum thrust me straight back into my father's still-outstretched arms. She tried to look defiant but all she really looked was defeated.

"Okay, just a few seconds more," she conceded.

Looking back on it now, with a certain maturity, I can really feel for my poor mum. She does all the hard work, puts in the hours, devotes almost her entire waking and barely sleeping life to her grizzly little daughter and the only person who can stop the crying just like that is the one person in the whole world the poor woman wouldn't wish to be seen dead with.

Then my dad said something that suddenly came to him, and he really didn't know from where. Maybe he read my mum's mind but that would be just too spooky for words. Yet, like the man himself, I do believe in magic and destiny and all weird stuff like that. I mean, isn't two people making a baby the most incredible magic in the world?

"Can't get a nanny, can you?"

Okay, so you can imagine my mum's reaction, can't you? A

man like this *daring* to say something like that, to a person like her, after all the history between them.

Well, you'd be wrong.

There was a comfy seat by the fire, just next to my empty pushchair, and my mum sank right back into it. I had seen her exhausted before. And frustrated. And exasperated. And really cross. But this was the first time I had seen her demolished.

We sat down beside her, at the little table. Dad with his long legs stretched out in front of him. Me, a tiny but now quite chilled Emily, nestled in his powerful, East Anglian arms.

That was when he said it. The words that would change my life.

"I usually only work here nights."

"So?" said my mum, although I think she already sort of guessed what he was getting at. She's pretty bright even if a bit tricky at times. Well, more than a bit.

"So – well… I could, y'know, look after her during the day. While you worked."

My mum just stared at him.

"*You have got to be f***ing kidding me!*" (Which wasn't even my grannie's French.)

"I'm really good with kids, Francesca. Ask my friend Cliff. Ask my sisters. Ask anyone. And you can see right now, I'm pretty bloody good with ours."

I gave an extra satisfied gurgle, because every little helps.

"*But – you're a man!*" spluttered my mum.

My dad smiled. "There's just no fooling you academic types. Didn't exactly bother you in Cambridge, did it?"

It could have just been the fire but I'm sure my tired but still lovely, flame-haired mother had begun to blush.

"And men can be nannies now, Francesca. They're called 'mannies'."

"Yes, I do know what they're bloody called! But they're not normally the father of the child."

81

"And that would be our secret. Barman's honour."

She rolled her eyes at that bit.

"Hey, I never sold those photos to the papers, did I, despite all your fears about me. And I'll take them down from the bar. None of your posh friends and family will ever know. About your bit of rough. They'll just think you've gone all woke and trendy."

After that he stopped talking and just stared at my mum. With those big brown eyes you could get lost in.

Mum gazed at him, holding me with such gentle love, and she saw clearly, if still reluctantly, a father and daughter already bonded. But I do also believe, as she looked across the table at him, that perhaps she was recalling just a bit of what she saw the very first time they met (even though he was putting on one hell of an act back then).

And I think she saw too the worn-out guy who was there at the hospital day after day, the 'act' all gone, determined and vulnerable and desperate with worry. The bloke who handled my grannie like an expert. The person who was already a devoted but desolate father, to some kid way off in New Zealand. My half-brother.

My dad and I waited, hardly breathing. Well, of course, I breathed, or I'd have gone blue again, but you know what I mean.

The wait seemed to last ages. It was only interrupted by one of the customers at the deserted bar.

"Any danger of us getting another pint, Don?"

"Be right with you, Harry," shouted my dad. Then he turned back to Mum, clearly wanting some sort of answer, even if it wasn't the one he most desired.

"One month," said my mum. "Just until I find someone."

My dad nodded, stood up and handed me back to my mum. And do you know what – I didn't cry once the whole rest of that afternoon.

Now, you're probably thinking my mum and dad finally got together and we're all living by now as one sweet, happy, slightly mismatched family.

Well, no. Not exactly.

But what I will say is that my dad's nanny/manny job has lasted way over a month. Or a year. Or a decade.

And my mum's doing really well at work. And with me.

I have two parents now. Even if they're not together so much of the time. Even if they go out or even stay in with other people now and then.

I think they kind of get on with each other. They might even respect each other. I'd go so far as to say that they're friends.

As for more than friends? Well, of this I can't really be certain.

But let's say I'm working on it. Hey, I've not done badly so far.

Two hopeful signs: my mum makes a mean Negroni. And my dad sort of likes *Citizen Kane*.

BETTER LATE

The crash came in the middle of the night. Although, of course, it's always 'the middle of the night' when something happens that is so shattering it awakens everyone around it in dark, swirling, switch-scrabbling panic.

Because they all knew that this was something beyond awful, something bound to happen, yet the one thing they hoped and prayed never would.

It began with a scream. For some the scream never ended.

DO I HEAR ONE?

*D*avid Ramsden is learning to speak Finnish.

There is no particular reason for him to do so; he has no intention of ever going there. The country, like the language, sounds particularly dark and cold and he prefers his holidays, if he ever bothers to take them, in places that don't disturb his equilibrium. Like Devon, or at least the northern part. Anyway, when you've lived in the Cotswolds for every one of your forty-four years, why would you wish to venture further afield?

He is learning Finnish to keep his brain active during the many car journeys he is compelled to take for work and as something to occupy his mind on his bracing morning strolls in the hills around Cheltenham. David isn't particularly fond of music, but neither is he comfortable with leaving his mind wholly disengaged, because he knows that such vacancies furnish opportunity for unsettling thoughts, premonitions of danger and hazard, to sneak in like mice through a rotten skirting board. You can't think of anything else when you're learning Finnish.

'Could you please speak more slowly?' says the amiable Fin on the cassette in his car. She is an old car, a Volvo, but she is safe and solid, and she knows the Gloucestershire roads by heart. '*Voisitko puhua hitaammin?*'

"*Voisitko puhua hitaammin?*" repeats David Ramsden quite accurately, realising that this is clearly a most useful phrase for a first-timer in, say, Helsinki, where he knows he will never be.

He is on a narrow country road near Winchcombe, a road he hasn't had cause to visit for a while but one which he rather likes, with its coil of sharp curves you have to take really slowly and fields in whose uncomplicated lushness you could really lose yourself, if you didn't have to keep your eyes fixed firmly on the road at all times.

So the bang comes as rather a surprise.

Something has smacked hard against his driver-side door, just as he is carefully rounding a particularly treacherous bend. David Ramsden halts immediately with an unpleasant screech and turns to look out of his window. He can see nothing save for a rather grim Victorian house on the corner, shrouded in laurel, with peeling windows and a 'For Sale' sign on its front lawn. It is, he realises, his final destination, and he wonders sadly if this might also be the case for whatever he has hit.

"Oh my God!" he yelps. Then adds, "*Hyvanen aika,*" priding himself on his foresight in having looked this up just the day before.

He repeats both phrases with mounting alarm as a small, wizened face suddenly rises up from the wheel end of his side window. The body attached to it is clearly hoisting itself painfully upwards, using his door handle for leverage. He has never seen this face before and, indeed, he has never seen a face like it, suffused as it is with what he can only suppose is terror in its most raw and primal form. A terror redolent, he senses immediately, of far more than simply banging into a slow-moving and very old Volvo.

"Are you *him*?" enquires the troubled face.

David notices that the voice, even through the closed window, is still remarkably strong. As he winds the window down, the elderly woman claws tightly onto its uppermost edge, until she realises that this is sending her in entirely the unintended direction, and she has to keep clambering back up to prevent herself from sinking into a small heap beside his front wheel.

"*Ramsden? Are you Mr Ramsden?*" She infuses the words with such frantic desperation that he would have offered an immediate 'yes' had he even been someone entirely different. He wonders for a brief moment how being different might feel but dismisses it in light of more pressing concerns, especially when she adds, "*Thank God you've come!*"

David Ramsden knows that auctioneers and house-clearers are not the most despised members of humanity, but only rarely are the heavens invoked to celebrate their arrival, so he can only wonder what else might be going on here. He tries to open the door, hoping that the woman will take this as a signal to rise and move away. When she glides round with it, light as a feather, he finds himself slipping swiftly out to support her, before she is crushed against the chassis like a tiny bird.

It is only when the old woman is safely – and, for him, embarrassingly – in his arms that she points back to the crumbling house behind her.

"You going in, then?" she asks, her feverish eyes searing into his own, as if this is more a challenge than an invitation. David courteously gestures 'after you', but a disturbingly violent shake of her wispy yet wild grey head dictates that he had better lead the way.

As he walks to her open door, David can't help thinking that the lady, clearly his new client, really is a very odd person. So he will probably not ask this Mrs Eileen Ballard of Winchcombe, Glos, why her house, on such a pleasant spring day, is so chillingly cold.

DO I HEAR TWO?

"*One Victorian burr walnut Sutherland table on turned underframe…*"

"Can't you go a bit faster!" says the old lady, who simply can't keep still.

David is too polite to say anything, but the woman's antics really are putting him off. She's like a senile squirrel that has found its way into a house but hasn't the brains, or is just too petrified, to find the safe route out. He wonders if, when he plays it back, the tape from his pocket Dictaphone will have picked up all the sighs, moans and tiny yelps emanating from the clearly troubled owner of the property in question.

"*Set of six Regency rose dining chairs, two with arms… very nice. Set of Charles and Diana ceremonial corgi cruets… not so nice.*" He turns to find Mrs Ballard almost up his backside. "Can't think why you'd want to leave this place, madam," he says, by way of conversation. "Getting too big for you, is it?"

He finds that it is this personal touch that has made the establishment for which he works so successful, even if it hasn't been over-keen to share the burgeoning success with its head auctioneer.

"*A most desirable period residence in traditional Cotswold stone,*" quotes its elderly owner quietly. "*In need of some repair and modernisation. Delightfully unkempt English country garden…*"

"Exactly!" agrees David. "So, why…?"

"*I sodding hate it!*" says the old lady, her frightened face crumbling even more.

"…Georgian mahogany chest of drawers…"

From somewhere outside they hear the roar of what sounds like a motorbike. The old lady suddenly utters a short but piercing scream and clings to an Edwardian standard lamp as if the house is buckling beneath her.

"It's only a— Is everything alright, Mrs Ballard?"

David Ramsden has a strong feeling that everything is light years from alright. For a moment it makes him think of his own dear mother, who is probably about ten years younger than the lady quivering beside him, but who also lives on her own and has her little foibles. Although, of course, she has her only son close by and most probably always will. Even a brief marriage, he thinks to himself, took him only one small suburb away.

He wonders if Mrs Ballard has anyone close and dependable like him, but she doesn't seem in the mood for conversation. And, to be honest, he would really like to put some distance between the two of them. She is making him nervous, and he hates to feel unsettled. He finds it quite – well, unsettling.

"Is there anything up in the loft?" he asks, praying for a negative response. Curiously, some of his colleagues love lofts, but as he tells them – rather wittily, he thinks – there's no love loft with him.

He turns to catch the old lady in a wide-eyed stare, as if he has asked her whether she is still sexually active and happy to frolic. Finally, she nods far more rabidly than required.

"Would you care to show me?" he asks.

The nods, which hadn't yet fully stopped, convert immediately to head-shakes of equal vehemence. He wouldn't be surprised if the rabid thing fell off and rolled bloodily across the fading Axminster. But head intact, she simply points up the stairs, waving a bony arm skywards, and retreats into the kitchen, still shaking.

"*Old woman, late 1930s. Demented.*"

DO I HEAR THREE?

A *t least I can be on my own up here*, thinks David Ramsden, as he climbs up the potentially lethal wooden steps into the darkened Ballard loft.

He does wonder sometimes whether it's totally healthy to be on his own quite so much, but he assures himself that fortunately he has those rollicking times back in the auction house with his colleagues and their constant banter, some of which he actually understands. Then there are the auctions themselves, of course, and most of all, his long-widowed mum. His life is really so full.

A shower of dislodged wood shavings falls into his eye as he scrabbles for a light switch. He finally discovers it but there's either no bulb in place or the current resident has served its time. He's accustomed to this, which is why he never goes anywhere without his rechargeable torch. Switching it on, as he heaves himself up into a dim chamber that is even icier than the rooms below, he realises fairly swiftly that, like most lofts in his experience, it is not exactly an auctioneer's Shangri-La.

Trying not to rest his arms or legs on anything that might be concealing a rotting floorboard, he manages to make purchase on timber that feels reasonably sound. But, of course, you never really know. The hospitals are full of auctioneers who haven't paid due care and attention. At least, this is what his concerned mother has been telling him since he first began as a trainee in this most hazardous of professions.

David does occasionally wonder what occupations or activities the woman doesn't actually regard as fraught. He recalls her being the only mum amongst his classmates who wrote his teacher a 'please excuse' note for choir practice because of the potential damage to his larynx.

He begins his tentative foray into the semi-darkness.

The auctioneer assumes that the near-Arctic chill that is making him shiver beneath his ageing but still functional, leather-elbowed Dunn & Co jacket must be the wind seeping through what have to be pretty large gaps in the roof tiles. The dust motes swirling in the beam of his torch seem like a swarm of flying ants.

As he guides the trusty tool of his trade in narrow then ever more expansive circles, he spies several items of varying size, wrapped in old, yellowing sheets of newspaper. David knows that he will have to rummage through all of these parcels in due course but he's truly not expecting much.

This is not to say that treasures aren't occasionally found – these are the stuff of auctioneers' dreams, and indeed of anecdotes when they get together after another gruelling day at the coalface. Yet, spotting an early but highly distressed gramophone and a rusty three-wheeled pram, his hopes aren't terribly high. He realises after a few minutes that he should be inventory-ing into his machine and wonders why the old lady downstairs has unsettled him so much.

"*One child's buggy – broken. One vacuum cleaner – obsolete. Not exactly Tutankhamen's tomb…* don't type that bit, Avril. *One battered— AAAAGGGHH!*"

David recoils with a start, sending the torch beam whirling madly around the loft like a manic mirrorball in a deserted ballroom, as he glimpses a shadowy figure in the gloom.

He soon offers the machine and the universe a self-deprecating laugh.

"*One tailor's dummy!*" He shakes his head – that's definitely one for the lads. The old lady really has managed to put the wind up him. It strikes him, in a rare moment of self-perception, that this might not in truth be the most onerous of tasks.

"*Hello, Davey.*"

This time he freezes.

No frenetic torch beam. Not even a gasp. The instantly petrified auctioneer dares not turn round. He cannot bring himself to face the direction from which he senses that this greeting – if greeting it was – has emanated.

Finally, after several seconds glued to the unstable floorboards, he manages to send a few ragged words into the chill yet musty air.

"Who's-who's there? How do you know my name? Which is *David*, actually."

With a chuckle, the voice continues. David recognises a Gloucestershire accent, such as he himself has, only far more pronounced and distinctly younger.

"You wouldn't believe me if I told you."

With what feels like a massive effort, David Ramsden forces himself to turn very slowly around.

He sees a once-elegant, early Victorian chaise longue that has clearly fallen on hard and lumpy times. On it reclines a shadowy yet clearly languid figure. The rattled auctioneer can make out unfashionably long dark hair and what could be the glint of leather. And teeth which seem unusually white.

"I warn you," says David, "I'm a green belt in karate."

"You're an auctioneer at that lardy Harbottle and Webb."

"I could be both," challenges the auctioneer, before wondering how the younger man knows this – and what on earth 'lardy' means.

"Well, are you both?"

"No. Who *are* you?"

For the first time, David allows his torch to shine fully onto the figure.

The beam trembles along with his hand, but still manages to illuminate a striking young man, rather pale, who he reckons can't be more than twenty-one. David wonders why this particular number occurs to him – why not twenty or twenty-two? – but he doesn't linger on it, as he is too taken with how singularly mesmerising this figure is. With his roguishly blue eyes that seem to play with whatever light is available, two-day growth and tall, Brylcreemed quiff, he looks like a Cotswold James Dean, especially clad in his tight denims and a leather, bike-boy jacket, with the insignia of the 59 Club on his shoulder, whatever the hell that means.

There's a cocky bravado here, in the way the younger man is smiling directly upwards through the quivering torch beam at a bemused David. Yet curiously, despite this, he is looking almost as stunned and fearful as the older man currently gawping down at him.

"That's better," says the reclining man, sitting up for a clearer view. "I've been waiting for this, Davey." To David's surprise, the man's smile instantly fades, to be replaced with a desperate sadness that seems quite at odds with the youthfulness of his face. "I've been waiting for forty-four years."

David shakes his head. He knows now why this man is kept in the loft. It's for his own protection – the poor fellow has what they would call these days 'learning difficulties'. No wonder old Mrs Ballard appeared so disturbed.

"Forty-four?" repeats David. "Sorry, but you can't be more than – what? – twenty-one." That number again. "I can get you help. I know a first-class consultant in Tewkesbury." David turns to go – he has to proceed with his task. "He collects Georgian trephines – they used them for drilling holes in the skull. Not that I'm suggesting—"

The young man's laugh stops him. "You look so like your mummy."

David turns back. This is getting creepy, and he doesn't do creepy.

"How on earth do you know what my mum – my mother – looks like?"

"'Cos I married her," explains the young man. "I'm your dad."

DO I HEAR FOUR?

"*I*n for four, out for seven…"

David and the curious young man, who moments earlier had caused his older visitor to hyperventilate and almost pass out, are now to be discovered sitting side by side on the faded chaise longue, alongside the broken gramophone. David's head is practically inside the gaping mouth of the machine's brass horn, which is the closest thing to a paper-bag his helper could think of in the spur of the moment.

"What if you just breathed in and out without counting?" suggests the young man, whose name, if he really is who he says he is, which of course David knows is impossible, would be Rick. Rick Ramsden. The very late Rick Ramsden.

"I've been breathing in and out for longer than you have," echoes David from inside the gramophone. "In for four…" He shakes his head vigorously in disbelief then decides this might be less painful were he to remove himself completely from the vintage metal container. "No. This isn't real. I'm just exhausted, that's all," he tells himself. "You can't work at the cutting edge of Gloucestershire auctioneering without having the occasional meltdown."

He senses the young man beside him stand up, although strangely he feels no change in the distribution of the lump-ridden furniture on which they're both currently sitting. But the curious fellow is now laughing fit to bust.

"What's so funny?" asks the auctioneer.

"I was pulling your leg, sunshine! Bit cruel, I know. Using your poor dad like that. I'm just the old lady's son, Terry Ballard. Gave you a scare, eh? Woooohhhh! But you gotta learn to cool it, man. Life is too short."

David is beyond relieved. So much so that he even laughs with his new and clearly deranged acquaintance, something he is not given to doing on a regular basis.

"Oh, right," he says. "I don't know why you would do that, but never let it be said David Ramsden can't take a joke, eh?"

Rick holds out his hand and David reaches out gratefully to clasp it.

He starts to realise his error as his fingers discover that they're gripping nothing other than air. His fears confirm themselves when his body falls straight through that of the younger man and lands on the dusty floor, just missing a broken dolls' house. He immediately smacks his head on a stretch of rotting wood.

Noticing a small knothole in the crumbly floorboard, David realises that he can see right down into the small bedroom below.

Through the pain, he can hear elated laughter from behind him that verges on the demonic.

"*That was brilliant!*" exults Rick. "Did you see that? Splat! Right on my old whispering-hole! First laugh your old man's had since 1980."

David, who is also hysterical but not in a good way, picks himself up and immediately bangs his head on an unexpectedly low cross-beam. This time his deceased father doesn't laugh but seems genuinely concerned.

"Ow!" empathises the young and spectral figure. "Davey! You okay? You know what works on bumps? – dab of butter. Your poor mum taught me that. What a worrier that woman was."

"Still is," mutters David through the pain, which causes his young dad to smile and sigh.

Even the older chap – his son – can't help but recognise that beneath the sadness in this 'person', there is clearly some palpable relief here. The woman who had been made a widow so very prematurely is clearly still around.

For a moment, Rick Ramsden appears quite still, lost perhaps in the memory of an age gone by, when his world was young and ripe with time and possibilities. So it is a few moments before he realises that David has backed away towards the rickety staircase that leads down to relative sanity.

"NO! Don't go," pleads the dad. "Davey – *please*. We've only just met!"

Whilst lunacy is not an atmosphere in which he especially thrives, David finds himself halted mid-retreat by the tearful break in the young man's voice. Perhaps he will stay just a few more moments and then, of course, try to forget that this ever happened. Because, as he tells himself, he has quite sufficient going on in his life, without the surreal or the paranormal.

A thought occurs to him, one of many he supposes might reasonably flood in when confronted with your barely post-pubescent, long-dead father, whom you've never actually met in your entire life.

"How did… how did you…" He finds he can't quite get the words to form.

"How did I know it was you?"

David just nods.

Rick wanders over to another part of the loft, gesturing for David to follow with his torch. The young man pauses and indicates with a bony finger a large bundle on the floor, wrapped in fading newspaper. David recognises the wrapping as a rather old inside-spread from the regional weekly.

"Read it in the local rag, didn't I?" says Rick, with an enthusiasm that could only be described as boyish. "It's all I seem to get up here. Talk about purgatory." He smiles with what could almost be pride, as he recites from memory: "'David Ramsden of Harbottle and Webb…' – she named you 'David' after her old dad, I wanted to call you Harley – 'gave a very interesting talk at the Local History Society entitled "My Crazy Life as a Cotswold Auctioneer". Tea and biscuits were served.' Doubt that."

"They do a very good biscuit," protests David. "Oh. You mean… it *was* very interesting, actually." Something occurs to him that sends his head spinning even more. "*You* made *me* come here, didn't you?* You scared poor old Mrs Ballard so much that she just wanted to sell-up and scoot the hell away!"

"Calling Harbottle and Webb! Yeah. Wasn't sure it would work, but…" Rick suddenly begins to cry. "My own little lad. Right here. Beside me. After all these years." He wipes his eyes. "Sorry, son. Yes – even grown-ups cry sometimes."

For a brief moment, David is genuinely moved. Until reality kicks in.

"Oh, stop it!" He begins to smack his own head. "You're just a figment of my imagination." He ceases the smacking because he's not great with pain and he knows that his mum can spot a bruise anywhere.

"Ooh, 'figment'," mocks Rick. "Somebody got his eleven plus."

"I did, actually," counters David, sniffily. "*And* I went on to the grammar school. Then to the local university. Almost got a 2:1."

"Oh, Davey." Rick sighs. "I had such hopes for you."

"*What?* Didn't you hear…?" David finds himself strangely hurt by his newly encountered father's all-too-obvious disappointment. "Anyway, you never met me. Never even knew what sex I would be. If you hadn't gone and got yourself electrocuted at work, when poor Mum was only four months—"

He doesn't get to finish. The stunned look on Rick's face in that stone-cold loft freezes the words on his tongue.

"Is that what she told you – electrocuted?"

Suddenly David's phone, in the front pocket of his plain white and now not-so-crisp shirt, begins to vibrate.

"Bloody hell!" yelps Rick in alarm. "You're a fucking robot!"

David answers his mobile. "Ramsden. Hi, Quentin. No, still at the Ballard house."

Rick is just staring. "That is spooky!"

"Coming from you!" David turns back to the phone and sighs. "Yes, okay, I'll list it all tonight... I *do* know we have a big sale on tomorrow. I'll be in first thing, Quentin."

"That is never a telephone? Jesus!"

David puts it away, but Rick simply slips inside his son's body to take a better look. This is quite enough for the older and unwillingly invaded man.

"Okay, I'm going now. Got a—"

"Big sale tomorrow. I heard. I was sort of hoping for a footballer. Or a fighter pilot."

"I'm in line for a partnership! My boss is having a serious mull, even as we speak." David can see that Rick is seriously unimpressed and finds himself weirdly eager to correct this. "My life is-is just how I want it, thank you. I'm very settled. I'm in the Rotary Club!"

With this coup de grâce, David Ramsden edges away with as much dignity as he can muster. Nearing the loft ladder, he finally resolves fully to turn his back on the younger man, although this will mean his descending in the most hazardous manner for any auctioneer.

The cries behind him pummel his ears and his heart.

"Davey, son – you can't leave your old man. Not now... YOU CAN'T LEAVE YOUR FATHER!"

David, standing the wrong way on the ladder, twists his head uncomfortably backwards for one final retort, before he returns to normal, un-ghostly life.

"I never *knew* my dad. My dad's dead!"

"Then you should show him a bit more respect!"

Rick appears thoughtful for a moment, clearly not a look with which he is overly familiar.

"I oughta be in heaven," he continues, "not stuck here in a musty old house. There must be some reason why they're not letting me in."

"I can think of several."

"Don't leave me here on me ownsome, son. Not after I went and done all that scary stuff to make the old bat call you in." He can sense that this is having no effect on David, who is both resolute and shell-shocked. So Rick Ramsden decides, in his abject desperation, to change tack. "You NEED me!"

David stares at him one final time, before descending back to normality. He slams the loft-ladder shut with an angry crash.

He is almost in his Volvo before he wonders what his dad was doing in Mrs Ballard's house in the first place.

A little boy plays with wooden blocks in a sunlit English garden. Roses bloom all around him, but he knows to stay away from the sharp prickles and to keep on the grass.

Suddenly he feels himself swept off his feet by a gigantic, leather arm. The man swirls him around effortlessly with one hand, laughing as he does. In the other firm hand is a toy of some sort, zooming around along with him, just out of reach. The boy can't quite make it out – there are wheels perhaps, and a handlebar…

Now there comes a sound so loud that it frightens him. Is it coming from inside the big man's massive mouth, that deep, toothy cavern? Or is it the call of something far more scary?

DO I HEAR FIVE?

The roar behind him is so fierce and real that David Ramsden's unexpected road-time reverie vanishes in an instant.

Instinctively, he looks in his mirror. The country road is deserted, save for a distant tractor turning off down a dusty farm track between two fields of wheat. Yet the sound is growing stronger.

He thinks he must be going insane and simultaneously wonders what sane man wouldn't when confronted (possibly) with his barely out of adolescence yet long-dead dad, someone he had never even encountered in forty-four years of life, let alone in a creepy old house in Winchcombe. And, to cap it all, there is a person speaking in tongues from the inside of his Volvo! He soon realises, with some relief, that it is simply the current language tape continuing unperturbed.

Must have a holiday, he thinks to himself. *Nowhere foreign.*

The mighty roar is now almost on top of him. More than almost. It is as if this hellish sound is actually inside his car. Or inside his head. But it could, of course, be something right beside him, directly in his blind spot, eating up the road. That has to be it. Instinctively he swerves to avoid it, whatever it is, and ends up careering blindly into a ditch.

The next noise he hears, which could be five minutes later or considerably more, is that of a police siren. In his concussed state he has no idea whether to be relieved, embarrassed or just mightily pissed off.

*

"Not like you to be out of control, Mr Ramsden," says the driver of the police car, addressing a bruised and disgruntled David in his rear-view mirror.

David just shakes his head, realising as he sits in the passenger seat of this unfamiliar vehicle that the rest of his body is doing a similar amount of vigorous shaking, without any instruction from him.

"I was certain I had a vehicle of some sort right up my backside," he tells the older of the two Gloucestershire policemen, both of whom are local and known to him. "The roaring was just *so* loud." He realises that he doesn't sound hugely convincing.

Suddenly he hears another far scarier sound.

"*That was me!*" announces an elated voice right beside him. "That *so* loud mechanical roaring. Been practising that for years."

David jolts instantly, as if a spike has suddenly shot up through his seat. He spins round at a speed that causes the uniformed men in front, whose instincts are so much swifter than our own, to gaze at each other and wonder vaguely what's up with the poor sod.

"Oh God!" moans the shocked auctioneer. "*Oh no!*"

"These things happen, Mr R," says the younger policeman kindly, bemused by the man's overly dramatic reaction. "Not the end of the world."

David reckons that this could be a serious understatement as he watches his long-departed father bouncing around on the seat beside him with a glee he has previously associated only with overstimulated children or the mentally ill. At one point the rebounding young Ramsden's head surges right up into the sky, which is all the more impressive as the patrol car isn't a convertible.

"I'm FREE!" yelps an ecstatic Rick Ramsden, late of that dusty old house on the bend. "After forty-four crappy years. Dunno how, but what a blast!"

"This is a nightmare," mutters David.

"Oh, that old car'll be as good as new," reassures the police driver. "Those Volvos are like tanks. My mother-in-law drives one, more's the pity."

Rick leaps out of the half-open window of the patrol car and begins to race it at a ghostly clip, waving at David as he maintains an easy, sweat-free pace.

"Look at your old dad, son. He's still got it." The boy-racer can glimpse his son's unsurprisingly confused face as the younger man zooms back into the car through the rear-window. "Speed, pal. That's what life's all about. And death, come to think of it."

They reach a built-up area, rows of social housing on either side of the road, attempting to match the sandy Cotswold stone in colour if not in texture.

"This used to be all fields," says Rick, with some sadness. "Hello, world, Ricky's back. *Rick the Ram!*" He beams at his son, his long, flowing hair moving not a millimetre in the breeze. "Must be you that's done this, Davey!"

"No!" yells David, in serious denial. "I'm hallucinating! I DON'T BELIEVE IN GHOSTS!"

"You sure you don't want us to drop you at the hospital, Mr Ramsden?" says the driver, who isn't big on weird stuff.

Rick is now sitting on the driver's knee, running long, spectral fingers over the controls and puzzling over the integrated satnav.

"What the fuck?" he muses.

"Look," shouts David, who isn't a fan of bad language, "*why are you here?*"

"Why are any of us here?" responds the younger policeman, surprising even his colleague with a hitherto unrevealed existential bent.

Rick is back beside his son, stroking the far older man's face with wondrous, loving hands. Hands that David can't feel but still isn't thrilled about.

"It's gotta be you, son," he decides, trying to make sense of the miracle that has clearly just occurred. "Stands to reason. I'm here for YOU!"

"I never had a dad," insists David. "I don't *need* a dad."

"We all need a dad, Mr Ramsden," says the older policeman, who can't quite get a grip on the curious conversational structure currently at play but is game to try. "Y'know, someone to look up to."

Rick takes this as a playful instruction to lie flat on the roof of the moving police car and dangle his head upside down just beyond the windscreen, waving between the coppers to his long-lost and now joyfully discovered son.

Up until this morning, David Ramsden has never given much credence to either heaven or hell. Now at least one of these locations has gained a new believer.

DO I HEAR SIX?

The rattled auctioneer can almost hear the sigh of constabulary relief as the patrol car drives hurriedly away from the small, modern, semi-detached house in which David Ramsden chooses to live. A house deliberately lacking in any of those older, finer and more collectable elements that make up such a large part of the rest of his life.

"It's very you," says the ghostly figure beside him.

"Thank you," says David.

"Wasn't a compliment, son." His younger dad sighs. "Let's hope the little woman has made it a bit more homey inside."

He suddenly smacks David on the shoulder. The older man watches in morbid fascination as a ghostly hand disappears into his more corporeal body.

"Hey, how many grandkids have I got? Four, five, six? Do I hear 'Dave the Ram'?"

"There's no little woman," says David, moving to his front door but holding faint hope that he will be able to block his new and uninvited relative from home, hearth or head. "We're divorced."

"Oh," says Rick, in evident disappointment. "Take the kiddies with her, did she?"

David is silent for a moment. It tells Rick everything he needs to know but nothing that he wishes to hear.

"Ah. Okay. Right."

He stares at the charm-free house disappointedly. Through the picture window, Rick Ramsden can see a particularly uncluttered and boring living room and thinks almost wistfully of his loft, which may have been layered in dust and debris and the odd glob of pigeon shit, but at least had character.

Then the door to the room opens and a small, white-haired figure enters, pushing a vacuum cleaner.

"At least you got yourself a lady-who-does," says Rick proudly.

"I've got bad news for you," says David, who can't quite believe he's having this conversation. "That old lady with the Hoover used to be your wife."

This time it is the ghost who passes out, which isn't something David would have thought psychic phenomena actually do.

The old vacuum cleaner, which requires either a good service or a mercy killing, reminds David of the noise in his head that nearly did for him less than two hours earlier. He realises now – although he knows that any petrol-head or idiot would have worked it out far sooner – that the recent fateful roar had been the sound of a motorcycle, travelling at a terrifying and most probably illegal speed. How his late father had managed to replicate this awful noise he has no idea, nor indeed why the fatally electrocuted man would have wished to do so.

The woman who has always told David how hazardous such machines are – alongside, it has to be said, every other activity known to man (other than perhaps reading and origami) – hasn't heard him come in. A morbidly obese black cat, however, snoozing fartily on the sofa, suddenly leaps awake with its back arched, hair like furry porcupine quills, and launches itself in pure terror onto the old lady's shoulder, sending her off-course and into the – thankfully unkindled – fireplace.

"*Keith!*" shouts a horrified David from the doorway. "Get off Mummy now! Down, boy."

The large cat descends somewhat sullenly and slinks into the corner, becoming a cowering black furball and eyeing its master with new and unfamiliar suspicion.

"Hello, David," says his startled mother, switching off the machine. She is about to interrogate him on his early arrival when she notices his face. "Are you alright, my darling? You're as white as a sheet." She looks out of the window. "I didn't hear your car – where is it?"

For a moment David thinks he might be alone, then realises that his fellow traveller has revived (in his own way) and is now standing right beside him, mouth and eyes wide open, former garrulousness lost in a haze of remembrance or pure horror.

"Had a bit of an accident with the Volvo, Mum," says David, then immediately wishes he hadn't.

Mrs Ramsden is trying really hard not to panic but failing utterly, as indeed her only son knew that she would.

"*Oh my God, David!* You're not hurt, are you? Did you go to the hospital? Mrs Creeley's older sister in Cirencester thought she was perfectly okay after her accident until three weeks later when the whiplash killed her, just like that, by the feminine hygiene counter in Boots."

"Mum," he reassures the worried lady, who is by now hugging him and gently feeling his body for fractures, "I'm fine, really."

David can't help but wonder at this point whether he actually is fine and resolves to have himself checked out once this nightmare is over. He also muses, looking at the lanky, leather-clad spectre beside him, whether in truth it ever will be.

"Were you listening to an over-stimulating language?" chides his mother.

David just shrugs, his attention focused primarily on Rick. The young man has moved in closer to his own widow's lined but still rather pretty face and is checking out the woman's every feature with trembling, unfelt hands. From her attractively crooked little nose to her flashing and currently concerned hazel eyes, his spectral fingers wander, carefully avoiding the deeper wrinkles and a double chin.

"Is this really you, Wendy?" he asks her, tears forming in his own disbelieving eyes, but of course receives no reply.

"Have you taken your blood pressure, sweetheart?" asks Wendy of her son. "Remember, a sphygmomanometer is for life…"

David nods, as he joins in. "Not just for Christmas."

They both smile at this, their little joke.

Keith, in the meantime, is baring his sharp little teeth and making a noise like an angry growl, as he retreats even further into his corner.

"*Keith!*" berates Wendy. "It's only Daddy, who's come home perturbingly early today."

Rick looks at David in confusion, but the latter just shakes his head. There's a line of enquiry he has decided to pursue, and he is not going to allow anything dead or alive to interfere. He stares as meaningfully into his mother's eyes as his soft and somewhat pudgy face will allow.

"There was this motorbike," he begins.

His mother's entire body freezes, whilst she tries with her smile and her voice to remain unperturbed. The effect is both implausible and seriously disconcerting.

"Motorbike?" she throws off over-lightly, picking up a feather-duster to keep her hands from shaking.

Rick walks around Wendy, his leathers glistening in a light whose source David can't quite discern.

"Yes, Wendy," he says, although he knows that she can't hear him. "A Triumph T120 Bonneville, actually. With five-speed gear—"

"Those machines, they shouldn't be on the road!" says the pensioner. She lifts a small vase and gives it an unnecessary wipe.

"You didn't say that when you were keeping my bum

nice and toasty en route to the Ace Caff," chuckles Rick, remembering. "With your little hands wandering and the Beast on his own bike just feet ahead of us."

"*What*?" yelps David, receiving a look of total confusion from his mum.

"So where did you see this motorbike, did you say?" she asks casually, as if she isn't terribly bothered.

David remains silent for a moment, then answers quietly, "Old Mrs Ballard's house. That little Victorian, right on the corner of Finster Road."

The vase his mother is dusting slips from her hands and disintegrates with a crash on the fireplace's tiled surround. Keith shakes his head and leaves the room.

"Oh, yes?" she says, bending down to pick up the shards with trembling fingers. "Silly old me!"

David stops her before blood is spilled.

"That did it, old son," chirps Rick. "You never forget where your old man kicked the bucket."

As David Ramsden gasps in full realisation, his late father moves noiselessly over to the shaking woman. She is trying desperately to hold it together and not shatter into as many pieces as the vase.

"Remember, Wendy, that awful Monday? After we'd had our little row…"

Wendy walks right through her late husband and out into the kitchen. "Now, you just put your feet up, David," she urges. "I'll fetch the dustpan and brush."

Rick watches her go, shaking his head. "Why did she lie to her own son all these years?"

"So he wouldn't turn out like you?" suggests his son.

"Well, that bit worked," agrees Rick, sadly.

David checks himself out in the mirror above the fireplace and nods approvingly. He sees nothing there to be ashamed of. Rick joins him and sees no reflection of himself at all.

"Shame. I was bloody good-looking." He looks at his son. "You've got my, er, well, you've got my ears. Yeah. And I can see your mum in you."

David turns to look at him.

"She used to be such a goer, that little woman. *Jesus!* Couldn't get enough of the old Ram-rod!"

"That's my mother you're talking about!"

Rick calls fruitlessly into the kitchen, "*I never stopped loving you, Wendy!*" He looks suddenly stricken. "We broke the bloody bed on our wedding night. That was just two days before I died."

David stares at him. "*What?*"

"Oh. Didn't she tell you – about her old dad and our 'shotgun'—"

"*Kanisteri me juoruta jokseenkin jokin jokin!*"

Rick moves over to his son, hands outstretched in strangling mode.

"My God, if I could just shake some ruddy life into you!"

In an instant, Keith, protective interests revved to the max, is back in the room and leaping straight at Rick. With nothing to break his journey, the overweight cat flies straight through the unwelcome spirit and stuns himself on the living-room window.

"Should've worn a helmet," says Rick.

David isn't quite sure whether the younger man is talking about the cat or himself.

DO I HEAR SEVEN?

"*Born to be wi-i-ld...*"

"Will you SHUT UP!" screams David from his spot next to his dead father on the main bedroom's double bed.

He wonders, for a moment, why he is scrunching up at one end – it's not like ghosts take up that much space. *Indeed*, he thinks, *all they are is space*. Yet David still feels, as he tries to plough through the sheaf of work papers on his lap, that he is now sharing his precious room with a seriously uninvited guest, who appears to have no intention of moving on. And who, indeed, finds sleep surplus to requirements.

"I need my rest for tomorrow's—"

"Big sale," completes Rick. "So what is it, Chippendale chamber pots?"

"Assorted memorabilia, fifties through seventies. Not my type of thing, but needs must."

David ponders for a moment on why he is justifying his working day to a ghost but reasons that this isn't just any ghost. And, to be honest, it's not entirely unpleasant to be discussing his career with his father, after all these silent years, the way he assumes most sons are wont to do.

He recalls his long-ago schooldays, the sadness he felt when boys went on about their dads, or indeed, went off with them. Fishing trips, football matches, cycle rides. He remembers how fathers would stand in the cold, breath curling like woodsmoke, punching the air as their lad scored a goal or a try. Or how they'd sit in the summertime sun, surreptitiously sipping beers, while their offspring smacked a six. Of course, his mum had always given him a note for games, but perhaps had his dad been around those '*please excuse David*'s might have remained unwritten.

It's not as if his mother ever asks him for details about his job – it's rarely more than a vague 'had a nice day, love?'. Just occasionally she will tell him a fact that she has read, such as in the United States last year more people lost their lives to furniture than to terrorism, so he had better be careful of those Victorian armoires.

"I'd like to go to sleep now," he tells Rick, "if it's all the same to you. I've got to be up at seven."

"Want me to tell you a bedtime story?"

"I'm forty-four!"

Rick looks over at the older man and smiles tenderly. "Never too late, son. You know, Davey, I may not have lived long, but at least I've lived."

David can see where this is going, where this might forever go, and he suddenly feels that he has had enough.

"*Can't you see?* I'm doing just fine. Good job, nice house, stable life. So, nothing to worry about anymore – you can go now, cheerio, rest in peace."

He switches off the light, only to find that his late father glows in the dark.

"Bugger," he says.

"Do you know something, David," resumes Rick a few minutes later, silently snapping his fingers, "I reckon I have been sent here *especially* to give you the benefit of my experience."

"Well, if I ever need to know how to smash headfirst into a brick wall, you'll be the first person I'll call. Meantime, I'm going to sleep. Play dead!"

"As the Beast said to the Ram, 'you can sleep when you're six feet under'."

Despite himself, David switches on the light once more.

"The Beast? The Ram! Is this some sort of hippy fairy tale?"

"The Beast weren't no fairy, boy." Rick smiles. "And Rick the Ram ain't no hippy. Bravest biker I ever knew was old Beastie. No one could touch him on that Norton of his. I remember one moonlit night – the road down to Oxford. Picture the scene, son..."

"No!" protests David. "No picturing. No scene! Can't you take a hint? What are you waiting for?"

Rick looks thoughtful. "Dunno. Some sort of sign?"

"I'll give you a bloody sign!"

"Now, now, no tantrums! We've got forty-four years to catch up on. How did the breastfeeding go?"

David looks at his father for what he hopes is the final time and switches off the light once more.

Yet even in the dark, as his own eyes are closing on this most gobsmacking of days, he notices a tiny smile on the younger man's face, a smile disconcertingly abundant in mischief and cunning. And the trace, too, of a perturbing glint in his eye – almost as if Rick Ramsden knows something that David Ramsden doesn't.

But of course, this is impossible. The man has been stuck in a musty loft since 1980.

David falls asleep, and dreams again of a little boy.

The bicycle is tiny, but to him it looks as high as a horse and just as daunting. He can hear the big man's laughter in his ears, ringing as loud and clear as the bell that is all he dares touch on this fearsome new object.

He wants to ask the laughing man about those little wheels, the ones he has seen on other 'starter bikes', the ones that keep the new rider from falling off and hurting himself on the cruel pavement.

There are no wheels.

Perhaps, *he thinks,* they are too expensive. *Yet he knows, as the big man lifts him up in the air and sets him firmly down on the tiny plastic saddle, that he is supposed to ride his new two-wheeler as just that.*

A big boy's bike.

He trusts the smiling man. Nothing bad will happen.

DO I HEAR EIGHT?

In the morning, as he slowly wakes, David Ramsden feels a lump at the bottom of his bed. It takes him a while to compute that, as his newly visiting father is currently both absent and weightless, it must be Keith, who is very far from either.

With a sense of relief that is not quite as potent as he might have anticipated but nonetheless real, he starts his day. As always, he talks things through with the cat, who listens without interruption or criticism, unlike his ex-wife or indeed his mother, who will fuss over him until she dies and quite possibly, given his recent experience, thereafter.

Yet perhaps yesterday was simply a dream, like the curious ones he is currently having, as there is no shred of evidence that his late father was ever here. Not that ghosts are known to leave an abundance of reminders. He has heard of something called ectoplasm but has no idea what it is, although it sounds disgusting and something his mother would probably hoover up before anyone could trip over it.

"And my talk to the Local History Society *was* interesting," he tells Keith defensively. "Mrs Harkness herself cheered, dementia or no dementia."

He showers swiftly, dons his most rakish cavalry twill, gulps down the healthy (if binding) muesli his mother makes by the barrel-load and heads for the door. It is only when he begins to talk Finnish that he recalls he has no car.

He returns inside and calls a taxi.

The Montpelier district of Cheltenham is one of the most fashionable and attractive in this historically white (in every sense) Georgian spa town. David Ramsden feels a great sense of pride that he works here, and that people know him by name. See how he nods to shopkeepers and local businessmen and watch how they nod cursorily back. Respect like this doesn't arrive fully wrapped overnight. It has to be diligently earned and prudently maintained.

There is an uncharacteristic lightness to his step this morning and not just because of the unfamiliar pleasure of having been driven by local taxi to work. Yet he can't quite puzzle out whether this is due to the extraordinary encounter he (possibly) had yesterday or the fact that it has left no visible trace today.

He even dares to gaze in the window of that new lingerie shop which just opened, to the disapproval of some of Montpelier's older residents. An unbelievably well-proportioned mannequin is wearing a policewoman's uniform that he is quite certain is yet to be officially sanctioned, unbuttoned as it is to reveal not entirely regulation lacy underwear.

David Ramsden regards himself as a man of the world, so whilst he might be intrigued, he is hardly shocked. He is more shocked, however, to see his late father standing in the same window, very close to the female PC, with a disgustingly leery look on his face.

This is how Elspeth Martin finds David, when she passes the new shop on her way to her job at the auction house.

"Morning, Mr Ramsden."

David catches her reflection in the window. It is a second or two before he can turn round, somewhat sheepishly, to greet her.

"Oh. Elspeth. Good morning."

"*She's a black girl!*" yells the stunned figure in the window, pointing at the colleague.

"We've got black people in Montpelier now!" retorts David, almost proudly.

"I *know!*" says Elspeth. "Isn't it exciting! Er – see you at work then."

"You're in there, son," says Rick, walking in and out of the policewoman. "Boss and secretary. I won't stand in your way."

"Elspeth is a Fine Arts graduate and a trainee auctioneer. And what's more…" He notices passers-by staring at the conservatively dressed man berating thin air, so he swiftly whips out his phone. "And what's more," he repeats, "the bidding will only start at eight thousand."

"Didn't no one tell you it's rude to ignore your elders?"

"You're not elder, actually. And I'd just rather my customers didn't think their local auctioneer is drunk or losing it."

"Got it." Rick nods.

He leaps out of the window and takes in the passing throng. He notices an unshaven man approaching, dishevelled and looking like he's talking to himself.

"Phone in his ear, right?"

"No, he's drunk and losing it. Morning, Neville."

Rick isn't listening. He currently stands in the middle of the road, allowing cars, of which he has never seen the like but adores on sight, to pass right through him. He's allowing young men and women to do likewise, as they cross this same road, and is clearly fascinated by the tattoos and the face furniture. He beams at David as if all his birthdays have come at once and this brave and exciting new world was created just for him.

"So, that Elspeth bird," he calls to the pavement, where David is gently edging away from the lingerie shop, "is she seeing anyone?"

"She's married, actually. To Sandy. Short for Alexandra."

"*Fucking hell!*" says Rick, but not before a few delicious moments have passed.

"You're really not going to cope here," says David. "Things have moved on."

Rick is right next to him, watching the world – mostly female – go by.

"You ain't moved anywhere, lad. You're stuck on the hard shoulder. But Daddy's here. Just waiting for that sign."

"Here's a sign for you," says David and thrusts two uncharacteristically spread fingers right up his late father's nose. Or into thin air, depending on how you and the bemused population of Montpelier choose to look at it.

The morning had started out so well.

DO I HEAR NINE?

The 'Why the Hell Did I Throw Mine Away?' sale is being prepared. At least, this is what the employees of Harbottle and Webb call it, as they dust and polish myriad items of fifties-to-seventies memorabilia scattered throughout the cavernous, brick-lined viewing chamber.

As David walks in, a stooped, white-haired old man slumps slowly past him, laboriously hefting a gleaming jukebox to the rear of the vast room. David finds it painful to watch as this frail but dignified gentleman, who should be enjoying his retirement by now, struggles to find a safe berth for the precious but bulky object. A fag dangles from his mouth, the ash almost as long as its host.

"Here," says David, moving towards him, "I'll take that for you."

"*Leave it!*" comes a voice like a chainsaw from a nearby office.

"Morning, Quentin," says David, stopping mid-assist. The old man shrugs and shuffles off.

"*Quentin bloody Harbottle!*" yelps Rick, staring at the portly owner with his drinker's face and belly. "Of course! He was a poncey mod with a scooter back in the seventies. You're working for a poncey mod!"

This is not entirely news to David, at least the poncey bit. Yet he finds himself taking umbrage at a father who has never shown the least interest in his son's world, owing to a totally avoidable early interment, now passing uninformed judgment on the people by whom his only living heir chooses to be employed.

"You look like a distressed commode," says the employer, scrutinising David through unattractively bleary eyes.

"Pillock!" mutters Rick.

"Sorry, Quentin," says David, ignoring his father. "I was doing the Ballard list until the early hours. I'd better just go help poor old—"

"Future partners, chummy, do not heft. Get on with what I pay you for."

As soon as the irascible man strides off, Rick is in there.

"You gonna let him talk to you like that, Davey?"

"He gave me the job." David knows that he is looking, and probably sounding, like a ventriloquist and finds himself wondering whether he could still do it whilst drinking a glass of water. "I owe him a lot."

"Not your bollocks, son. A man's gotta stand up for himself, or he's no son of mine."

"Some threat," responds the son of his, but Rick is already prancing around the auction room in unashamed wonder, gazing at objects of nostalgia as if that magical childhood world he so unwillingly left long ago has been carefully preserved just for him.

He glides in and out of familiar Oxo tins and Ercol recliners and Dansette record players, passes through Mickey Mouse dial phones and Agas and Subbuteo sets. He even has fun trying to leap out of 'modern' Swedish wardrobes and scare people, but when he realises they can't see him and really couldn't care less, some – yet by no means all – of the fun wears off.

Meanwhile the ash-stained and very elderly gentleman is still shifting objects excruciatingly slowly into the yard, each one appearing to send his poor bending back another centimetre closer towards the ground, where he will doubtless lay in entirety before long.

"How's your delightful mother?" calls Quentin Harbottle from his office, without regard for those other employees who might be listening.

"Oh. Er… she's fine, thank you, Quentin."

"She tell you about our intimate little dinner the other night? She fought all the way." He smiles. "For her son, that is."

Rick is out of his wardrobe in a flash. "He's after my little Wendy? The randy old— Over my dead body!"

This time he whizzes all over the shop, bouncing angrily off walls and windows, shooting out via the ceiling and back through the door again. David thinks he is simply showing off but has to admit that it's quite impressive.

Suddenly there's a huge crash from outside, followed by a mournful, drawn-out groan.

"Go and help him." Quentin sighs. "Shoot him if necessary."

David rushes outside into the yard, followed by Rick, who is still glaring at the senior partner.

They find the aged man struggling under the weight of a vintage but lovingly well-restored motorcycle, minus its name badge and number. Despite its years, it looks like a gleaming baby compared to the decrepit body pinned and wriggling beneath.

David rushes to hoist the classic but potentially lethal machine off his writhing colleague.

"I've died and gone to heaven," exclaims Rick, as he watches the rescue take place.

"I wish," says David.

He manages to shift the motorcycle sufficiently for its victim to raise himself up, although the shocked man doesn't seem hugely keen.

"You know what this is, don't you?" asks Rick rhetorically.

"It's an old Triumph T120 Bonneville," says David.

Rick stares at him, as if his little boy just began talking in Serbo-Croat. (Which, interestingly, is the next one on David's list – language number nine – but Rick is unlikely to know this.)

"She's a 'Bonnie' alright." Rick sighs. "In fact, just like…" David notices that Rick is finding it hard to finish the sentence and believes that he may know why. "She is *so* beautiful."

His father is clearly choked as the emotion wells up, giving if not colour to his cheeks then at least an interesting change of pallor. But David is more surprised to see that the incident is having an equally profound effect on the poor shifter.

"Had her in the shed for donkey's years," explains the old man. David realises that this is actually the first time he has seen this admittedly splendid object, although he has catalogued other equally lethal examples in the past. "Then a few months back I had the notion to restore her." He looks at the auctioneer pleadingly. "I was thinking we might put her into the sale today, David. If it's okay with you, of course. And the boss. See, I need the cash."

David looks almost embarrassed. "Ah. Well, I'm not sure – it's just that I don't know that Quentin would exactly approve of his staff just…" He hears a loud cough beside him and looks at Rick, who is staring at him quite sternly – in fact, as sternly as a twenty-one-year-old hell-raiser of possibly arrested development might stare. "I'm certain we can fit her in."

"Thanks, lad," says the bruised but clearly much-relieved dogsbody. He strokes the Triumph with what can only be perceived as a true and profound love. "Real beauty, she was. In her day. Until…" He shakes his head and David can discern a deeply genuine sadness. "Never mind. I hope whoever ends up with her lets me visit her now and again."

The emotion is too much for him. His rheumy eyes seem on the cusp of streaming. Brusquely, the old man picks up the bike and wheels it proudly, if shakily, away.

This time David doesn't hang back. "Here, I'll help you, Walter." And they both carry it together.

He hears the sudden intake of breath behind him.

"*Walter?*" repeats the ghost, in a shaky croak. "Walt— Oh my God – it's the Beast!"

"THE BEAST?!" screams David, causing Walter, aka the Beast, to drop his end of the proudly restored Triumph T120 Bonneville onto David's left foot.

"Nobody's called me that since…" The old man sniffs the dusty air. "Can anyone smell Brylcreem?"

Instinctively, Rick runs a delicate hand over his quiff. "Beastie, what did I *do* to you?" he moans, as he tries to caress the bike. His hands pass gently through it. "You kept my bike! You kept Bonnie all these years? But you never told Davey here, did you, about what happened that awful night?" The answer occurs to Rick, and he shakes his head. "Wendy must've sworn you and every last soul in this ruddy town to secrecy." He turns to his awestruck son. "Davey, my boy," he says in a portentous whisper. "I think we just had our sign."

David stares into his father's weepy yet curiously suspect smile and has a horrible feeling that this will all end in tears.

DO I HEAR TEN?

"*I am NOT buying a bloody motorbike!*"

The chairs are out, and the buyers are in. Hyper-vigilant men and women of all ages, Gloucestershire gentry in Burberry and Barbour, local dealers with pockets full of catalogues and blarney, cash and hip flasks. The latter glint under lights positioned to show off lots to their best advantage and afford auctioneers notice of bidding at its most discreet.

David Ramsden would rather not be seen talking to himself as he walks to the podium, but he finds that he just can't let this go. Fortunately, there is so much hubbub in the crowded room, the chatter of anticipation melding with fake indifference, that he isn't noticed. He wonders vaguely whether this is what tinnitus is like – a constant, annoying buzzing in his ear. Although tinnitus probably isn't life-threatening, whereas Rick Ramsden most definitely is.

"*I couldn't buy it anyway. I'm the bloody auctioneer!*"

Rick points upwards to the cheap chandeliers and the high-timbered roof. Or perhaps beyond.

"But *He* wants you to, son. That's why *He* sent me the Beast."

"Nonsense! Old Walter Carstairs has been here forever. And Mum never said you were religious!"

"Being dead can change a man, David. You have to listen to what *He* says."

"God wants me to buy a sodding Triumph?"

David thinks he may have said this just a bit too loud, as the background noises instantly fade down. Many of the familiar faces have known him for years but never realised that he was one of those who based their decisions on diktats from above. It immediately changes their long-held perceptions of him and has them churning over past encounters, to see how they conform to this faintly disconcerting world-view.

Then she walks into the room.

David has never seen anyone like her in his life.

Possibly because people like her don't usually frequent auction rooms and people like him – well, exactly like him – rarely venture outside them, except perhaps to visit houses for valuations. Yet, at the same time, something about her is hugely familiar, especially since yesterday, because she is dressed entirely in leathers, as if she has just stepped off a motorcycle of her own. And she holds a bright red helmet confidently in her hand, as other women might carry an accessory that perfectly defines who they are and without which they would never countenance being seen at all.

She is not beautiful, or at least not in a way that David, who admittedly knows little about these things, has defined beauty up until now. Yet there is a freshness and an honesty about this young woman, a compelling directness in the way she strides down the aisle towards him, past rows of bemused customers, staring unblinkingly into his astonished face with eyes he would categorise professionally as lapis lazuli blue, under short hair as black as her jacket. No-nonsense practicality, an economy of movement, seem to inform every muscle of her body, as it flexes under the hugging tightness of apparel that she may wear for safety yet which, in this arena, reads distinctly like a statement.

"Hello, doll face, and who, might I ask, are you?" says Rick, adding a hugely extended whistle of approval that makes David think with some relief how far the representatives of his sex have come. Yet he finds himself staring at her in a way that causes him to wonder if there's still some way to go. It's not attraction, surely. Not towards a young biker in perhaps her late twenties. Rather a fascination, as if in the hours since 10.00 yesterday morning, he has entered a peculiarly alternate realm.

But he still knows that the gaze he is offering, reflected in her own slightly combative eyes, is one of cool disdain. Despite her bravado, she seems as if she has walked into totally the wrong place – almost into a different social stratum, and everyone else in that suddenly stilled room feels the same.

"Hear you got a Bonnie," says the young woman, in an accent more upmarket than he was expecting, from his admittedly limited knowledge of the Gloucestershire biking fraternity. "Triumph T120 Bonneville?"

David stares at her in amazement. "How on Earth…?" he responds. "It's not even in the catalogue!"

She shrugs. "Small town. You hear things. And Walter comes into where I work."

"And where is that?" asks David, thinking a supermarket perhaps, or a charity shop, but then he hears a loud coughing start up behind him. He turns to see Quentin, who is muttering that it could be fun to have an auction sometime soon.

"*Don't let her get it, Davey!*" says Rick. "Take it off the shelf for later. Don't let that beauty get away. The bike, I mean."

David turns to his father, with a smile that is almost cruel, then back to the newcomer.

"Could you tell me your name, Miss?"

"Gosforth. Daisy Gosforth."

David believes that he hears a loud gasp from beside him, which has obviously to be something basic and intimately involved with sex. So he simply removes his beloved gavel from its felt-lined box and offers the expectant crowd a firm but welcoming nod.

He doesn't notice the surprisingly gentle smile Rick Ramsden is now affording the auction room's newest and most unexpected arrival.

DO I HEAR ELEVEN?

*I*t is 11.00 at night and Rick Ramsden is still crying.

"For pity's sake, man."

"'Dad'. At least call me 'dad'."

"Will no one rid me of this troublesome ghost!" says David, which he can't help thinking is rather clever, although he knows instinctively that this will fall on dead ears. He also feels more tired than he believes he has ever been, save for that time when his ex-wife spent the entire night listing the reasons why she was leaving him and that his imploring her not to in five different Eastern European languages was just compounding the problem.

What bothers David Ramsden the most, as he sits in his favourite and only armchair, nursing a larger supermarket Scotch than he has drunk in years, is that there appears to be a disturbing sense of normality setting in. It no longer feels quite so surreal to be sharing his home, every waking moment and most of the sleepy ones, with the spirit of his juvenile, twenty-one-year-old father, an emanation who can talk only about women and bikes and women on bikes and, bewilderingly, women who *are* bikes. Or, of course, how his only son is squandering his precious birthright.

Yet David really does wish that he could find a way to send Rick Ramsden back to purgatory or heaven or at least up again into his Ballard loft. It's not like you can Google it – and he caught *Poltergeist* once by accident on the TV, so he's not going anywhere near *that*. He'd also like a still vaguely concussed Keith to come back in from under the garden shed.

Right now, however, he'd simply settle for a way to stop Rick the Ram bawling his head off.

"*It's a flaming bike!*" cries David in frustration. "The weird young woman wanted it, she bought it, she's got it. She's happy, Quentin is satisfied and Walter, formerly known as the Beast, is ecstatic. Job done."

"But it was meant for *you*, Davey. Your inheritance. It was the one thing I could give to you. That has to be why Beastie was fixing it up."

David shakes his head in disbelief but finding that it still hurts from the accident, he stops.

"What was I going to bloody do with it – frame it on the wall? Oh, I know, I could have had it turned into a modern sculpture and planted it on your grave."

Rick stops crying. "You'd do that for me? Nice thought, son. But, actually, I wanted you to ride it."

For a long moment David Ramsden is lost for words.

"You have got to be bloody joking," he says, finally.

"You wouldn't have been on your own – I'd have been there to teach you."

"Bit like Captain Smith of the Titanic giving sailing lessons."

The ghost heaves an enormous sigh. "I'd have been better off staying in my little loft. You are such a disappointment."

David is surprised to discover how much this hurts. It has to be some sort of nadir when even the dead don't have a good word for you. But it makes him more determined than ever to return to the status quo. He's way behind on his Finnish.

"Okay," he says, finally. "What would it take to get you out of my hair and back into that loft?"

"Would you still come visit me?"

"Not sure how the new owners would feel – if it ever gets sold – but we'll see. Now, what am I bid for your disappearance?"

"You've got that bird's address – the leather girl?"

"She's not a 'bird' – and Elspeth must have it written down. For our books."

"Then take me to see my bike one last time."

DO I HEAR TWELVE?

"Well, I never expected this," says Rick Ramsden, gazing in awe at the shop window. "I think I've died—"

"And gone to heaven," completes David, staring along with him. "I really wish you'd stop saying that."

David thinks that this is the most dispiriting retail establishment he has ever been cajoled into visiting, save perhaps for those dress shops with his mum when he was a little kid and had no dad to be left with. It is only a small shop, yet motorcycles and their enthusiasts take up almost every inch.

Displayed in those rare corners where machines are not erect, propped or dangling are gleaming helmets, crisp new leathers and all the accoutrements of the roaring road. There's even a black T-shirt that proclaims in white lettering on its back, *'If you can read this, the bitch has fallen off'*, which David doesn't understand, but is pretty certain wouldn't be a favourite of the young manager, one Ms Daisy Gosforth.

"Didn't think I'd see *you* in here," says the young woman, from behind her mysteriously cluttered counter. She is still in black but not this time in leather.

"Nor I you," says an intrigued Rick, after which the silence grows even more uncomfortable. He tries to nudge his son, without success. "Say something, boy. Be sociable."

"Why?" demands David, then sees the quizzical look on the young woman's face. "Why – it's all part of our service. At

Harbottle and Webb. To see if our purchasers are completely happy."

"Well, I am," she says, "completely happy. Thanks. Though I wasn't so happy with the look you gave me when I came into your place yesterday."

"Ah. What look?" Although he believes he does recall the look.

"You know. The old 'what's someone like you doing in a lardy place like this?' look."

"Lardy?" repeats David. He's already come across that curious word quite recently but can't recall where. Was it something to do with baking?

"Short for la-de-da," explains Rick. "Ain't heard that for years! Well, *go on*, man!"

In an ensuing lull, David finds himself moving closer to the counter and the young woman. As if unable to shift his gaze, he stares unblinkingly into her unusually blue eyes, and the tiny piercings in her nose and ears that he hadn't noticed before. *Why do people do this?* he wonders. A face would be fine without them. *Well, at least this one would*, he decides. He has known some that could only be improved with wire mesh.

"Anything else?" she enquires, as the silence persists.

"You've got bloody pins in your face!" cries Rick, who clearly hadn't noticed them either.

"You've got bloody pins in your face!" repeats David instinctively, as if this had been a prompt and not simply an observation. But swiftly added, "Which is totally fine by me," an addendum that doesn't really ease the situation.

He glares at the ghost. That, he decides, was a final line crossed. Or, as his mother would say, for reasons best known to herself, 'a fridge too far'. *I should be at work*, he tells himself, *not on the other side of town, insulting innocent young women with metallised faces in bike shops.* He really has had his fill of Rick Ramsden.

"Phew!" says Daisy Gosforth. "I'll certainly sleep easier tonight, knowing you approve. Anything else you wanted? Latest *Bikers' Monthly*?"

It is now, at this most unexpected of junctures, that Rick Ramsden says something to change David's life and world forever.

"If she lets you and me ride her Bonnie, just the one last glorious time, Davey, I'll be out of your hair for good and all," he promises. And this time he sounds totally sincere. "I'll have passed something small but fine on, from father to son, and my job will be done." He smiles, almost embarrassed by his earnestness. "Sounded like a poem, didn't it?"

David looks directly into Rick's pale eyes. He's not going to repeat the mistake of talking rubbish out loud, but the stare he's drilling into the far younger and only slightly deader man's face is one that demands total reassurance. The ghost simply nods. A deceased man's word is his bond.

David Ramsden turns back to the young woman and moves even closer, until he is leaning on the counter. Quietly, as if he doesn't want anyone else to hear, he gently murmurs words into her intriguing face that he never thought he would hear himself say in a million years.

"I want to ride your bike," he whispers.

He expects a response with an element of surprise in it, but not quite as much element as he receives.

"Get out of my shop, you fucking perve!" says Daisy Gosforth, quietly but firmly.

*

It takes David Ramsden a good twelve minutes to convince Daisy Gosforth of his innocence.

Twelve minutes which aren't aided by the sound of almost hysterical ghostly laughter shooting directly into his left earhole.

Hearing the spirit of one's long-deceased parent talk about wetting himself, a phenomenon even David suspects goes way beyond the most outer of limits, is an experience he will not easily forget.

David is finally rewarded when the young woman agrees – somewhat reluctantly, it has to said – to meet him this coming Sunday at an ageing and long-abandoned airfield on the outskirts of town. It turns out that the never-less-than-surprising Ms Gosforth is a qualified motorcycle instructor, a calling she combines most efficiently with running the shop.

"Well, we'd better get you geared up first, hadn't we?" she says, with an enthusiasm even her future pupil can detect as containing more than a note of amusement. She points with a small but wiry hand to an array of clothing that David Ramsden wouldn't normally be seen dead in, although he feels that this could be exactly the state in which he might soon be found. "And I have to tell you, an old Triumph T120 Bonneville, however lovingly restored, is so not a starter bike for a guy like you."

"It's gotta be my old bike, Davey," urges the voice beside him, "or I'll haunt you until the end of your days, morning to night, Cotswolds and beyond the A40."

"Yes, okay," hisses David to the air around him, ignoring his previous vow. "That has to be the bike, Ms Gosforth."

"I'll need you to fill in a form," says Daisy, handing him some printed sheets from a drawer under the counter. She taps them firmly. "There's a big section on health." Staring straight at him, she adds, "I'd pay particular attention to the mental health bit."

David's cheeks grow red, as the insinuation slaps him. "Are you suggesting I've got... problems?"

"You're a middle-aged auctioneer who suddenly, out of the blue, decides he simply has to ride a powerful vintage bike he only just saw the day before. No, you're firing on all cylinders."

"You're in there, Davey!" says Rick Ramsden, which even in all the surrounding madness has to be the barmiest thing David has heard all day. Yet he feels he has no choice, if he wants his old life back.

One session should hopefully do it. He will just have to go along for the ride.

DO I HEAR THIRTEEN?

*A*t least the weather is fine, thinks David Ramsden, clutching at straws, as he drives his newly repaired Volvo to the old airfield. His 'Fin-Begin' tape is playing at full blast, if only to drown out the overexcited rambling from the seat beside him.

'*Kuinka paljon kalaa on*?' says the tape.

"*Kuinka paljon kalaa on*?" repeats David.

"What the hell is that?" exclaims the Fin-Beginner's father finally. "And can't you go any faster?"

David switches off the tape. "No. And it means 'how much is the fish?' in Finnish. It's very useful."

"Going to Finland, are you?"

"Why would I do that?"

"Jeez. Aren't you just a bit fired-up, son, about this morning?"

"You're the one who's a bit 'fired-up'. You didn't stop talking about it all night. I'm a bit terrified-up, if you must know."

"There's nothing to it, bike-riding." Rick laughs. "Easy as falling off a log."

"Or smashing into a wall."

"If there's one thing I'm gonna teach you before I leave, it's to stop being so negative."

"Perhaps it's being so negative that's kept me alive twice as long as you. Why were you riding at such speed round the corner that night?" David can't even look at Rick. "You were about to become a dad. *My* dad."

"Practising, son. Naturally."

"Practising? For what – oblivion!"

"Don't, Davey. The ladies don't go for cynicism. I was practising for the Isle of Man TT."

"What on earth is that?"

"Only one of the most dangerous sporting events in the world."

"Well, that's responsible. Didn't even make it to the bloody ferry, did you?"

"No." Rick pauses for a moment. "But there's still time."

David Ramsden turns to stare at the ghost of his late father, who is sitting there in the seat beside him looking paler and more agitated than his son has ever seen him, yet also, curiously, more determined.

"Keep your eyes on the road, son. We're here."

There are around a dozen motorcycles and dutifully helmeted riders at the airfield and as many instructors, male and female, yet David spots Daisy straight away. And it isn't just because she is standing beside the gleaming Triumph, a sight over which he can hear his rapt companion immediately begin to slaver. At least, he assumes the 'hello, baby' and 'hi, you little beauty' are addressed to the bike.

David can't help noticing that whilst she is possibly the most practical and down-to-earth person he has ever come across, there is something curiously otherworldly about Daisy Gosforth, as if she is firmly rooted on this planet, yet inextricably linked to somewhere and something beyond. He can't quite explain it and thinks perhaps it is because he has never met anyone, young or old, who appears so comfortable and almost unnaturally serene in their own skin, seemingly untouched by the earthly forces surrounding her.

He also can't help but notice once again, berating himself even as his eyes remain stubbornly fixed, how well that skin is contained within worn, but undeniably fetching, motorcycle leathers. He puts this uncharacteristically crude observation, directed at someone who is so far removed from his limited social (and even more limited imaginative) circle, down to the strain of the occasion. And, of course, the fact that he is being driven round the bend at almost exactly the same speed as his clearly possessed father took that fatal curve so many years ago.

"Good enough to eat, that one is," mutters the ex-biker beside him, reminding David gratefully how much attitudes have moved on. He just wishes he wasn't thinking exactly the same and supposes the difference is that these days you just don't express it out loud.

David never had robot toys as a child and doesn't go to those movies in which robots play a major role. Yet, as he struggles stiffly out of the Volvo, clad in his spanking new – and to him, ridiculously expensive – leathers, he feels that he is moving and creaking exactly like a machine designed to function as a working human but leaving plenty room for more work to be done.

"Morning, Mr Ramsden," says Daisy Gosforth, moving towards him. The professionally welcoming smile can't quite cloak the apprehension on her make-up-free and enviably unlined face. "Are you sure?" she asks gently.

"Too tight?" he asks, assuming she is questioning his dress sense.

"Probably, but I meant about all this. You know. The Triumph."

David doesn't say anything until a voice beside him says, "Unless you don't want a sound night's sleep ever again, tell her you're more than sure."

"I'm more than sure, Ms Gosforth," says David, without much conviction. "I've never been more certain of anything in my life."

"And it has to be *that* Triumph," comes the prompt.

"And it has to be *that* Triumph," repeats David, adding,

"although, I've done my research and I do realise that I must go to full licence to be legally permitted to ride this one on the roads." He can't believe he is actually spouting this rubbish and that he should be demanding practical instruction on the one machine that is specifically programmed to kill Ramsdens.

"Fine," she says, shaking her head. They walk across the recently restored tarmac towards the threatening machine. "Okay. Well, I normally start my pupils off by comparing and contrasting riding a motorcycle with riding a bicycle, so…" She is about to elaborate on this when she notices his face. "What's wrong, Mr Ramsden?… Mister…?" The first lines begin to appear on her brow as the horrible truth dawns. "Can't ride a bike, can you?"

David shakes his head. "My mother wouldn't let me near the things. I could never work out why – well, not until last week."

"Oh shit," says the spectral voice beside him, adding ominously, "I might be here longer than we thought."

DO I HEAR FOURTEEN?

The difference between learning to ride a motorcycle and taking lessons in driving a car is, of course, that the practising biker will eventually need to confront the highways entirely on his own.

David Ramsden, however, is never on his own.

At each point on his journey, from that first tentative mounting, an almost invisible passenger rides pillion, whispering fervid and occasionally crude instructions into the ear of his apprehensive but strangely determined son.

Yet something almost as momentous, and possibly even more surprising, is happening to David. It occurs on the very first lesson, when he manages to un-creak his encased legs sufficiently to clamber onto the huge and terrifying machine. He was once lifted onto a mangy donkey on a seaside day trip in a rare moment of abandon by his over-cautious mummy, and began immediately to cry, because he suddenly found himself helpless and unimaginably far off the ground. He feels much the same right now.

For about five seconds.

It could be the encouraging, if certifiably overexcited, voice in his ear that only he can hear. But he doesn't think so.

Something is happening to him, something deep inside, not just corporeally but within his very soul and essence. His inner Dave. And it occurs the moment this terrifying machine, on which he has been sitting with understandable reluctance bordering on an almost existential dread, bursts suddenly into roaring life.

To the utter astonishment of his instructor, himself and most probably everyone around him, David discovers that he has a natural sense of balance; more than that, an instantaneous, almost inexplicable affinity with the machine that now throbs so powerfully and unforgivingly beneath him, like a tiger straining at the leash. As if somehow his own ignition has simultaneously been switched on.

It scares the shit out of him! Yet somehow – not.

This state of affairs, however, comes as absolutely no surprise to his late father, who always knew his progeny would have biker's genes. What comes as more of a surprise is that David, rather than feeling stolidly hostile to this turn of events, finds himself curiously elated – even as this same elation is probably sending his hypertension off the charts.

He gradually senses that the undisguised admiration of those other new learners around him, most of whom are at least twenty years his junior, isn't purely for the exquisitely restored 1974 Triumph T120 Bonneville.

"Well, I never thought I'd find myself gobsmacked," says Daisy Gosforth, shaking her head, as the first lesson draws to an end. "If I didn't know better, Mr Ramsden, I'd say you were a born biker. Are you sure you haven't done this before?"

David is sitting on the Triumph and shaking his head, wondering for a moment if he might be possessed or schizophrenic or victim perhaps of multiple personality disorder, like someone he once saw on a documentary, before his mum switched it back to *Emmerdale*. But he can sense the shake of another equally triumphant yet completely weightless head directly behind his own.

When Daisy moves off incredulously to write something on her chart, David turns to Rick.

"It's you, isn't it? Keeping me upright."

"I'm a ruddy ghost, sunshine. This was all your own work. Born to ride, you are."

"Don't be ridiculous," scoffs son-of-ghost. "This is just to get you off my back, you understand. Literally."

"If you say so. And a Ramsden always keeps his promise."

David doubts this with every fibre of his being but holds his own counsel.

"Oh God, Davey, did you not feel the thrum?"

"The what?"

Somewhere, David Ramsden knows full well what his transported dad is on about, although he dares not admit it. Not yet. Perhaps not ever. Because it frightens the timid middle-aged auctioneer still in him to death.

"*The thrum!*" enthuses Rick. "You know – the throb of her. The sensation of man and machine as one. The not knowing where she starts and you ruddy finish. It's better than sex, Davey, even with your mum. Although, mind you, sometimes riding her wasn't unlike—"

"*That's my mother you're talking about!*" yells the outraged son.

Daisy, who happens now to be making a very swift phone call, looks back at him in puzzlement.

"No, it's my mum I'm talking to. She's not been well." She ends the call and returns to the bike. "Why would I talk about yours?"

"No reason," says David. "Shall we book another lesson, Ms Gosforth? Saturday the fourteenth? And I hope she gets better soon."

"Thanks. And sure, if you want. Can I ask you something, Mr Ramsden?"

"David," whispers Rick.

"David," mutters David, a bit shyly.

"David… why are you doing this?"

He looks at her. "When I have enough adventure in my life…?"

"*What?*" yelps Rick. Daisy seems a bit lost for words. The man doesn't appear to be attempting sarcasm.

"If I told you, Ms Gosforth," says David, "you wouldn't believe me."

"Oh, I'm sure I would."

He takes off his helmet and she looks into his pale grey eyes. There's a disarming, crinkly warmth to them that she hadn't quite spotted before. And they are currently wide open.

"No, you wouldn't," he insists.

Despite her usual cynicism, she finds that she is drawn to the almost painful innocence of the man, as if life has managed to pass him by without leaving a trace, save for the natural effect of years rolling inexorably on. Somehow she knows instinctively that if this David Ramsden did tell her something, however bizarre, she would believe him.

"Okay, well, let me get my calendar," she says, tapping into her phone.

David unzips every zip in his new leathers, save thankfully his fly, until he finds his own small pocket diary.

He can't feel the nudge his father wants to give but knows that there is an excited virtual-nudger beside him.

What perturbs David most about the morning is that he is actually looking forward to the next encounter. Whether it's with Bonneville, Triumph or Gosforth, Daisy he is not entirely certain. He finds either scenario equally disconcerting. For a man who has just discovered an unexpectedly acute sense of balance, he feels in grave peril of disturbing a long-established and reputedly comfortable equilibrium.

So he won't think too much about it, and simply let the days crawl by until the next invigorating lesson.

DO I HEAR FIFTEEN?

The days between lessons do indeed crawl, as if in defiance of the escalation in speed occurring with some regularity on the converted airfield.

Finally, David tells himself that if he takes on more instruction with Daisy, perhaps early mornings or even the occasional lunch hour, it will accelerate the departure of what is most haunting him.

In his rare but precious quiet moments, he wonders if what is most haunting him may not be his late father after all. And this is what disturbs him most.

There is a part of David that is genuinely beginning, against every sane instinct, to share the surging excitement Rick Ramsden feels each time the fatherly ghost sits on that old Triumph, behind (or sometimes even in front of) his son. *The deceased biker's sheer transparency*, David thinks with something bordering almost on affection, *isn't simply a feature of his spectral state.*

"For the first time in my life, son, I'm proud of you," says Rick, as they stroll down the busy street towards the auction house, some weeks after their first 'spin'.

David is less self-conscious about talking to his father in public now, mainly because he is wearing those earphones he recently observed on more worldly souls, with a microphone built-in.

"Weren't you proud when you read about my success in the auctioneering field?"

"I was excited to read about you. 'Course I was. Y'know, that you were alive and still shacked-up nearby. But be honest, Davey, what father could say he's proud of a son who's an auctioneer?"

"Most fathers, actually."

"Not when their boys were born to be bikers," insists Rick. "Just ask your new lady friend." Before David can protest at either of these notions, which are too ridiculous even to countenance, Rick has a revelation that sends him leaping high into the Cotswold air, where he lingers until he can calm down. "*Of course!*"

"Of course *what*?"

"Bloody hellfire! Your mum was riding pillion with me until she was four months gone! It's all making sense now. *You were there, Davey!* And, blow me – you were conceived in my bloody bike shed! Right next to the Bonnie! My Wendy popped in wearing her tight little T-shirt and spanking new hotpants that steamy Sunday morning. Just when I was polishing my—"

"AAHHH… ummmm… ooooohhhhh…"

If the worthies of Cheltenham wonder why their local auctioneer has burst loudly into a song which sounds vaguely foreign, with choreography to match, they wisely keep it to themselves – at least until they can pass the news on to everyone who might be interested.

Unfortunately, Quentin is one of those interested.

And a fortnight after this, when David is up to three lessons a week with a bemused yet curiously never-bored Daisy Gosforth, the older man strolls corpulently over to David's desk and asks his senior auctioneer to join him for a lunchtime drink.

David grabs his new leather jacket from the rack beside him. Which is probably his first mistake.

"What the hell is *that*?" asks Quentin, pointing to the garment as if it has just been sliced off an available cow.

"Do you like it? I bought it for— for a change."

"It has tassels, David," the older man mutters. "We need to talk."

"Wanker," says Rick, and David knows that for once his dad isn't talking about him.

*

The old Tudor pub, with its high ceilings and minstrel gallery, might readily be described in local guidebooks as characterful. Yet as David and Rick look around, they can see that it is mostly full of characters with whom they wouldn't wish to spend that much time. The tourists are okay, the Ramsdens kindly concede, as are those who pop in now and then for the overpriced gourmet food, but it's the regulars with whom David is finding less and less affinity.

In the past he has been able to do small talk with relative ease, simply by making a show of listening avidly to the beer-guzzlers and borderline alcoholics, whilst they loudly rabbited on about themselves or foreigners. But these days, to his astonishment, he feels a desperate yearning to tell them about his other life, a life in which they would be at best disinterested or at worst appalled. He has recently read in newspapers about people who 'identify' as something or other, whilst first impressions might signal quite the reverse. He wonders, as he gazes at his spectral father, whether he is beginning to identify as – God forbid – a 'biker'.

Thankfully, he is not totally lacking in perception and finds himself almost hoping that his boss will simply tell him to grow up, pull himself together and stop pissing around.

Quentin has downed his first lunchtime pint, but probably not his last, before he even contemplates speaking to his head auctioneer, who nervously sips a large lime and soda.

Of course, someone else won't shut up.

"I can't bear the thought, Davey."

David dares not ask Rick which unbearable thought, although he's pretty sure he knows and that elaboration is on its way.

"That porky old fart's grubby hands all over my little Wend. Bad enough she looks like my granny – or at least like her old bat of a mum – but she deserves better in her old age."

"How's your lovely mother?" asks the porky old fart finally.

"You probably know as much as I do, Quentin," says David. "I haven't seen a lot of Mum lately." Which is true, what with living twenty-four-seven with his exhausting dead dad and trying to conceal exactly how he currently spends his free time (which he knows might send his poor mother to an early grave).

"She's been through a lot in her life, David. You don't want to be upsetting her even more, do you?"

"No, of course not," he says, suspicion growing swiftly as to where this conversation will lead.

"Well then, grow up, pull yourself together and stop pissing around."

There you go.

It is becoming increasingly apparent to David that the entire world has been aware for years of how his father died and that there has been a ruthlessly observed conspiracy of silence. He feels quite angry, which is not a common emotion for him, or hasn't been until Rick Ramsden came roaring back onto the scene.

As Quentin stares at him, David suddenly realises exactly what is going on here. At age forty-four and a half, he is finally rebelling.

It might be around thirty years too late, decades beyond the acknowledged time when most males go through it, but it has to be better than nothing. He has heard of mid-life crises, so he suspects he could also be having one of those, save for the fact that he is slowly beginning to realise that he may not actually have had a life to be in the midst of. Or perhaps, appropriately, it has been one only half-lived.

"Get on that stupid ruddy bike again and you can whistle for your partnership," threatens Quentin.

So, of course, Rick Ramsden begins to whistle. Something David could have predicted a mile off.

What David couldn't have predicted from any distance is that he himself would whistle too. Right into Quentin's glowering face.

The portly man, glass frozen halfway to his rubbery lips, is too shocked to respond. So David – who is, of course, equally shocked – turns to his father. He assumes, quite naturally, that the younger man will be beside himself that his son has finally grown a pair. He is surprised to find Rick Ramsden shaking even more than he himself is.

"Can we get out of here, please, son?" says Rick, rather quietly for him. "I-I never expected this."

David, deciding that he is hardly likely to astonish his stunned and reddening boss more than he just did, sidles away to continue his apparent conversation with thin air.

"*What?*" he addresses the ether. "Never expected that your milksop son would finally stand up to his bully of a boss?"

"No. Well, yeah. Respect for that, son." Rick reduces his quavering voice to a whisper. "But this is something much worse."

"What could be worse than a man losing everything he's ever achieved or striven for his whole life in a moment he may later – well, in about five seconds – regard as total madness?"

"Davey," says the shivering spectre, "I think this old pub is haunted. I've just seen a bloody ghost."

DO I HEAR SIXTEEN?

*I*f there is one place David Ramsden would never have expected to find himself, especially on a working Thursday afternoon prior to a full day's auctioneering, it is in the poky back room of a small motorcycle shop on the outskirts of the town in which he has lived, or at least existed, all of his life.

And, quite as unpredictably, he is drinking coffee, a caffeinated beverage off which he has been warned since childhood, as it leads to excess excitability and micturition, whilst being the sworn enemy of nourishing sleep.

This shows the full extent of the hedonistic mire into which the man has unwittingly sunk. But, as he tells the young woman sitting beside him, who had temporarily quit her front-desk post fifteen minutes earlier to minister to her never-less-than-bewildering pupil, if an angel like him can't raise a little hell now and then, he is unfit to wear the jacket.

"David," she says to him, gently but firmly, "babe, do you not think you're sort of running a little bit before you can walk?"

No one has ever called him 'babe' before, or at least not that he can remember, and it confuses him, as it confuses the unseen but ever-present figure beside him. Indeed, when David glances at his father's youthful face, he wonders at the look of deep puzzlement upon it, as if the man is slowly working something out. To David, however, all now seems crystal clear.

"No, Daisy, I really don't think I am. I've had what I believe they call an epiphany. It's time for me to cast off the shackles of responsibility," he announces poetically, although it does sound like something he might once have read, "and start the life I was born to lead."

"So you're going to leave your job?"

"Don't be ridiculous. Why would I do that?!"

"Oh sorry, I just thought—"

"No, I'm going to apologise profusely to Quentin then explain to him that if he wants the best auctioneer in Gloucestershire – in fact, dare I say, in the whole of the Cotswolds, including the Oxfordshire borders – he has to accept that he's also getting the first auctioneer in history to win the Isle of Man TT."

"That's my boy!" exults Rick, then pauses. If a ghost can be seen to go pale, this one does. "*WHAT?*"

Daisy says nothing, at least not immediately. To David's astonishment, yet by no means displeasure, she reaches out and takes both his trembling hands in her own small but noticeably firm ones.

"David?" she says.

He just nods. It's all he can do. He's sitting down yet everything is going too fast for him.

"Are you listening?"

He nods, again.

Finally, she utters the words he would never expect Ms Daisy Gosforth, nor indeed any confident woman of any description – or, to be totally honest, any woman at all – to say to him.

"Can I take you out to dinner tonight?"

David Ramsden is understandably speechless. And, for once, his father is too.

DO I HEAR SEVENTEEN?

The establishment to which Daisy Gosforth has invited David Ramsden on this sultry, late spring evening, perched on a major road just outside Tewkesbury, is not one that he already knows. This could be because he rarely ventures inside restaurants of any description, unless he has to make a professional assessment, preferring a homemade sandwich for lunch and quite often also for dinner.

This particular evening, however, he puts the unfamiliarity down to the rendezvous of choice being a bikers' café and, of course, he is not yet fully a biker. So he could only ever have arrived here in his old Volvo, which would stand out in the car park in a way that might make him, at best, self-conscious and, at worst, terrified.

Which is exactly what his Volvo does. To his slight disappointment, Daisy has arranged to meet him here at the café, rather than accepting his invitation to escort her. Perhaps she had known that he might be too intimidated by the array of bikes, with leathery-faced and jacketed smokers milling beside them, and would simply decide to drive them both on and away as swiftly as possible.

To the passenger who takes up no room and needs no invitation, Syd's Place is the Savoy. And the fact that Syd is a voluptuous lady biker only adds to Rick Ramsden's joy. He wishes that this 'gaff' had been here in his time – he'd never have gone home. David reckons if his dad tells him he thinks he has died and gone to heaven one more time, he will undoubtedly arrange it.

Ramsden Jr is sufficiently nervous as it is. The last time David went out on a proper date was with his ex-wife – and look how well that worked out. The fact that Daisy Gosforth actually invited him in person has sent him into a state of inner turmoil the like of which he hasn't known since he discovered an early Thomas Girtin watercolour in a run-down Tudor cottage near Painswick. And that was sixteen years ago.

David Ramsden reckons that he must have washed and showered at least three times. On observing his fellow guests, as he enters the steamy room (confusingly famed, according to its blackboards, for its all-day and all-night breakfasts), he muses that this gives him a lead of at least three on the majority. He immediately berates himself for being judgmental, especially as he will undoubtedly be one of their number ere long.

David would like to engage them in some biker talk and just wishes that he hadn't chosen to wear his best suit, the one he dons when accompanying his mother to church or a funeral. He supposes he should have realised that a place called Syd's would probably not be the classiest of eateries, although who really knows nowadays? But he doubts anyway that Daisy Gosforth is exactly flush with cash, especially not when she has just forked out on his dad's old Bonnie. (Not that he will allow her to pay the bill, he isn't that modern.)

Curiously, as he looks around the room and at the bemused diners staring up at him (most of whom assume he is either lost, slumming or a sanitary inspector), he realises that he doesn't feel overly daunted, choice of wardrobe aside, in talking motorcycles. He reckons that this is because bikes have formed a particularly large part of any recent discussions at home with his dad – discussions which, to his own surprise, he has grown almost to enjoy.

To be honest, David had thought that Rick Ramsden might have been a tad more gracious about an incredibly fired-up son wanting to finish the job his dad had started: competing in the notorious race that had so long ago eluded him. The son puts this down to sadness and regret, and perhaps just a tinge of totally understandable yet still rather petty jealousy.

On a more positive note, David Ramsden does know that his father is more than a little impressed with the incredible progress his lad has been making. And, of course, both men fully acknowledge that it is the constant voice in his ear, albeit infuriating at times, that has been helping David to blossom so swiftly into a two-wheeled knight of the road. This and the fact, childish though it might seem, that he wants to make Ms Daisy Gosforth proud of him.

Surely, he thinks, *to train a pupil up to those standards that David fully intends to attain must be like, say, a piano teacher coaching a youngster to first place in the International Tchaikovsky Competition. Only better.*

Who would have thought that he, staid and conservative (and just possibly a tad dull) David Ramsden, could find something in common with such a lovely young woman? He wonders if, on this very special and pleasantly mellow evening, they might become something more than simply teacher and pupil. The odds are not unpromising.

He also wonders where the hell she is.

"Reckon she stood you up?" asks Rick, as they sit down at a wooden table. "You can't let this one go, son. Birds like that come round once in a lifetime. Y'know, I really think I can smell that bacon."

Suddenly all the doubts that David has been trying frantically to park alongside his old Volvo come karooming back in with the speed he intends one day to reach on the Bonnie.

Ten minutes later, just when he has had to apologise yet again to a very pleasant server with a heavily tattooed face and an increasingly sympathetic expression, and explain that he is waiting for a friend who has probably become delayed in traffic, Daisy Gosforth walks in.

"Told you she'd be here," says Rick, although he never said anything of the sort.

David's relief and delight that his 'date', if this is indeed what she is, has finally turned up (a delight reflected in the faces of other customers) is somewhat thrown by the fact that she is holding two motorcycle helmets in her gloved hands. *Has she brought someone with her?* he wonders, his heart plummeting down to his sturdy brogues.

Daisy doesn't say anything. She just tosses one of the helmets to David then turns back to the door. He looks to his father, totally perplexed as to what is going on and exactly what he is expected to do. It could be a modern mating ritual that hasn't as yet appeared on his admittedly outmoded radar.

"She wants us to go with her," decides Rick, a man of the (nether)world.

"*Us?*" says David, who has already stood up, because this is what you do for ladies.

"I'm as intrigued as you are, sunshine. Thought we was gonna have a nice quiet dinner, just the three of us, with some good bike talk."

"So did I," says David, making for the door. The remaining clientele heave a communal sigh of relief. The suited guy talking to himself was starting to become a touch worrisome.

They aren't the only ones who are troubled. By the time David joins Daisy outside, she is on her Triumph Bonneville. The bike that he has, after so many lessons, curiously begun to regard as his own. Or, at least, as part of the family.

"*Get on!*" she tells David, which sounds very much like an order, one which clearly he will not be permitted to refuse. And indeed, why would he wish to, as it would mean riding on a machine that he has grown to love, whilst holding on tight to the woman he… well, he's not sure what his feelings are, but he knows they are nothing like he has ever felt before.

How strange, he thinks, *for someone who has just begun to relish speed, to feel that things are going far too fast.*

DO I HEAR EIGHTEEN?

"Put your arms round me," commands Daisy Gosforth. "Don't want you falling off."

Sporting the brand new helmet, which is just his size, David is able to climb onto the back of the now familiar bike with commendable adroitness. But the usual confidence he exudes on Bonnie completely deserts him when he finds himself in such close proximity to the head and body of his teacher, whose form he greatly admires and whose particular scent he can inhale even through all her layers of protective clothing.

This understandable hesitancy isn't shared by his late father, whose hands and body are rolling around the oblivious young woman with a zest that only the still-lustful dead can muster. He winks at David as he urges his son to do, if not exactly the same, some acceptable twenty-first-century equivalent.

"I remember when your mummy was just seventeen—"

"Oh, grow up!" cries David, as his rider starts the engine. He instantly realises, of course, that growing up was one of many opportunities sadly denied to his father by the very bike on which they're now sitting. Fortunately Daisy doesn't hear.

"Come on then, David," cries Daisy. "And hang on for dear sodding life!"

Whilst this doesn't sound quite the language David Ramsden would expect from a conscientious bike-trainer, it certainly makes its point. Tentatively, he stretches his worsted arms out until his fingers are clasped firmly around the young woman's taut waist. He finds himself thinking of his father and mother that hot morning in the bike shed, then decides that he won't go there.

"Ready?" she cries above the roar.

"I'll say," cries Rick.

"Where are we going?" enquires David, thinking that perhaps she knows a more intimate, less middle-of-the-A-road sort of place, where his smartest suit might find fellow travellers and he can discover whether this really is a date after all.

"You wouldn't believe me if I told you."

He wonders where he has heard this before.

*

The pure exhilaration David Ramsden feels when powering the Bonnie down an airfield at full pelt is as nothing compared to the vomit-inducing sensation of riding pillion with a biker who appears to know no fear. Especially on roads where caution is not only advised but almost mandatory.

He can't as yet understand why Daisy Gosforth feels impelled to travel quite so fast. His only assumption is that she has made reservations at somewhere rather exclusive and that these are not the sort of people to hold a table for even a second beyond the diarised time. But then why arrange to meet him at Syd's? Unless this is a very 'in' biker joke to which he is not yet, but happily soon will be, party.

David knows that he won't be overheard if he whispers into a nearby phantom ear.

"Dad, why are we going so fast?"

Silence. From one all-too-rarely silent source. For an unexpected reason.

"I'm moved, son," says Rick gently, after a few moments.

"Yes, I'm moved too," says David, not understanding. "My bloody bowels most of all. Answer my question."

Rick can't talk. He's too choked to make a sound. Finally he manages, "I'm moved, son, because you just called me 'dad'."

"Did I?" said David, genuinely surprised.

But then he too finds himself unable to speak, as he recognises *exactly* where they are.

It's the same road he drove along just a few short weeks and a lifetime ago. He was in the old Volvo and well into his Finnish when, about a mile or two further on, beyond a few tight and winding corners, a (justifiably) horrified old lady ran smack into his side.

He can tell by the intake of ghostly breath that his father recognises it too. They look at each other, but neither says a thing. No need.

The speed at which Daisy is taking the curves makes David more terrified than he has ever been in his life. Not that he has ever done anything the least bit terrifying, but his mother has made quite certain that he remains terrified of absolutely anything he might do. He can't for a moment believe that his 'date' is staying within those speed limits on which she has insisted at every lesson she has given him.

David suddenly wonders if the young woman is going slowly – or, indeed, quite rapidly – insane. And whether he is a contributory factor. He doubts it. Why would anyone like her go mad over someone like him?

Yet why also should Ms Daisy Gosforth wish to send one of her most innocent pupils careering at over 100mph round the Cotswold bends, their fragile heads and bodies now at such an angle as to be sailing almost parallel to the most treacherous road in the area?

He tries to yell into her nearest ear but her helmet, the rabid scream of the engine and perhaps her downright contrariness make any warnings futile.

It is with particular horror – amidst all the terrors of this impending night – that David sees the fatal bend coming up.

He can only pray that Daisy Gosforth sees it too, because so far she's offering him precious little evidence. Indeed, it feels to him that the young woman is going to smash headlong into the very same bend at which—

"NO!" screams David Ramsden.

"FUCKKK!" screams young Rick, the older.

The brickwork, which must have been replaced at the time of that fatal crash, is looking like it might soon need replacing again. Because Daisy and David – and, of course, Rick – are charging straight for it.

History is going to repeat itself. Incredibly loudly. And bloodily. And—

And yet it doesn't.

A nanosecond before the inevitable and undoubtedly fatal crash, Daisy executes the most exquisite glide, front wheel rearing like an obedient stallion, back wheel eating up the grass verge bordering the deadly wall, until she can safely land and screech to a screaming halt some good distance ahead.

"We're here!" she cries, as the roar dies down and two generations of Ramsdens begin to cry.

DO I HEAR NINETEEN?

Sitting on the low front wall of a now deserted old house, eating chunky homemade sandwiches which his host has been storing in her leather pocket, is not how David Ramsden had expected the evening to unfold.

To be fair, he has been far too on-edge to hold out any expectations whatsoever. So the novice biker/shit-scared passenger is forced to admit, as his heart rate and blood pressure return almost to normal – although they may never fully do so – that this isn't the worst of outcomes. (The expression he has heard about some eating establishments – that people would *kill* for a table – has a hitherto unappreciated resonance.)

Finally, he has to ask, "Ms Gosforth… Daisy…?"

She stops him with a nod. "I know: 'What the fuck was all that about?'."

"Well, I wasn't going to—"

"Yeah, what the fuck was all that about?" echoes Rick, who *was* going to. He still feels curiously hungry. Must be from the sight of those all-day breakfasts at Syd's.

"You were going too fast, David."

He stares at her.

He wasn't the rider who nearly killed them both… so she must mean their relationship. But he's not sure there even is one – and anyway, wasn't it she who asked him?

"I'm confused, Daisy."

"Can I tell you a story?"

He just nods.

"You won't believe a word of it, so take it as a fairy tale. Although," she pauses and looks back up at the darkened house, "although it's probably more of a ghost story."

This time it's David and Rick who exchange glances.

"About eighteen years ago, when I was a little girl, I lived in this house." She points to a small front bedroom but neither man can take their eyes off her face, a face that appears to be growing younger by the second. "That bedroom, right up there."

David hears a gasp, which is more like a shocked sniff. As if the 'person' beside him suddenly knows exactly what's coming.

"Oh my God!" whispers Ramsden senior.

"There was a little hole in the ceiling," continues Daisy.

David recalls that small knothole, last spied when he had collapsed onto the rotten timbers in Mrs Eileen Ballard's dusty loft.

"And I was sure that someone was whispering to me through it as I slept."

"It was totally dark, son. I only whispered – I never peeked," insists Rick, although the thought hadn't even occurred. "I never thought she'd hear me."

"It was a young voice," she continues, "the voice of a young man. A local man, I think. And he told me how, about twenty-five years earlier, he'd been practising on his bike for the big race – it was a Bonnie T120, like the one I just bought – and he'd crashed really badly. Well, as badly as it gets. Into this very wall we're sitting on."

"Or the wall that this one replaced," corrects David pedantically, but Daisy doesn't hear him. She's a little girl again, back in her tiny, doll-strewn bedroom. Listening to a ghost.

"He was going *way* too fast, poor guy. And not wearing a helmet. And doing a lot of other daft things young men do when they think they're immortal." She looks at David. "Older men too."

David can hardly speak. "So, what did you do?"

She seems puzzled. "Do? I didn't do anything, David. I was a child. I forgot all about it."

"No, you didn't," says Rick. But now he's smiling, and his eyes are wide open.

"Well, I thought I'd forgotten. But look where I ended up. Look at what I'm doing. I hated school, although I'm far from stupid." She pauses, as if waiting.

Rick gives his son as near to a nudge as he can manage.

"Far from it," agrees David. "You're one of the brightest people I know."

"Exactly. And thank you. It was only when I saw the Bonnie – y'know, the one Walter was restoring – that it all came shooting back. And I had to have it. Hey, maybe it was even the same one!" She shakes her head at the lunacy of the notion.

"But why…" He finds himself too confused to complete the thought.

"Why did I nearly kill us both?"

He just nods.

"I wanted to warn you. The way he – it, whatever it was – warned me."

"Warn me? About what?"

"Well, about taking risks. Okay, I know we all have to take risks in our lives—"

"I don't," says David. "Well, I haven't until now."

"There are risks and risks, David. I mean, accepting my invite this evening was a risk."

"I'll bloody say," says Rick, still panting.

"But wanting to ride a bike round the most dangerous circuit in the world? At your age? Just because you've discovered some – I dunno – hidden aptitude." She stares at him with those scarily honest yet curiously knowing blue eyes, and he feels the stare exposing his soul. "How stupid is that!"

"Very stupid?"

"Wasn't actually a question. But yes, very stupid. You knew somewhere that you needed… well, something else in your life. But surely not *this!*"

"Did you ever try to find out who the man was?"

"I told you, I'd forgotten. Or at least my conscious mind had. I suppose I could try now. But poor guy, he must have killed himself over forty years ago. Why bother?"

David can sense a movement beside him.

Rick is bouncing up and down, shouting into the young woman's glowing face as loud as he can.

"I *knew* it. I knew in my water it was you!"

"Rubbish!" responds David.

He watches the hurt rise on her face, like one of those sudden and unexpected allergic reactions his mother has always warned him about. And the pain in his own heart is unbearable.

"*No* – Daisy! I wasn't talking to— You're right, Daisy. I'm sure you are… What did you mean, I needed something else in my life?" He looks around, as if for guidance. He can't understand why his reckless young dad is suddenly looking so – hard to admit, but undeniable – very wise. "What did I need, Daisy?"

"You needed me, David Ramsden."

The silence around them and between them is quite beautiful. Until a voice right next to him cries, "*Result!*"

"Daisy Gosforth," says David Ramsden, wondering if he might be going slightly insane, yet curiously not feeling too worked up about it. "There's somebody I'd like you to meet."

DO I HEAR TWENTY?

The loft feels far less chilly this morning as David Ramsden slides opens the hatch and clambers back up for his second ever visit. He observes contentedly that he is taking the dodgy ladder with a lighter spring to his step, hoisting himself onto the fraying timbers with the sprightliness of an auctioneer half his age.

"Are you sure you want to stay up here... again?" he asks the figure just ahead of him.

"It's my home, Davey," replies his father, looking around as he hops into the dark, familiar chamber. "Until my maker sees fit to—"

"Yes, well, all in good time."

They sit down beside each other on the old chaise longue. Neither speaks for a while, which is a huge strain on at least one of the parties. Finally, David has to say what has been on his mind.

"You never wanted me to try for that race, did you?"

"And bloody kill yourself? 'Course not, son."

"Then why—"

"I wanted you to *meet* people. Not stuffy ones like... well, like you. Real, decent people."

"Like bikers."

"Yeah. And like Daisy. She was my sign, son. Well, her and the Bonnie. I wanted to see you happy, Davey. I wanted you to have what I missed." He looks at his son, who is still wearing his leather jacket. "And I don't mean a trophy."

"You mean a life."

"And a kid."

"Well," David nods, with a shy smile, "maybe you'll get your wish."

"When are you two moving in?"

"The nineteenth. When the sale goes through." He shakes his head. "I'll say one thing – when a house is haunted, you don't exactly have to fight off other buyers."

"See how parents can help their kids onto the property ladder! So, what does your mum reckon about you and our Miss Gosforth?"

"What do you think?" David's sigh of frustration seems to reverberate around the dusty loft. "Daisy isn't exactly what she envisioned."

"She'll come round. Hey, would you like me to talk to her?"

David stares at the man and suddenly begins to laugh in a way that he doesn't think he has properly laughed in his entire life.

"One day," he says, when he recovers. "Perhaps. Maybe."

"*Are you two going to be up there all day?*" calls Daisy Gosforth from the landing. "I'm not cleaning this dustbowl on my own."

"Coming, my love," calls her fiancé, the auctioneer. "So, Dad," he says, smiling at the younger and more deceased man, "you okay?"

"Couldn't be happier. You know where I am, Davey. Until He—"

"Yeah. I do. And you know where we are. Or will be very soon. Just don't scare us away. Or peek!"

"On yer bike, son!" The ghost of the late Rick Ramsden laughs. "On yer bike."

PENALTY!

THE GAME

I've heard it said that the best friends we can ever have are the ones we make in childhood. Because with them we share the most potent memories. You know, those formative experiences and emotions that have made us what we are today.

That's certainly true of me and George and Adrian and Clinky, fast friends and closest buddies to this very day, almost seventy years on. I *know!* I can hardly believe it myself.

We all met in the junior school of our local grammar on the North East Coast, way back when we were just seven years old. But we truly bonded forever when we were at the advanced age of eleven, in our first year of the seniors. And I honestly believe that it was all because of the dramatic events surrounding the Car-Washing Maniac of Number 43. (Who's probably long gone by now, God rest him and his shammy leather. This was, after all, the late fifties. You remember – when the world was still in black and white.)

It began on an ordinary Sunday morning in late autumn.

We didn't go to church in our family. Our dad told us that God was everywhere, but especially – on a good day – at the municipal golf course. And the funny thing was, as I recall, it never rained on a Sunday. Or if it did, it would get it over with by breakfast and not start again until after tea, when we were watching the telly. Sort of a gentleman's agreement.

Everything would start when I'd scoot out the front door

of our little house first thing, often even before my mum and dad had fully woken up. We lived in a tiny cul de sac. (Actually that reminds me of a joke my dad would tell. About the Geordie coalman who went to France for his holidays then came back and asked his customers if they wanted their nutty slack '*coal de sack* or *a la cart*'. I never understood it then and it's not exactly a rib-tickler now. But it's still nice to remember it.) Anyway, that's when I went round the corner on a morning to pick up George.

No idea why old George – or young George as he was then – couldn't just shoot round that same corner to pick me up. I lived closer to our final destination (and he was a little whirlwind in those short grey trousers he always wore) but I suppose this was just the way things were.

"*Achtung, donner und blitzen, der Englische pig dog,*" he'd yell as he charged at me, like in the war comics we both read.

I'd immediately fall to the ground screaming, "*Aaarrgghh!!*" Every time. Without fail.

"I'm going to be a Desert Rat, when I'm twenty," George would announce as we'd run round to fetch Adrian, "like my Uncle Sidney's mate."

George was my best friend, my blood brother, sixer to my seconder, Johnson to my Boswell. He was exactly four and one third months older than me and about ten years wiser.

"If you dropped a cat out of an aeroplane from 30,000 feet, it'd land on its paws and run away. Think Adrian's got any sweets?"

It was always Adrian's mum, as I recall, who opened their door. And she always had the biggest smile for us, as if we were this terrific surprise, even though we turned up at this same time every single weekend.

Of course, Adrian was right behind her, in his newly washed and pressed soccer kit. He wasn't just the tallest of the four of us, he was by far the sportiest. He didn't have any ambitions, however, to be our 'leader'. But that said, you couldn't ever lead Adrian where he didn't want to go.

"Don't be late," warned his mum, handing each of us a gobstopper. "Your cousin Beryl is coming for lunch."

As we ran off down the path – I don't think we ever actually walked anywhere, except maybe into morning assembly – Adrian said, "She keeps w-wanting to show me her kn-kn-knickers." We knew he meant Cousin Beryl, not his mum.

Adrian had a bit of a stutter. Still does but it doesn't seem to have stopped him getting where he wanted to go in life. Which was medicine actually, not sport. Football was the most important thing in our lives back then – playing and watching – but it never occurred to any of us to do it for a living. Passion didn't equate with flair.

"*Come on, you buggers!*" said George, who thrived on impatience and relished action. "*He'll* be starting soon." 'He', of course, being the Maniac of what and you-know-where.

To get to the street in question – the street where both Clinky and the Car-Washer hung out (although never together) – we had to crawl through enemy lines and evade at least one Gestapo lookout. Occasionally George would instruct us to flatten ourselves against a hedge or a wall, for no other reason than this was of course what you did.

Finally and inevitably we arrived at Rokeby Road. Our soccer pitch. Our Wembley Stadium. One small suburban road, outwardly very ordinary, but with a tall and glorious red-brick wall at the end of it, a goal-in-waiting if ever there was one. And there, as ever, parked just outside a modest and rather ordinary semi-detached house quite near to the wall itself, was the car.

A dusty old 1956 Coronation Blue Ford Consul Mk1.

A motor car desperately in need of a jolly good clean.

It was sitting there quite serenely, in its regular parking place, just like it always did on a Sunday morning. Settled in a street with not that many cars, because not everyone had a car in those days. A popular, average, medium-sized saloon, with enough 1950s dust and grime on it to write your English compo.

"He hasn't started yet," observed George, the anticipation already building in his voice.

We had one more house to visit. Probably the most important one. Not because its youngest occupant was our finest player. Not by a long chalk. Clinky was simply the one with the ball.

I rang the bell and a lady for whom the term long-suffering might well have been coined eventually came to the door.

"Hello, Robert," she said wearily. "Hello, lads."

"Is Clinky up, Mrs Washburn?" I asked politely.

The woman sighed and called up the stairs. "*Neville!*"

Of course Clinky wasn't his real name. What parent calls their child 'Clinky'? But we all called him that because he was the first boy in our class to be put into detention. Or 'clink', as it was known. It wasn't even his fault – our maths teacher had an unfortunate lisp and when he asked a question Clinky came out in unwitting sympathy. The floor was wet with algebra.

"Here I am!" announced Clinky finally, at the doorway.

"Where's the ball?" asked George.

We stood there another five minutes until our pal returned with a fine, white, plastic football, which he proceeded to mishead dramatically into the hall mirror then mis-knee painfully up to his chin. Sometimes I think we only played with him because it was his ball, but I don't reckon he ever cottoned on. He's a maths teacher and deputy head himself now. Well, a contentedly retired one. (In case you thought he might have been a soccer legend or manager or something.)

"Can I be on *your* team today, Adrian?" he asked.

Adrian, who was probably the sweetest amongst us and perhaps still is – he was a paediatric cardiologist until relatively recently – just nodded. Clinky kept on beaming, even as his attention turned to the car.

In fact all our attentions were on the car. And on the still firmly closed, white-panelled door of number 43.

We decided to sit down on the low brick wall that bordered Clinky's house. The house directly opposite the vehicle of the moment.

And wait.

*

Every Sunday morning we sat and waited on that same front wall. Me, George, Adrian and Clinky (who was still holding the white plastic ball). We looked like a very small team photo. Sitting and waiting. For that white-panelled door to open and for the aforementioned Maniac to emerge.

Finally – and quite inevitably – the door began to move.

I still recall us nudging each other. We always nudged each other, four little boys in shorts of varying styles and freshness, with cold scabby knees and beating hearts. Our eyes would widen in anticipation. Our mouths would gape.

And out he would come.

He was a nondescript man of medium height, with ruddy cheeks and thin, mean-looking eyes. He had precious little hair on his head, save near and out of his ears, and a small moustache that was sort of silver and trimmed almost to invisibility. He always wore the same shapeless grey trousers, with an equally baggy pale blue cardigan. And bottoming off this glittering ensemble was a well-worn pair of black, plastic wellingtons.

He proceeded to walk the length of his narrow path, as he always did, with his head bent low, almost like he was scrutinising the concrete, whilst daring his eyes at their peril to lift and look at anything remotely on the horizon. Certainly not up at the dusty car. It was if he was saving this joy, this enchantment beyond compare, until the very last moment.

Dangling from his right hand was a big yellow bucket full of soapy water. In his other hairy fist was clutched a large cloth carrier bag, which we knew contained an impressive assortment of the finest sponges, bits of rag, shammy leathers (or chamois leathers, as I learnt much later they were officially called) and various tins of polish.

He came to a pause at his front gate.

Then and only then did he allow his glinting head to lift towards the sun, his eyes to stare straight ahead over his gate of wrought iron. It was as if he was trying to catch the dormant car unawares.

Immediately his face would become suffused with an ecstatic glow, a transcendence that I bet even his poor wife had never seen, although, of course, I have no way of knowing this for certain. Indeed, the neighbours in the street all said that the man loved that car far more than he loved his missus. We didn't find that curious at the time – we had seen his missus. Do you know, I don't think we ever caught his name. To us he was always just the Car-Washing Maniac at Number 43.

The routine was always the same. He would approach the car like a besotted yet still tentative suitor, caress it featheringly from bonnet to boot and then very delicately run a finger along its dusty roof, savouring the weekly muck and grime, worshipping the deceased insects, perhaps pausing en route to flick away an errant leaf or acorn.

This was when the fun began.

This was when we started to bounce the ball.

And his adoring hand would freeze in mid-stroke.

As ever, he would look across at we four little miscreants sitting on the wall. By this time it would be George who had possession of the ball. George was undisputed master of the taunting bounce.

The car-washer's face was a tableau of hate and fear.

This was our cue to hoist ourselves briskly up from Clinky's wall and over to the infinitely larger one, on which you could still see, from previous weeks, the outline of a goalmouth scratched out with a sharp stone.

Although our backs were by this time turned to him, we knew that the man was waving his damp sponge at us, as he made his threat of the week.

"I'm warning youse all, you little sods," he addressed us in his usual neighbourly fashion. "If that blasted ball goes anywhere near this machine, there'll be ructions. I shan't tell you twice."

"Bet he will," muttered Adrian. "He's like a g-g-gramophone record."

"It's my street as much as his," protested George. "I'm a ratepayer."

I had no idea what a ratepayer was. I doubt George did either. He probably does now, what with him being a retired solicitor. (Fortunately, what was to happen later this particular, memorable week didn't cast a notable blight on his future career.)

As we began to kick the ball around, admittedly a bit hesitantly, Clinky shared with us his mum's opinion that the Maniac deliberately drove his car around all day Saturday, in town and in the country, over hill and dale and 'B' roads, getting it nicely 'clarty' and dusty, simply so that he could clean it like billy-o to sublime and pristine perfection on a Sunday.

"C'mon," said George, "forget about him. Let's pick teams."

Which we did, even though this particular Sunday it had already been most graciously decided. So for once the words 'I suppose I'd better have Clinky' didn't need to be uttered.

"Right," announced Adrian, taking charge before George could claim his territory. "Ten shots and swap. Most g-goals wins. We'll be attackers. Clinky, don't shoot until I t-tell you." To which Clinky waved obligingly, although we all knew that the chances of his taking this strategy onboard were pretty minimal.

I took up my defensive position, as the de facto goalie, knowing that George would be on the attack regardless. We could tell that Adrian was already preparing to shoot, before George could do one of his celebrated and often quite lethal tackles. Clinky stayed on the left wing, despite being a right footer.

"That's it, Adrian. Go on – shoot!" he cried. Several times in fact.

Which Adrian did. The first ball hit the wall with a thud, just above my head and the goalpost, and bounced towards the car. We could see the man watching it angrily. Daring it to even try.

The game went on like this. You could almost smell the tension in the street. Eventually, after the requisite ten shots, five of which found their mark, we changed sides and Clinky was in goal. Not for long, inevitably. The air was thick with sounds of triumph (from me and George) and abject apologies (from Clinky).

You could almost follow the progress of our game by its reflected glory in the ever more gleaming bodywork of the man's 1956 Consul. The car-washer's face was like a flashing traffic light – green for smoothly transported and red for paralysed with fear.

It was always the same. The battle on the soccer pitch was nothing compared to the war of nerves going on around it. The man wasn't going to move his car, and we would have had a hell of a job shifting our wall. (Although I might have been up for it a few years later – I went into property and construction.) If I'm totally honest, looking back, I reckon that this is what gave our game its special edge. You never really knew what was going to happen.

And that particular Sunday something certainly did.

It properly started after about half an hour, when Adrian, back in defence, tackled a powerfully oncoming George. My best friend went down clutching his ankle. It all looked a bit theatrical to me but, as he was my teammate, I prudently kept my own counsel.

"*P-penalty!*" yelped the grounded victim.

Adrian looked mortified. He wasn't a dirty player but nor was he a suspicious one. So he immediately conceded.

George, having made a miraculous, practically Lourdes-like recovery, lined up against Clinky in goal. The latter took up the posture we had all seen a thousand times on TV and at the local ground and did the usual jumping around. We all knew this had precious little to do with the inevitable outcome but to no one's surprise more than his own, Clinky dived in the unexpected direction just as George tried to wrongfoot him by doing the same.

It was a spectacular save. And there was truly only one way Clinky could express his almost overwhelming elation, not to mention utter surprise. With an exultant yelp, he gave the once white, now quite filthy, plastic ball a triumphant boot into the air.

Within seconds, the elation on his face had turned to horror.

Our mutual, albeit more muted, excitement transformed just as swiftly to fear.

The ball, still in the air on its victory roll, was heading unstoppably towards the car.

The car.

The Maniac was too busy polishing his already immaculate and buffed-to-buggery rear bumpers to take instant notice of the lethal sphere's inexorable trajectory.

But he certainly took it on board when the ball in question happily bounced onto the Ford's gleaming bonnet then unexpectedly upwards towards its gleaming roof. It now proceeded to glide sleekly and mercilessly across that immaculate surface, before smoothly descending the car's newly washed rear window like a hockey-puck along the ice. It ended up by spectacularly careering off the balding head of the man himself, leaving on this and every other shiny point of contact an almost circular dust spot, finally splashing with triumphant aplomb into his dirty yellow bucket.

We were all transfixed, our mouths hanging open.

As I recall, the man was pretty speechless too. But once the shock had worn off, he simply grabbed the ball with both trembling hands from where it had so splashily settled and tried to tear it mercilessly apart.

We all realised that we had to do or say something. Which we did, all at once.

"Very sorry, Mr, er…" I think I heard Clinky say 'Maniac' but thankfully it was only to himself.

"*Sorry*? I'll give you bloody sorry!" roared the man, his face growing redder and more choleric by the second. "Sorry isn't anywhere near good enough! Oh no, not by a long chalk!"

With this, he drew back his cardiganed, car-scrubbing arm and lobbed the offending ball right over his side gate and out of sight. It was quite an impressive throw, as I still recall.

"*There!*" He smiled cruelly. "What do you have to say about *that*, eh? EH? And it's never coming back. Oh no. Never ever! Again! And I'll do the same with the next one. Your footballing days in this street are over! For good!"

We just looked at each other. George was seething but Adrian remained his usual stoic self. I think I had so many emotions flying around I didn't know which one to go with, but I was distracted mostly by Clinky starting to cry. After all, it was his ball and his kick.

"That's not f-fair!" said Adrian, finally.

"It really isn't," said I, pretty feebly.

"He's crossed a line, that man," said George, but I don't think any of us knew what that meant.

"I'll tell my dad," whimpered Clinky. "He's a policeman."

"He's got a fruit shop," I said, to which my friend just shrugged.

Then George said something that changed the whole tenor of our hitherto helpless moaning.

"Don't tell anyone about this. Not even your mums or dads." He looked back at the man, who was devoting himself once again, with an angry vigour, to his special Sunday 'date'. "He's not going to get away with this. No way! The bugger's going to pay the penalty."

"What sort of penalty?" I asked.

"No idea," said George. "But I'm already working on it."

And knowing George, I truly believed that he was.

PENALTY TIME

"I t's got to be something really *really* d-d-dreadful," decided Adrian, as we walked back towards his house.

"Yeah," agreed Clinky. "Couldn't we just ask him if we could please have our ball back?"

One by one, or maybe in unison (it was a long time ago!), we each shook our respective heads. Eventually Clinky agreed with us.

"No. Okay. So what should we do now then?" he asked, quite reasonably. Then added, "George?"

George began to walk off towards his house. "I'm going home. To work on my plan."

"Yeah," I agreed, "so am I," although I didn't have a thought in my head other than anger and disappointment. And of course Sunday lunch.

"I've got to see Cousin B-Beryl." Adrian sighed. "And her kn-nickers."

"Okay. Well, see you at school tomorrow," said a smiling Clinky, who was the sort of person whose cheery demeanour couldn't be dented for long, even by a confiscated football. But inside we knew that he was probably pretty gutted, as they say today. "Will you have thought of something by tomorrow, George?" he inquired hopefully.

We all turned round to see the Car-Washer still glaring at us through his wing mirror.

"Bound to," said George.

*

"We could garrotte him with piano wire," suggested George, as the four of us walked to school the following day. (In those days, we walked everywhere, at any time. Day or night.) "The way the Frenchies did in the Resistance."

"Where do you get piano wire?" I asked, not unreasonably.

"From a p-p-piano, twit!"

Tentatively, I broached the question, as we reached the gates of our school: "Did you think of anything else, George?"

"'Course I did," said my wise old friend, disdainfully. "There's a thing they do in Japan. It's called Harry Kiwi. They slit each other's bellies with massive sharp swords and all their guts spill out on the carpet and the lino. Then they chop each other's heads off."

I hesitated to ask, but felt I had to, "How can they chop each other's heads off? I mean if you've just had your own head chopped off, you can't very well—"

Adrian, who could see George starting to become really angry that logic of all things should be so casually dumped over his inspired proposal, tried to move us on in a spirit of amicable collaboration.

"Maybe we could b-blackmail him. You do it with bits of old n-newspaper."

I really felt I should offer a suggestion of my own. But it had to make sense.

"*Kidnap!* We don't give him back until he gives us the ball." I realised I probably hadn't thought this one through quite sufficiently. "Until his *wife* gives us the ball."

"She'll probably be glad we've got him," said George, as we walked into the classroom, already stuffed with thirty, less vengeful boys. I could tell by the furrowing of his brows that his mind was still set on ultra-violence. He had already progressed to excruciating, mouth-foaming, stomach-exploding poison by the time our first lesson began.

Whenever I read in the paper about some unsolved crime, I like to think that George could have done it. He had the most highly developed criminal mind of any eleven-year-old I've ever met. So we knew for sure that he'd come up with something. Even if it took all week.

In fact, it took until Latin class, which was our last and most turgid period on the following Wednesday. (I could really see why it was a dead language – it was sucking the life out of us.) All the lessons prior to this had seen a fairly constant flurry of hastily hand-scrawled notes being passed surreptitiously, mostly from George to me and then onwards to Adrian and Clinky. These were met with equally surreptitious shakes of the head or mouths locked open in puzzlement-stroke-horror. Whilst unquestionably imaginative, none of the suggestions were the least bit feasible and several would have got us sent to reform school or locked up somewhere for life.

But it was only a matter of time.

I still recall the moment I read the actual winner. I wanted to leap up in the air and scream 'YES!', as indeed one should when confronted with genius. But I restricted myself to a solemn nod.

Unfortunately, however, the crumpled note of perfection chose to land on Clinky's desk just as a question from our rather stern Latin master assailed him.

"Washburn, please conjugate the Latin verb 'to work'."

I doubt Clinky even heard. He was too busy deciphering the note. The teacher only fully noticed him when the smile on my friend's face began to spread from ear to ear. He beamed at George and gave him two lusty thumbs up.

"Washburn," repeated the teacher. "I said conjugate the Latin verb 'to work'. I believe I even said 'please'."

No response.

"You see, class," announced the man, "verbs conjugate but Washburn declines."

Clinky heard this and was jolted out of his elation. "Sorry, sir, can you repeat the question, please?"

"Perhaps you would like to repeat it yourself, Mr Washburn. After school, tomorrow, five hundred times." With this, he picked up the crumpled note from Clinky's desk.

Another detention. But this time I do believe even Clinky would have reckoned that it was worth it.

And I'll never forget the look of utter bewilderment on our teacher's face when the poor man finally unfurled and read George's triumphantly hand-scribbled note.

*

Once he had come up with it, there was no stopping our dear friend.

He planned Operation Penalty, as I'm proud to say I myself named it, with all the skill and precision of a military operation. Or, perhaps, more accurately, the minute attention to detail of a major heist.

It was on the Thursday evening, outside the local scout hut, as we were scooting home in the dark from our weekly meeting, that George gave us the final instruction. (Kids regularly did night-time scoots in those days and played until all hours in the street. And we're all still here.)

"Next Saturday night. We strike. Pass it on."

Such was the authoritative charisma of George that, although we all heard exactly what he said, we each chose to pass the message on to our closest neighbour. Even Clinky, who was at the end of the line, passed it on to the scoutmaster's Alsatian.

The following day, in the school showers after rugby, when it was clear that George had been up nights doing even more meticulous planning, the cryptic instruction came: "Wear boot polish and gloves."

Perhaps it was our current nakedness that caused Clinky's confusion.

"Not j-just boot polish and g-gloves," clarified Adrian, to the most puzzled member of our gang, who then received a perhaps clearer instruction from George.

"Clinky, your house will be our operational HQ."

Once Clinky had absorbed this with some pride, we learnt that the whole devilish operation was to commence at exactly midnight on the upcoming Saturday.

"Synthesise your watches," said George, which I wasn't certain was exactly right, but I think we all knew what he meant.

*

Saturdays are funny things when you're eleven. They take about a month to come and, at most, half an hour to pass. But this Saturday was different. This Saturday would have got into the *Guinness Book*, no question. Every minute had ninety seconds to it. And I counted them all.

It was George's specific instruction that the four of us shouldn't be seen together on the days leading up to the big event. I wasn't quite certain why this should be, as everyone in the area knew that we were a 'gang' of sorts, albeit a relatively non-antisocial (pro-social?) and totally unthreatening one.

"Not seeing your pals this afternoon?" asked my mum.

To which I just shook my head.

"Want to come to the match with me?" asked my dad, to which I readily agreed in the hope that it might take my mind off the fraught activities of the upcoming midnight.

It didn't. Even though we won, and I had a Tizer and some chips.

Finally, the witching hour decided to come. (We were doing *Macbeth* in English that year.) I had already anticipated it by going to bed at the usual time but with my clothes still on. And not falling asleep. Which, to be honest, wasn't too tricky, as my heart was beating far too fast for slumber.

I used a torch to check my new Timex watch, then padded over to my desk, which was actually my grandma's old pine dressing-table, and eased out from one of its drawers a tin of black Cherry Blossom shoe polish I'd purloined earlier from a cupboard downstairs. Shining my torch onto the nearby mirror, I spread the polish thickly over my face. Then I put on some old and suitably dark woolly gloves and my United supporters woolly hat.

The final item – and probably the most important – was the small haversack resting by my bed. As I slung it on my back, I could hear the vital tools pre-loaded inside begin to rattle.

Trying to avoid the creaking floorboard on the landing, I slipped out of my room. But another floorboard had clearly decided to become the new creaker, and it caused my dad to open his bedroom door. I ran swiftly into the toilet.

"Robert, are you alright?" he said sleepily.

"Yes, thanks," I said, offering up a lavatorial grunt. "Uh, that's better."

"Straight back to bed now."

I heard his door close as I flushed. Then, gripping my bag tightly so that there were no more clunks, I tiptoed down the stairs and gently opened our front door.

Every click, creak or crackle sounded to my ears like an explosion, but I managed to leave the house undetected.

My watch read 11.55.

I ran as quietly as I could down the deserted road, keeping as close to the hedges and as far away from street lighting as possible.

When I was just a little way from George's house, a figure suddenly leapt out from another garden and gave me the shock of my life. It was, of course, my Machiavellian mate, completely black-faced and black-clad, wearing a full haversack that rattled in sympathy with my own.

"11.56. Dead on!" he said, with an approving nod.

We ran to collect Adrian. Typically he was already jogging on the spot outside his house. He nodded seriously to us, fully aware of the gravity of the situation and the enormous risks we were all taking.

Dodging in and out of the lamplight, we made our curious but determined way along the street, looking like child refugees from that hugely popular telly show of the time, *The Black and White Minstrel Show*.

Of course, when we arrived at Clinky's, the lad was nowhere to be seen. The three of us just looked at each other. We couldn't very well shout or ring the bell. And his bedroom faced the back, so we'd have a hard job hitting his window with a pebble. Although, at this stage, I was feeling that a brick might work for me.

After about five helpless minutes, which seemed to us like a lifetime, the Washburn front door opened and Clinky emerged. He was wearing a white Aran pullover, red mittens and a face covered in mid-tan shoe polish. We just stared at him.

"What happened to your f-face?" asked Adrian.

"We ran out of black," explained Clinky. The pullover required no explanation. He was just an idiot, but a warm one.

Dragging our eyes away from our almost luminous friend, we scanned the midnight street. It was totally deserted. Not a single light was on in any of the houses.

"Right," George sighed, "let's get on with it. Men, unzip your bags."

We did as we were told and each of us removed our own pre-specified tool of revenge.

"Take up your positions."

The four of us, gear in hand, walked across the road towards our target. The familiar and dastardly 1956 Ford Consul. Our bête currently ever so noir.

"You're a fine bunch of men," said George. "I'm proud to be leading you. Now get to work."

Which we did. With fear-laden gusto.

I was absolutely convinced that every clank, scratch, scrape and bang could be heard a mile away and that it was only a matter of time before the town's entire constabulary would be onto us.

We never realised that it would take us so long.

I suppose some of this was because our hands were shaking so much. From the cold, from terror and just from plain exhaustion. It was way past our bedtimes. And, of course, having Clinky didn't make it any easier.

"I need to go to the toilet, George."

"You should've gone before."

"I didn't need to go before."

Suddenly, we saw the lights of a car.

"Down, men!" ordered George.

As we threw ourselves madly onto the ground, the car's headlights just skimmed the top of our heads. We heard a screech of tyres then the headlights receded.

"He's just t-turning," said Adrian, in some relief.

"I don't need to go to the toilet now, George," said Clinky.

We resumed our task.

I heard myself whispering to Adrian, beneath the clatter and the clanking, "Adrian, do you think he'll know it was us?"

"I b-b-bloody well hope so."

We looked up at the Maniac's darkened bedroom window as we heard a final metallic clank.

*

The following morning, another typical Sunday, saw us sitting in the autumn sunshine on Clinky's wall once more. And staring bleary-eyed across the road. We all four of us looked like death warmed up; yet, inside our heads and bodies, we were so alive you could probably get electric shocks off us.

Finally, after what seemed like a lifetime, the white-panelled door directly opposite us slowly began to open. Number 43 was on the move.

"Here he comes," whispered George, although there was no one around to hear us.

The householder emerged. Dressed, as ever, in his Sunday worst, with his head bent directly down like he was fascinated by his own wellies.

We just stared at him, our minds almost engorged with anticipation and pure, hardly unreasonable fear. After all, we had never done anything of this magnitude (or criminality) in our entire lives.

Not a single breath emerged from any of our open mouths into the autumnal Northumbrian air, as the man stopped and began to lift his eyes upwards towards the holy Consul. We watched as that weekly smile of total, puppy-like adoration washed over his normally miserable face.

Then just as suddenly vanished.

The round and ruddy countenance of the middle-aged gentleman at number 43 appeared to pale, shatter and dissolve before our eyes. That regular Sunday-morning look of joyous anticipation replaced in an instant by one of singular heartbreak. He just shook his head, as if he couldn't quite comprehend what was happening.

His beautiful motor car had been transformed overnight into an object of horror and shame. It was no longer a trusty, reliable companion, covered and layered with a week's hard-earned dust and grime. It was now a car that looked almost professionally valeted, pristine and reeking of spit 'n' polish, gleaming all too brilliantly in the matutinal sun. Incredibly, miraculously, impossibly spotless. Groomed to perfection.

Cleaned to buggery. A vehicle that was indeed so showroom-proud that it almost seemed brand new.

I'll never forget the look the man threw us as we watched in silence from our little wall. It was the look of someone whose life and Sundays were suddenly robbed of all meaning. It was the look of a man bereft.

And all he received in return was four rather satisfied little smiles.

*

If you were to ask me today, '*Robert, have you ever been completely, utterly content?*', I'd have to say to you, 'yes'. Several times. Our wedding. The birth of our children. Their nuptials. The arrival of our grandkids. But maybe never more so than that day the four of us – George, Adrian, Clinky and I – scored the decisive penalty against the Car-Washing Maniac of Number 43. The magical day that our friendship, which still happily flourishes even in our dotage, reached its ultimate high.

(By the way, we did finally get our ball back. And the only cars we've ever cleaned since that day have been our own. But not every Sunday.)

SKI-ING!

THE CREMATION

*W*hilst quite often, in his more idle moments, Matt Brownridge had daydreamed that both his parents might topple over a cliff, or, better yet, the Clifton Suspension Bridge, he did not actively contemplate killing them until some days after his 'Uncle' Clive's cremation. Looking back from where he is now, however, Matt would have to admit that his parents' behaviour at that sad event must have added at least some fuel to the flame.

Matt and his younger sister Janie, who begrudgingly shared a small and uncomfortable rented flat in one of Bristol's more perilous suburbs, had each made a very special effort to look respectable for the dear man's last farewell. It was the least they could do.

Matt was wearing a shiny black shirt which he truly felt hit the funereal dress code bang on, even though Clive Dawkins wasn't known to be a fascist. He had even managed to retrieve his old Scout tie from the back of an overstuffed drawer, which he reckoned, despite the unidentifiable but stubbornly permanent stains, would still be a fitting tribute to the deceased, who, after all, had been his scoutmaster for so many of his formative years.

Matt wasn't quite certain how to explain the outfit to his boss when he returned to work later on, especially as had told the man that he was having a wisdom tooth extracted, but as he worked in telesales, he reasoned that it shouldn't be too much of a problem (although he might have to alter his voice a little, to allow for the after-effects of the anaesthetic).

Janie, on the other hand, had gone to town. After all, she had a reputation to uphold. A reputation that, unfortunately, quite unbeknownst to her, or at least blithely ignored, was for designing the most hideous and appalling outfits, not simply for home consumption but in the forlorn aspiration of future sales and fame. The fact that she had never managed to convince a soul that her designs were anything other than misguided and that no one aside from herself had, in all these years, even worn so much as a fascinator with her signature on it did not seem to deter her one bit.

She honestly reckoned that she looked the business when they entered the crematorium. This was only confirmed by the many glances and double takes being hurled at her jet-black crushed velvet outfit with the trellised, blue-leather back, thick taffeta underlay, a lacy Victorian collar, not unlike the sort dogs wear to stop them scratching a wounded ear, and random yellow splotches that looked like a seagull flying overhead had lost his breakfast. The expansive hat resembled something a person might wear at Royal Ascot, if they wanted to frighten the horses.

The siblings hadn't been able to sit next to their parents at the service, as Ray and Bobbi Brownridge had already parked themselves on either side of the grieving widow, forcing the late Clive's surviving blood kin to find spaces further down.

"Typical!" muttered Matt, to which Janie and several others nearby simply nodded, although Janie's head movements were beginning to prove a health hazard to anyone in her vicinity.

From their seats further to the rear, the siblings could watch their father's podgy hand slide snakily but purposefully around the quivering back of the bereaved lady, in order to fondle the fleshy shoulder of his unnaturally blonde wife.

"Dunno why he doesn't just bend her over the coffin and have done with it," said Janie, trying her best to tamp down unruly taffeta.

They had no idea, as the late Clive Dawkins glided into the flames to the strains of 'If You're Happy and You Know It', echoed by the dozens of now fully grown ex-Scouts amongst the attendees, that the worst was very much yet to come.

*

The line of friends and relatives arriving from the crematorium, to comfort the widow and stock up on free drink and open sandwiches, stretched out of the front door and down the narrow drive of the small and slightly neglected Dawkins semi.

The Brownridges dutifully, if not entirely patiently, waited their turn behind a seemingly endless conga line of former scouts and parents. Through the open doorway, they could see that the walls of the crowded little hall were festooned with Scout memorabilia. Photos of smiling troops over the years, all with the uniformed and ever-ebullient deceased at the helm, vied with browning snapshots from historic bare-knee jamborees and gang shows, with a framed collection of woggles taking pride of place. Even the wreath with Clive's name on it was done as a massive Scout badge for life-saving.

The words 'thank you for coming' were beginning to sound like a mantra as a teary Denise Dawkins greeted each of her guests in turn.

"It would have meant a lot to Clive. He loved his little boys and girls," she said, adding, a bit unnecessarily, "but in a good way."

By the time that the Brownridges, now quite ravenous, entered the house, Matt could see that his father was looking unusually shaken. The jowls on his fleshy face, normally stretched tight in smiles of overweening self-satisfaction, now hung so low it was as if he was beginning to melt. He had removed his hands from whatever part of his wife's still bounteous anatomy he had currently chosen to pet and was wringing them with what Matt could only think was anxiety, an emotion as alien to the man, in Matt's experience, as compassion, empathy or basic humanity.

"He's such a softy," murmured Bobbi Brownridge to her children, tapping her life partner's visibly shaking hands in total adoration. She didn't notice the look exchanged between her offspring and might not have understood it even if she had.

When it was their turn, Ray was of course first to speak. Unclamping his now clammy hands, he lay them down heavily on top of those of his grieving hostess.

"What can I say, Denise, love? What CAN I say?" He sighed and shook his head. "In the circumstances, I've cancelled my big birthday party on Saturday. Sixty-eight – hard to believe, eh? No, don't try to change my mind. I insist. Least I can do. So we won't be needing poor Clive's karaoke machine after all. Not that he'll be— drinks through here, are they?"

Bobbi was attempting to tidy her son's unruly hair when she realised that it was her turn to offer solace.

"It was a lovely cremation, dear – that dress is so you. And see, I told you Boots' waterproof eyeliner was a good buy."

"Thank you, Bobbi," said Denise Dawkins, sounding as if she almost meant it, but then her attention was captured and held hostage by Janie and that dress. "Hello, Janie, love. Thank you for coming. Is that one you made yourself?"

Beaming at this, Janie simply nodded and gave a little twirl, assuming the inevitable compliment was only a nanosecond behind.

"Oh Matty," said the older woman, moving on down the line with a wobble in her voice, "you were always one of his favourites. Clive was determined you'd get at least one badge on that little sleeve of yours before you left the troop. Still, badges aren't everything, eh?"

At this, she began to sob. Matt, who was himself feeling quite upset, offered a clumsy but comforting tap on her shoulder, only to watch the widow's slightly unkempt, silvery-grey head spin round, along with everyone else's, as a large and gleaming white Tesla pulled up noiselessly outside the house.

Their interest only grew as a good-looking and very nattily dressed young man stepped briskly out, clutching the biggest bouquet of flowers the onlookers had ever seen.

"*Ohhh, he made it!*" gushed Denise, offering up her first real smile of the day.

The young man, who appeared of a similar age to Matt and to many of the other ex-scouts, swished in, ignoring the line, and presented the huge bouquet with a theatrical flourish to the now beaming widow.

"Sorry I missed the send-off, Mrs D," said the new arrival quite loudly. "Bloody Cathay Pacific! First class doesn't get you here any quicker. Ha!"

"Oh Gourlay," said the woman, thrusting the flowers at Janie so that she could better clasp the newcomer's neatly manicured hand with both her own. "You were always his absolute favourite. No question. He would have been so pleased if he was here."

"He is, Mrs D," said the young man, tapping the heart beneath his glimmering silk jacket. "He is." He suddenly sensed someone next to him, staring uneasily. "*Matt Brownridge?* Hey, long time no see! How's things, pal?"

Matt reacted as if he had only just clocked the new guy's arrival, even as, all around him, people were calling out the young man's name.

"*Gourlay?*" he said. "Bloody hell!"

"You're looking… the same," said Gourlay. "Catch you later, eh? Don't neck all the Scotch!"

Matt Brownridge watched the newcomer – who, he had to admit, had not grown any uglier – with something approaching, if not absolutely identical in every conceivable way, to envy as the super-confident young man glided effortlessly through the admiring throng and into the packed living room.

Matt muttered to his sister, whose head he could just see poking out above the huge floral tribute in her care, that only one thing could make the day worse: their father deciding to make one of his speeches.

The entire bouquet shuddered in agreement.

*

"When I heard about old Clive keeling over like that into the local scouts' Nights Away campfire – almost as if he was preparing for today's main event – I thought: '*isn't life bloody unfair?*'."

Matt and Janie exchanged despairing looks. They each pondered to themselves that whilst they might frequently disagree on so many things, occasionally to the point of drawing blood, this was something on which the siblings had always been firmly united.

Beyond the dusty French windows and the guzzling crowd, they could see a small Scout tent in the garden. Some young and enthusiastic present-day Scouts, boys and girls, were building a fire.

"Just sixty-four years old." Ray Brownridge sighed, shaking his large and steadily reddening head. "Four years younger than me; although, of course, he looked a lot older. *And I'm the one with the dodgy ticker!* Well, I won't kid you – the shock nearly killed me. Ask my still gorgeous, ex-flight attendant wife here – the stew with a view, the hostess with the mostess – didn't it, Bobbi? Didn't it nearly top me off?"

As all eyes turned to the questionably still gorgeous Bobbi Brownridge, as if expecting her to guide them with her large, red-taloned hands smoothly to the nearest exits, she nodded concernedly.

"Clive had so much still to do," continued the orator. "I don't mean grandkids, 'cos sadly he and Denise weren't blessed with children – mind you, Denise, I have to tell you, they're a bit of a mixed blessing. And they cost a bloody fortune!"

At this, he nodded towards his own mortified offspring, who consequently attracted the attention of the crowd. Janie immediately shifted the flowers she was still holding so that her dress could be more easily admired. The crowd, as one, looked away.

"But, of course, not having single-handedly built up a business of his own, from practically nothing, against all the odds, with almost his bare bloody hands, poor Clivey was struggling to make ends meet." He looked around the room. "Clearly. Thank God for life insurance, eh, Denise?"

Now it was Denise's turn to look away.

"Oh. Anyway, they do say you always remember where you were when you heard tragic news. Not that Clive was a Kennedy or anything. Far from it. Well, yours truly was concluding a really successful deal for a fleet of new minicabs, so we can be even quicker to your door – 'no delay, just call BobRay' – and the bastards were trying to claim that ten cars didn't qualify for a bulk discount. So I told 'em—"

He paused for a moment as he noticed Bobbi making a gesture that airline passengers might not immediately recognise, encouraging him to move it along.

"Eh? Okay. Anyway," he continued, speeding up to his empathic conclusion, "then I heard that Clive was dead and somehow a three per cent discount just didn't seem to matter. So we left it at two and a half. Now, Ray Brownridge is not a religious man… but I think that sometimes we all need to sit down and ask ourselves: 'am I truly on the right and best path?'. And that's what Clive's untimely death has done for me." He raised his glass heavenwards. "So, thanks, Clivey. I owe you one, mate."

Sensing an exhortation to continue drinking or simply an opportunity to shut the garrulous man up, the attendees swiftly raised their glasses – "To Clive!"

Denise Dawkins stepped smartly in. "Thank you, Ray. That was very moving. In its own way. Now, everybody, please stay – there's lots of food. And the current twenty-third troop have made a campfire outside as a tribute to my dear Clive, so if anyone wants baked potatoes or toasty marshmallows – although most of you seem quite full enough…"

Janie shuffled even closer to Matt. "I've got to get back to work!" she whispered. "Mrs Edwards will kill me. I had to tell her it was *Dad's* cremation to get the morning off. But even then…"

Matt was only paying half-attention. "Yeah, yeah. Hang on. I just need a word with Gourlay."

Suddenly, Ray was part of the conversation. "Well, it looks like *he's* done alright for himself," he observed, nodding at the flashy young man in the silk jacket.

"Maybe he works for his dad," said Matt, bitterly.

"Oh, that old chestnut," groaned Ray. "Maybe he's halfway ruddy competent."

Matt glared at his father, then wandered off in disgust. He bumped into Gourlay at the food table, surrounded by admirers. So he took out his phone and began tapping.

"Well, Matt," said Gourlay, when he could tear himself away from the crowd, "did you become a plastic surgeon?"

"Eh? Oh no. I was out by one A-level. Grrr! I'm running a shit-hot sales team now. Living the dream. So, you're not still on your uncle's fish stall then?"

"No. No, I was, Matt, years ago. Good memory. But I made a bit of money, managed it wisely, dabbled a little in the property market – then my folks pegged out within two months of each other, bless 'em, and I inherited £973,000 and a bloody huge house. *Result!*"

Matt had nothing to say to this, so, with a final gaze into Gourlay's remarkably satisfied and unblemished face, he decided to leave. But Gourlay apparently had one more observation to make.

"Mind you, *your* parents look in pretty good nick, don't they?"

Matt followed Gourlay's gaze to where Ray and Bobbi were sharing a joke and a party-size pig in a blanket. They watched as Ray's pastry-free hand slid almost of its own volition up and down Bobbi's tightly encased back, but mostly down. Matt swivelled away to look for his sister, who wasn't hard to find, and dragged her towards the door.

In the garden, the Scouts' tent was just catching fire.

*

The battered old Nissan Micra looked even more dejected, parked as it was between Gourlay's huge Tesla and one of their father's gleaming 'BobRay' limos. Before Janie could gather up all her taffeta and fully struggle in, barely avoiding her back-trellis getting caught in the door handles, they heard the familiar clack of a pair of high heels under serious stress.

"Janie, pet, are you doing anything tonight? No, of course you're not."

"I might be," she told her mother, unconvincingly.

"Well, as you know, it's your dad's and my line-dancing night. He needs cheering up after what his old friend went and did. The poor man's bereft. Can you just pop round to the house and give Rumpleteazer his insulin injection?"

"Can't you do it yourself?"

"Now, sweetie, you know that it has to be at exactly 8.00 at night. His poor little pussy pancreas takes no prisoners."

She was about to turn on her best funereal heels and see if there was any pudding when she remembered something that was clearly important.

"Oh! Nearly forgot! Daddy says we're all going out for dinner tomorrow, to his favourite Thai restaurant. For his birthday. Just the four of us." If she noticed that her children appeared several degrees less than ecstatic, she didn't let it ruffle her. In fact, her whole face began to glow with secret excitement. "He's got something to tell you. Something I think might just make you both really happy!"

"We're adopted?" said Matt, but his mother had already turned to go back to the house.

*

It was some considerable time before the siblings were able to discuss this new and potentially life-changing development with the wild speculation it merited, because Matt found himself having to concentrate far harder than anticipated on his driving. Janie, in the seat beside him, was feverishly struggling to change out of her mourning weeds and into her work clothes. She was all arms and legs and taffeta.

Finally she decided to begin the conversation through the layers of material stuck around her head.

"It had better be something bloody good, this 'thing' of theirs. The hours I've put in with that diabetic sodding cat."

"Janie—"

"*And* the fetching *and* the carrying *and* the shopping *and* the taking things back 'cos she still thinks she's a size ten and skipping down the aisle of her bloody Pan Am 747—"

"Hoy!" said Matt, concerned that his sister's seismic rage was causing her arms to flail around with more abandon than even a frenzied change of outfits might demand. "I dunno, Janie. You saw Dad today. I've never seen him so emotional. Not even when he forgot the password for his bitcoins."

"Huh!" said Janie, sceptically.

"Mum said it would make us happy. What d'you think would?"

"Dad investing in my talent! *Janie Fashions*. For women with flair."

"Yeah – that'll happen! No, I reckon he's finally taking me into the business. He needs someone younger, sharper. Someone with his fingers on the pulse."

"Your pulse must've moved a lot lower down."

"Or – hey, I know," enthused Matt, excitedly, "he's giving us each a wad of money for separate flats."

"Don't you like living with me? Sharing stuff. Splitting the rent."

"No."

"Oh. Well, don't build your hopes up." Janie sniffed. "You heard them. They can't stop telling the world what a big disappointment we are. She even does it on Mumsnet!"

Matt suddenly ducked to avoid being blinded by an airborne, wooden-toggled cardigan and nearly hit an elderly woman on a zebra crossing.

"*Jesus!* They don't moan about us *all* the time."

"He called our cousin Daniel the son he never had!"

"Yeah, okay. But we're family, Janie! Okay, the way they're always snogging and groping and baby-talking each other is—"

"Is repellent. No other word. Revolting! Yucky!" She began to do a passable imitation of her father, complete with hand movements. "'Check out those jumbos!'"

"Well, okay, but there *are* other elements to being a good parent."

"Name one!" challenged Janie, still attempting to fasten her weaponised cardigan.

"Well," said Matt, recalling smug Gourlay with his Tesla and his first-class air tickets, "building up a legacy. You know, something solid to pass on to your kids. Especially when times are hard. As they bloody are now." He sensed his sister's dismissive shrug but pressed on with his theme. "One day, it'll all be ours, Janie. The big, tasteless house; the thriving minicab business; the investments! That's a serious load of dosh. So, cut the randy old farts some slack. Nobody lives forever."

He pulled up outside the smart little shop where Janie worked and offered a sigh of relief that the journey had been completed in relative safety. Swivelling round and lurching over to the back seat, Janie grabbed a huge, black portfolio case, bulging to bursting point, and swung it briskly towards her.

It knocked her brother's head flat into his steering wheel.

*

The SUE E. GENEROUS dress shop in Clifton specialised in elegant fashion for the more ample form, and its owner, Mrs Susan Edwards, clearly lived her vision. Her one disappointment was that her staff, especially the reed-like Janie, didn't make a bit more of an effort in this regard.

Despite the bulky cardigan into which Janie was still struggling, as she bustled through the extra-wide shop doorway with her outsized portfolio gripped tightly under one arm, it was abundantly – or perhaps not so abundantly – clear to Mrs Edwards and all her clientele that there was precious little underneath. Had Janie been more superstitious, or simply more observant, she might have noticed that burly customers all around her, hovering near the extended dressing rooms or shuffling through the plus-size racks, were giving her the 'evil eye'.

To her employee's surprise, the often less than gracious Mrs E chose for once to be sympathetic.

"How *is* your mother, Janie?"

"Fine, why?" replied Janie, momentarily forgetting the lie. "Oh. Well, you know."

"It's a difficult time," agreed her boss, putting a discarded winter coat back onto its reinforced hanger. "But we all have difficult times. I've lost a filling; my poor husband's got his piles again; and Mrs Goring needs someone to help her out of her jeans. Mind you, you'd need a bloody can opener. Quarts and pint pots, if you get my drift."

Janie suddenly whipped the hefty portfolio from its by now rather damp lodging place and began to unzip it on the nearby counter.

"Er, actually, Mrs Edwards, I thought you might want to take a look at some of my new designs."

"Why in God's name would I want to do that?"

"I'll go see to Mrs Goring," said the deflated salesgirl, zipping herself up once again.

"Haven't you forgotten something?" called Mrs Edwards.

Janie sighed and shuffled across to a free-standing pine wardrobe beside the till. Opening it, she lifted out an industrial-size bar of Cadbury's Fruit & Nut from a large pile of the same.

"*I won't put on weight, Mrs Edwards!*" she protested. "Even if I hoovered up the shelves as well. It's my metabolism!"

"There is such a thing as company loyalty, you know, Janie Brownridge!"

Janie ripped away the wrapping and bit off a massive chunk of calories. Then she stomped grumpily off to release Mrs Goring once again from denim hell.

*

Allow me to intervene here, if I may. You have no idea who I am, but you will soon enough. I'd like to chat to you a wee bit about death.

Death. Le mort. Il morte. The Great Equalizer. He comes to all of us in the end. Some of us sooner rather than later.

That's where I come in. I've hastened the passage of seventeen human beings in my time. Plus one rabid shih tzu. And three hedge-fund managers.

207

But this here now is, in its own way, the chilling wee tale of what ended my illustrious career. A story in which I'm not even the main protagonist – thank Christ. Oh, and in case you were wondering, it wasn't me who topped the poor old scoutmaster. Although I would have, had someone asked me nicely.

Just saying.

But you know, it's in the ashes of disappointment that we find the sparks to fire our dreams. Oh, would you listen to that? As my man Flaubert would say – get le mot juste.

I'll be back. The name's Struan by the way. Means 'small stream' in my native Scottish. Which sounds a wee bit personal, if you ask me, but there you go.

THE CAMEL'S BACK

*M*att Brownridge was already in a bad mood when he and his family rolled up at the Thai restaurant just outside of town in one of his father's flashiest and unnecessarily large limos. Mr Cracknell, his boss in telesales, had pointed out to him that his record over the past six months in nailing new contracts was far outpaced by customers cancelling their existing orders immediately after his having spoken to them. He had been given three months to alter the balance.

Matt was finding it hard even to acknowledge his father's driver, a man who had known him since childhood and had only ever been kind to him. Not merely kind but often, Matt was pretty sure, quietly sympathetic to his and Janie's plight.

As they emerged from the car and headed towards the restaurant, Janie entangled in a creation that defied description and Ray with his hand lightly squeezing his wife's right buttock, they heard the driver cry, "Have a good one, birthday boy!"

Ray removed his hand from its favourite resting place in order to respond with a jaunty air-golf swing. Matt and Janie exchanged a look of dread intermingled, in this particular instance, with the unusual but not altogether noxious tang of nervous anticipation.

The charming young Thai woman who greeted them at the door offered an open smile and a disarming bow.

A thought suddenly struck Matt Brownridge. "Oh shit! Do you think Dad is going to do his usual pronouncing all his 'R's like 'L's ?" he whispered fearfully to Janie.

"God, I hope not. The man really thinks he's being friendly. Just try to cough if you hear him going for one," muttered his sister, eyeing their parent with suspicion. "Now would be good."

Ray Brownridge tapped the young woman on her slender arm and began to speak.

Matt's sudden hacking cough managed to obscure the potentially boorish greeting.

"One down, ninety-six to go!" muttered Matt, blowing his nose unnecessarily.

*

After almost a full bottle of champagne, shared not entirely or even vaguely equally, Ray Brownridge was in full, unedifying flow. Waiters were hovering nearby with jasmine tea and attentive smiles. Matt could tell, and he assumed Janie could too, that beneath the excessive courtesy, they were seriously unimpressed.

He did sense, however, that his spasmodic but inordinately loud coughing was being noted with gratitude as well as sympathy.

"...And just the other day," said Ray, his voice amplified to grand cru, "I read about this bloke who uses vegetable oil as fuel for his fleet of lorries. Swear to God! *Vegetable oil!*" At this point in his story, he chose to include the waiters with a touch of cod-Japanese.

Fortunately, Matt managed once again to cover the unreconstructed racism from their father with a whole series of booming staccato coughs.

"Raryngitis!" explained Ray helpfully, when the hacking died down, which sort of defeated the purpose.

Meantime, a riveted Bobbi had picked up a large edamame bean and was studiously squeezing it at one end.

"So, if you just…?" From the other end, three of the hard little vegetables shot out over the heads of the waiters and bounced off a decorative wooden sculpture. "Oopsie," apologised the bean-shooter. "Everyone alright?"

With the wit that was already endearing him to one and all, Ray addressed the waiting staff. "Lucky you're a squitty lot or she would have had your eyes out!"

Matt and Janie shrank into their chairs, trying to smile at the waiters in an 'I'm not at all like him and am as equally appalled as you are, if not more so' kind of way. But Bobbi just laughed.

"Ray, you're embarrassing your children."

"That's the only point in having ruddy children! Especially these two little losers." He punched both children matily and grinned at them. "Joking! You'll do – well, you'll have to. Eat up. Anyway, the thing of it is, you could squeeze a few courgettes or swedes or something and – *and power your whole fleet for a week!* Save a bloody fortune! If the government didn't slap a tax on it." He snapped his fingers at the nearest waiter. "But knowing this current bunch, they'd have civil servants sniffing your exhaust pipes just to see if the car starts farting!"

"That's fascinating, Father," said Matt, digging into seams of sarcasm he hadn't mined for some time.

"You should really put all this down in a book, Dad," added Janie, "before you forget it."

"If I only had the time, Janie, love," said their father, who was as blissfully resistant to sarcasm as he was to disapproval. "Ah! Here come the tea-wallahs!"

Ignoring this cultural misappropriation or just plain boorishness, the waiters set down sizzling platters of food on the table's hotplates, plus a small pot of jasmine tea for Ray and an identical one for Matt. Before Matt could reach for his, another waiter slipped in and hurriedly swapped the two teapots around, all the while smiling knowingly at the younger man.

As confusion gave way to satisfaction and a pleasantly filling stomach, Matt decided to get down to the business of the evening. Because surely there was no pleasure in it... although, who really knew? Perhaps tonight would change everything.

Yet he was forced to ask himself, as his own devil's advocate, did he really *want* to work with his father, if indeed this was to be the meat of the surprise? Granted, it had to afford more prospects than his current soulless employment, especially after Mr Cracknell's recent threat. *But to see this person every single day?*

He found himself trying out counter-arguments. That the ignorant man was simply the product of his humble and quite possibly brutal upbringing, a reflection of his age and background, just another representative of the narrow society, un-diverse milieu and waspish golf clubs in which he chose to mix, even in this unavoidably multicultural environment. An aging citizen, with no friends other than those sharing his own outmoded beliefs and culture, who had been led to believe, by people who really should have known better, including some in high places, that the nation was overrun with scrounging immigrants and foreigners, doggedly after his hospital beds, his benefits, his jobs, his wife.

Matt would have deemed the man irredeemable, but he had a certain growing confidence that this evening might just prove him wrong.

Janie, meantime, was pondering how she might make it up to the poor, smiling yet undoubtedly deeply offended staff. She was thinking homemade ties and scarves, perhaps integrating symbols of their ancient culture with some of their signature dishes.

This inevitably led her to wondering whether their father's big surprise might involve a workshop of her own, in a flat or even a tiny house. To think – no more working on kitchen tables as the sounds of her brother's latest violent action series on Netflix vied with the clatter of her near-obsolescent sewing machine.

Finally, Matt could stand it no longer. "So, birthday boy, you said you had something to tell us?"

"Something that would cheer us up," encouraged Janie.

Ray Brownridge gave one of his trademark self-satisfied and not entirely food-free smiles.

Clasping Bobbi's hand as it was halfway to her mouth, he said, "Indeed I have, my dears. No, indeed *we* have."

The younger pair found themselves shuffling closer to their dad, even though there was no dialling down in the big man's delivery. He sipped his tea and sighed pleasurably.

"This is great, pal," he said to a passing waiter, as the kids suffered through their own waiting. "What do you put in it?"

"Secret. Big secret," said the man, with a gentle smile.

"Inscrutable to the end." Raymond Brownridge smiled. "Right – to business." He paused for a moment, gathering his thoughts.

Matt and Janie exchanged a look, but unlike its myriad predecessors, one not totally suffused with distaste.

"Well," began their host with some gravity, "poor old Clive's untimely death has made your lovely mother and me think really carefully." He ran a few sweet 'n' sour fingers through his hair in a gesture clearly designed to imply careful thinking. "No need to tell you of all people that we've worked bloody hard over the years. We – well, mostly me – have made all this money, what with the thriving business and the lovely house, savings, shrewd investments, tax dodges etcetera. All despite the bloody downturn and the government's punitive frame of mind! But okay, spade a spade, let's face it, we're no spring chickens – especially me with my dodgy ticker—"

Bobbi suddenly interrupted him. "Ooh, have you taken your warfarin?" As he nodded, she offered up her sauciest smile.

"Well, you'd better double your medication tonight, Daddy – for your big birthday treat!"

The kids looked like they were about to vomit but for once attempted a collaborative smile. Which unfortunately only encouraged him.

"Will I need that oxygen mask again? *'Doors to manual!'* Anyway, as I said, me and your dear mum, we're never gonna be able to spend it all, are we?" He paused, as if allowing for smiles of blissful anticipation. "*But we're gonna have a bloody good try!*"

The ensuing silence surprised even the waiters, let alone the other customers, as they all assumed the noisy, red-faced man was going to bang on in a similar vein all night.

"What?" said Matt, eventually.

"Sorry?" added Janie, in a voice so small that she wondered if she had actually spoken at all.

"What Daddy is trying to say," elaborated their beaming mother, "is – well, you only live once. *Crappy diem!* as they say in France. So that's what we're gonna do. We're gonna sell the business, put the house on the market—"

"Cash in all our investments," added Ray, gleefully, "buy a brand new, top-of-the-line Roller, go on loads of luxury holidays, stay only at the best five-star hotels, eat truckloads of cordon blue, drink astronomically priced wines…"

As if they had completed the verse and were now into the rousing chorus, they finished the anthem in glorious unison: "And SPEND, SPEND, SPEND!"

This time, the silence was even more fierce than its predecessor.

"*You bastards!*" cried Janie, after a few gobsmacked seconds, ignoring the other fascinated-whilst-repelled tables, her large brown eyes pooling.

Matt tried to calm her down, noticing at the same time a curious puzzlement rising on the faces of his hitherto almost ecstatic parents.

"Pardon?" said Ray.

"Have we said something to upset you, love?" said Bobbi.

"What about setting me up in business? *Janie Fashions*?"

"Or me eventually taking over BobRay Cars?" added Matt, who felt he should have his share of ire at the nothing being offered.

"We said we wanted to *spend* our hard-earned money," explained their father, "not piss it up the wall. We've bankrolled you two rascals for over thirty years. And I reckon it's probably held you both back. So, now we're giving you the most precious gift a parent can offer their children. We are giving you *your independence*." He gestured to the waiters. "Like we gave that lot."

"They're Thai, Dad. We never colonised Thailand."

Ray just grunted at this irrelevance and waved his empty bottle of bubbly at a member of staff.

"But what about *us*?" persisted his shell-shocked daughter.

"If you spend it all," said Matt, almost in tears himself, both of anger and pure panic, "we'll have no visible means of support."

"Like one of my strapless evening-dungarees," amplified Janie, unnecessarily.

Ray Brownridge shook his head in genuine bewilderment. "Am I hearing right? Is this all you can do – think about yourselves? Dear Lord – tonight is meant to be a celebration!"

Matt immediately stood and grabbed Janie's arm. "*Let's go, Janie!*"

Janie stared at Matt, then at her parents and finally at her still unfinished plate. Despite all appearances, she loved her food and didn't actually go out that often. Even a couple of hours in the company of her appalling family could be worth it if the meal was good, and this one had been particularly tasty. Admittedly, the jasmine tea was potentially suspect, but she was hoping not.

Feeling that Matt's livid eyes were still firmly on her, she selected the least sticky item on her plate and shoved it with a polka-dot, day-gloved hand into her quivering mouth.

"Coming," she mumbled. But she could hear their father calling after them in what sounded more like confusion than rage. "Oi! What about the bill?"

Matt and Janie both turned back in disbelief.

"It's my birthday!" explained the sixty-eight-year old, reasonably.

With a sigh, Matt returned to the table, opened his wallet and dropped a couple of £20 notes into their father's rice. He then looked at Janie, who realised that he was requiring her to repeat the gesture.

Sharing a sizeable portion of disappointment seasoned with incredulity, Ray and Bobbi moved their chairs even closer. As their children departed, the magnanimous couple clasped adoring hands.

"*Kids!* They'll get over it," he reassured his bemused spouse. "Now, I wonder if this lot have got any of those 'how-to-spend-a-bloody-fortune' cookies! Ha! Get it?"

As his eyes were fixed firmly on his favourite person in the world, the older man didn't notice the kids in question bumping into an old friend at the door.

"*Matt! Janie!* Well, hello again," said Gourlay. He turned to introduce his dinner companion, a deeply tanned and stunningly dressed young woman. "You haven't met my beautiful wife Dorita, have you? We bumped into each other on Copacabana Beach. And then kept bumping."

Matt Brownridge hadn't thought he could feel more pissed off this evening than he already was, but even in this he had been proved wrong.

"Why don't you go boil your head?" he said, gazing briefly into Gourlay's impossibly blue eyes, and stomped crossly out of the door.

Janie, ever the peacemaker, smiled up at Dorita. "*Love* that frock, babe! I've got just the cardy to go with it."

"*Janie!*"

With an apologetic shrug, the younger sibling swiftly excused herself to the baffled couple and ran to her brother as nimbly as her three-quarter-length brocade kilt would allow.

*

Janie Brownridge didn't dare to look at her brother's face on their journey home, yet even its dusty reflection on the top deck of the bus was sufficient to chill her blood.

Gazing around at her fellow late-night passengers didn't help to ease her discomfort. If they weren't drunk and muttering to themselves, they were confused and muttering to themselves. One elderly man looked like he might have got on the bus as a child during the war and just stayed there going round and round.

"They could be us any minute," said Matt, without changing his gaze. "Homeless and hopeless."

"Who would *do* that to their own children – their own flesh and blood?" echoed Janie, mystified not simply by the recent momentous proclamation but by the sheer glee with which it had been uttered. "Okay, I know we haven't done everything they wanted us to do. I didn't marry any of the rich boys from Dad's golf club, although clearly I could have."

She could see her brother's eyebrows raise, even though his face was mostly a collage of flashing streetlights and kebab shop signs.

"I didn't play for England," matched Matt, more out of support for his sister than anything else, other than perhaps a curious urge not to be outdone in the parental disappointment stakes. A flashing ambulance added to the blues on his grim face.

"But we're nice people," protested Janie. "We're good people. Aren't we? I don't mean good like we go visit starving refugees in Africa – but I'm sure I would, if I was famous. I'm thinking a dashiki. Brown and green, so's not to clash with the flora and fauna – or the starving Africans."

"Jeez, Janie, it's not like we haven't put in the hours! Looked after them when they're sick or hungover."

"Listened to all their crap about the good old days, before Elon Musk and chlamydia."

For a moment, the window of the bus became for Matt like a screen, as if someone had made a Facebook-style slideshow of a singularly miserable life, for his edification alone: his tiny cubicle at work with a sombre Mr Cracknell glowering; Ray Brownridge laughing sweatily at the table, any table, as he gropes his adoring wife; Gourlay arriving at the Dawkins' house in his gleaming Tesla, flashing his gleaming teeth.

Meantime, he could hear his outraged little sister still wittering on.

"Okay, maybe all their hopes for us *haven't* been realised – as yet. But we've never been on drugs or drink or Just Stop Oil demonstrations. And – and Mum was so thrilled, wasn't she, when I was voted cutest baby in the nursery that she still tells people what a wonderful uterus she has. Not just tells."

She noticed that Matt's face had suddenly changed. The anger had been replaced with something that she could only describe as determination, not a quality of his with which she had hitherto been overly familiar.

"Matty? ...Matt?"

For the first time in this entire, mind-numbing journey, Matt Brownridge turned to his younger sibling and spoke directly into her quizzical face.

"Janie, I've got a plan. A now-or-never, once-in-a-lifetime, all-or-nothing plan."

"Suicide pact?"

"Eh? *No!* I was thinking more along the lines of – of homicide pact."

"Sorry?"

Her brother's voice lowered, as his face in the harsh strip lighting became like a rather scary mask.

"*They've got to die,*" he said.

"Who has?" asked Janie, a bit dimly.

"Who do you think? Jeez! Mum and Dad. *Mum and Dad have to die!*" How many times did he have to say it?

Now it was Janie's turn to watch as her own face in the window of the number X9 bus slowly took on an expression she had never so far observed in any mirror. It terrified her even to look at it.

*

Oh come on, guys. It's all very well expressing the thought – I mean, haven't we all done that at one time? But, in my experience, it's the execution that separates the men from the boys.

And, of course, the parents from their children.

SERIOUSLY?

The Brownridge siblings didn't discuss the previous night's dinner, or, indeed, the scary and almost surreal conversation that it precipitated, until the following morning, when it was almost time to go to work.

For most of their breakfast, Matt and Janie sat in unaccustomed silence, surrounded by peeling walls that were flimsy enough to broadcast from either side harassed neighbours threatening their kids on a daily basis with permanent screen bans. In every corner of the poky room, dressmaker's dummies hovered, looking almost embarrassed by what they were being made to wear. Matt's men-of-style magazines lay unopened beside his *Call of Duty* best tips and cheats guides.

Janie stood up and stuffed an absolutely final piece of toast in her mouth and then another one.

"Gotta go to work. *Matt?*"

Matt didn't respond. Janie wasn't even certain that he had heard her. Perhaps it was the mouthful of half-chewed toast that obscured things, but he did appear lost in thoughts that she could almost hear buzzing around his head (which she truly felt might be the best place for them).

"Can I have a lift – please?" She picked up two huge bags bulging with gaudy material. "I want to take a couple of dresses to show Mrs Edwards. I think she'll go for these. They're really beautiful. And really, *really* big. I've sat in circuses that used less fabric... *Matt!*"

He just stared at her. "I'm not going into work."

"Oh. Okay. What you going to do then?"

"Research."

"What, for a new job?" she said, supportively. "Well, it's about bloody time. You've been wasting your..."

As her brother's stare became more fixed, his eyes curiously narrowing, Janie began to gather what this rare foray into 'research' might truly entail.

"You weren't serious, last night – y'know, about what you said? No," she laughed nervously, "'course you weren't."

"Deadly," confirmed Matthew Brownridge.

Janie shook her head so vigorously that it began to hurt. "*We can't KILL mum and dad!*" Instinctively, she lowered her voice. "We can't kill mum n dad! I mean, sometimes I'd like to – but I bet everybody has these feelings. About their own parents, not about ours. Well, maybe about ours too, if they've met them. But it's just not what you do. Killing. Murder. Not people like us."

"You saw them last night – you heard what they said to the waiters. Well, what *he* said mostly, but she was laughing and nodding all the way. Like she always does."

"I know – it was disgusting and so racist. And – and the way he talks to women, and his staff. And to – well, everyone, really. Wherever he goes. But you can't kill people for that."

"People get 'cancelled' all the time."

"Not by making them dead. Are you really that woke?"

"Yes, I am actually," said Matt. "I'm very woke. I'm a woke warrior."

"So it's not about the money."

"Janie," he scoffed, "I am not *that* shallow." He paused for a moment. "Well, yes, it's about the money too, obviously. But they're all part of the same thing really, aren't they?"

"Are they?"

"Yes! It's all about how they treat other people. Like they're 'less' than them! Foreigners, employees…tradespeople. Anyone who's poor or deprived or homeless. *Offspring*! Janie – look at this place! I mean, look around. We're paying serious rent for what – a bloody skip with windows! We'll never be able to afford to buy a place of our own. Not on what we earn. Not with the state of the world. Nobody our age can these days."

"Yes, I know that but…?"

"The only way people like us – good, honest, hard-working, caring, non-racist people – can afford a decent home, a decent life, is to come into some money. And to come into some money, somebody close, somebody very close, has to – y'know – die."

"Well, there's the lottery. Mrs Jackson down the road—"

Matt chose not to give this lunacy credence, as he had always felt gambling was for losers, and, anyway, murder was so much more targeted.

"They *owe* us, Janie! God knows, they owe us. And now they're trying to welch. Do us out of what's rightly ours. '*Spend, spend, spend!*' Well, I for one am not gonna let 'em."

"But, Matt—"

"But nothing, Janie. No butting. If our rent goes up any higher, which of course it will, we'll be back in that awful bloody house living with Mum and Dad again. Two weeks of that and we'd kill them anyway."

Janie suddenly saw that there was no point in continuing the conversation. Which, of course, was really all that it was.

"See you tonight," she said, shuffling off with the overstuffed sacks to catch a bus and disgruntle the rush-hour passengers. "It's your turn to do supper."

As soon as she was out of the front door and the rustling had diminished, Matt rose with his coffee cup from the cluttered kitchen and walked determinedly into the equally cramped and tatty living room.

Setting his drink down carefully on an upturned wooden

box, he went over to an old chest of drawers and took out his complete collection of *CSI* box sets.

The research phase had begun.

*

The living room was in darkness, save for a flickering light, when Janie trudged home from work that evening, the bulging dress bags still in her hands.

On the table sat a huge pile of DVDs and an equally precarious collection of cigarette butts. Her bleary-eyed brother, sprawled on the sofa, barely acknowledged his sister's return.

"Have you been here all day?"

Matt didn't bother to answer. Nor did he shift his eyes from the cadaver-of-the-week currently onscreen.

"*CSI!* No! You've been watching your old *CSI* sets all day?"

Still nothing.

"You know the basic flaw in your masterplan, Matthew Brownridge?"

This time he deigned to shift at least one eye in her direction, although she would keep shuffling around, as if unable to stand still for one precious moment.

"THEY ALL GET BLOODY CAUGHT!"

Realising that his sister still needed some convincing and sensing now, as he turned further in her direction, that she wasn't so much shuffling as shaking, possibly from sheer terror, Matt switched the sound down.

"It's television," he protested, "not real life! They have to be caught in the end. It's a basic rule. But some of the plans are shit-hot."

Janie pulled up a sagging armchair and sank into it, which was both uncomfortable and disempowering. But at least she was blocking his view.

"Maybe we could just, y'know, *talk* to the both of them,"

she suggested, with a gentle smile. "Sort of tell them how upset we are." She ignored the disdainful snort, although the accompanying blast of old cigarettes lingered.

A change of subject seemed necessary; yet, she would have to admit, as it left her tremulous lips, that it wasn't exactly much of one.

"Had a call at work today. It was – er, Mum. Yes. She wants me to make one of my nice chocolate cakes for Dad's birthday – you know, the one he loves so much, with the Bacardi rum inside and the sprinkles. And the icing. And the Cadbury's flakes. A really big cake. As a sort of surprise, 'cos he's not having a party. Seeing as how Uncle Clive…"

"And, of course, you said yes."

"This time – yes," said Janie, sheepishly. "Yes, I did, Matt. But it's the last time. I told her so in no uncertain terms. Well, I implied.."

"In no uncertain terms."

"I will tell her – when I go round with the cake." Then she smiled, in a deliberate attempt to lighten the atmosphere, what with so many homicides still hovering in the ether. "Hey, maybe all that chocolate and butter and sugar will kill him – you know – what with his dodgy heart and stuff."

Matt just stared at her for a moment then suddenly leapt up from his chair as if it had just been plugged in. Grabbing her bony shoulders, he looked straight into her eyes. Rather large and sparkly brown eyes, but he wasn't assessing or admiring them. He was attempting to pierce right through them and engage her potentially homicidal brain.

"*What?*" he said and stared some more. "WHAT?" he repeated, but simply for effect, as he knew exactly what. His voice hit a pitch of unaccustomed excitement. "*Tomorrow* – Mum and Dad, what are they doing, exactly?"

"Dunno, exactly," replied Janie, still confused. "But I can guess."

They could both guess, even though the specifics of their guesses might not have been totally identical. But for certain, these itineraries all involved upmarket travel agents, the city's best and swishest shops and outlets, its finest hostelries and off-licences and an exclusive selection of luxury-car showrooms. Always laughing, always canoodling, always spending. The siblings imagined the bags and boxes mounting up in every room of their parents' sprawling house as the credit cards, and most probably the parents themselves, got joyously hammered.

The day after the big *CSI*-fest, during his lunch hour, Matt set off to do his own shopping. It was on a more narrowly focused and far less profligate scale, involving simply a tatty backstreet joke shop, an old-established ironmongers and, a touch embarrassingly, the make-up counter in a small neighbourhood pharmacy.

It was also considerably less fun.

FIRST BLOOD

*H*e was beginning to feel rather cold in his parents' en suite bathtub.

There was also a guest bathroom on the other side of the landing, but after some consideration, Matt had decided that the en suite was not only more appropriate for this endeavour but also most probably the only bathroom they ever used. He didn't want to remain somewhere undisturbed all night.

As he allowed more hot water to run over his slowly chilling toes, he gazed around the unnecessarily large room. Caricatures of the happy couple abounded, executed by talentless artists from several major cities and holiday resorts. But they all managed to amplify their father's large face and their mother's ample bosom, features which one might easily have assumed would defy exaggeration.

There were more potions and creams and unguents on display here than Matt had observed on his recent foray into the arcane world of female cosmetics, alongside a collection of mirrors that would make a funfair envious.

His only companion, on what was already proving to be a long, tedious afternoon, was the waterproof shower-radio, but even this didn't tame the nerves that any first-time murderer would quite naturally feel.

The fortunate aspect of all these mirrors was that Matt could periodically check out how he might appear to any unsuspecting

Brownridge strolling in. The arm dangling Marat-like over the side of the bathtub seemed to work and the blood dripping from a nasty wound on the wrist felt reasonably authentic, although it was beginning to dry a bit and might need to be replenished.

Fortunately, he had purchased several tubes from the joke shop, along with some fake scars and wounds, knowing that an efficient kill-machine must surely plan for every eventuality. The equally bloody carving knife on the edge of the bath was the real thing, even if the blood was not.

A ready supply of soothingly warm water did help just a bit to ease the would-be corpse's growing anxiety, but the downside of these regular and comforting infusions meant that after a couple of languorous hours, Matt fell fast asleep.

It was the chimes of the evening news at 6.00 that awakened him. That and the fact he was almost freezing to death. *Where the hell were they?* Surely the posh shops must be shutting by now. He tried to lift his bloody arm, but it had gone completely numb, so he had to lever it very gently away from the bath's edge with his other, un-distressed hand and flop it around until the circulation thankfully returned.

By now, Matt Brownridge was becoming royally fed-up and even more exasperated with his tardy parents. His crinkled but incredibly clean body looked like that of a ninety-year old, or so he assumed, as he had never actually seen a naked ninety-year-old and nor would he wish to, even if that person were married to him. Surely four and a half hours in a parent's tacky en suite bathroom was enough for any self-respecting killer. No one could accuse him – not even Mr Cracknell – of not taking his work seriously.

"*Where the fuck are you?*" he cried into the musty air and the condensated mirrors, glaring reproachfully at each and every inept caricature in turn. He wondered for a moment whether the obscenely happy couple had slipped away for the night. He wouldn't put it past the randy buggers.

"Well, okay then, sod you, Ray and Bobbi, enough is enough."

He lifted himself with some difficulty out of the cold bath and wiped the blood off the edges with a cloth he had brought with him expressly for this purpose. He then proceeded to do the same with his 'wounded' arm and the kitchen knife, slipping the latter into a small duffle bag.

Before getting dressed once more, he decided to nip out onto the landing, just in case he heard his father's car pulling up or saw the lights. He reckoned he'd have just sufficient time to re-blood and re-dangle in advance of them finally coming upstairs. And the whole afternoon in the bath wouldn't have been a complete washout.

He opened the bedroom door and moved somewhat damply over the fluffy Axminster to the head of the stairs.

"If you don't come back within the next five minutes, then tough!" he called out defiantly.

This was just before he noticed heads appearing on the other side of the front door's stained-glass panel.

"Oh shit!" he said, wondering how come he hadn't heard them but then realised that his ears were probably still utterly waterlogged.

Matt turned swiftly on his soggy heels to retreat back to the bathroom and resume bloody death.

Unfortunately, he hadn't noticed that, in the meantime, Rumpleteazer, his parents' unappealing and diabetic old tabby cat, had emerged from somewhere warm and cozy to see what on earth was going on.

Before he could stop himself, the dripping visitor had stepped with his full weight onto the inquisitive family pet. As the squashed tabby screeched and pulled away, a naked Matt found his damp foot slipping helplessly backwards over the newly alarmed fur. The front door opened just in time for Ray and Bobbi Brownridge, laden with bags and boxes, to see a fully grown and bare-arsed man bouncing wetly down their staircase, his shocked face and unprotected tackle banging step by painful step on the rough carpet, as he screamed his terrified head off. All this whilst one naked and still crinkly backside pointed defiantly upwards towards the ceiling.

Although Matt Brownridge was far too busy smacking head, knees and genitals with increasing torque to notice this, the stunned householders were actually not alone. A rather attractive and smartly dressed young woman was standing beside them, clutching a clipboard with one elegant, perfectly French-manicured hand, whilst the other hand was slowly reaching up to cover her shocked and extremely open mouth. Even this precaution didn't prevent a little scream sneaking out.

"So sorry, Siobhan," said Ray Brownridge to his guest. "This looks like our idiot son."

"*He doesn't come with the house!*" explained Bobbi Brownridge swiftly, because with estate agents, you have to ensure that they have every detail right.

Matt, who was not, at this juncture, fully aware of the new arrival, reached the bottom of the stairs with a final, agonising bump and realised that there was no alternative now but to turn painfully round. He could feel that his skin had been rubbed raw and that, this time, the blood pouring down his face hadn't come out of a tube.

He was just able to acknowledge that there was indeed a stranger in the house before he passed fully out onto the latest set of inheritance-draining purchases in the hallway.

"Do you think we ought to call an ambulance?" said a rather sweet but patently disturbed voice.

*

"*Of a broken heart!*" exclaimed Janie Brownridge a bit too loudly, as she sat by the hospital bed, offering more disbelief than sympathy. "*OF A...!*"

Matt found it quite difficult to turn his head, as the incident had done something rather weird to his neck. Janie was actually quite relieved – his face did look a bit of a mess. Yet beneath her disdain, she felt genuinely grateful, on her brother's behalf, that his vital equipment was simply bruised and swollen rather than rendered useless beyond repair. Not that, so far as she was aware, he used it much anyway, or at least not in company, but who knew what the future held once it had reverted to its natural colour and size?

"It happens," replied Matt, through the pain. His jaw felt like he had gone three rounds with Tyson Fury on an angry day.

"Dad gets a fatal coronary and Mum dies pretty swiftly after of a broken heart?" she persisted.

"They're very close."

"You're very stupid. Is it sore?"

Matt didn't feel this merited a reply.

"And who was this woman you flashed?"

"I *didn't* fl – her name's Siobhan. I think. She's Mum and Dad's new estate agent. From that smart place on the parade. She seemed very nice. When she stopped screaming. And hyperventilating."

"So you reckon you're in with a chance, do you?"

"Now that she's seen what I've got to offer." He could feel her wince, even though his head was still facing the other way. "It was a trial run, Janie! No harm done."

Janie looked around at the other patients. "Can you keep your voice down? *NO HARM DONE?!* What did Mum and Dad think you were up to?"

"I just told them our dodgy boiler had packed up again, so I came in to use their bath. And had one of my nosebleeds. That bloody cat is a health hazard." Now he could actually *hear* her shaking her head. It was like they were identical twins. "They weren't exactly sympathetic. Not even a sodding plaster! *Don't they care at all?*"

"Not much," said Janie with a sigh, after a moment's dispiriting thought. "Not unless we're useful."

"They really are selling the house, you know, Janie. And buying something far smaller and cheaper. *Our family home!* Our inheritance. For what – spending money! Pissing-up-the-wall money! Depriving their only kids of a decent life money!"

This time, when Janie looked at him, she couldn't help feeling a modicum of affection. She realised that she did indeed share his pain, although obviously not the sort going on down there. But to her surprise and, even more joltingly, to her concern, she found that she was also just beginning to share Matt's dream; a parent-free world in which she could be her own person, able to fulfil her own creative destiny without feeling the constant sense of disapproval and disappointment, not to mention total disinterest, that was starting to corrode her entire being.

Was it really so wrong to want to put down the two people who had been putting her down all her life?

At that moment, her phone rang. She saw the too-familiar number and sighed. As she rose from the hospital chair, she mumbled quietly, "If you want something done properly…"

"Sorry?" said Matt, but his sister wasn't quite certain whether this was a call for elaboration or simply an apology for getting himself into this mess.

She offered his pyjamaed back a gentle half-smile, which she was pretty sure he picked up round the front.

THEM'S THE BRAKES

*M*att Brownridge was still limping a few days later when he and Janie slipped furtively out onto the deserted street from their clapped-out car.

It was early in the morning, so Matt was pretty confident that he wouldn't bump into any of his parents' nosy neighbours. At this crucial point in the operation, he didn't wish to become entangled in more lies than were absolutely necessary. In fact, he didn't want anyone to know that he and Janie were there at all, which was why they had arrived at dawn and parked a few streets away from the scene of the (God-willing) crime.

To his relief, their parents' main car, a huge and wasteful urban tractor, was on the street right outside the house, while their mother's smaller car and a spare from the BobRay fleet shared the large driveway. Not so heartening was the glaring 'For Sale' sign in the front garden.

Matt looked at Janie, who was dressed in clothes as dark and inconspicuous as his but a fair bit grubbier, as it was she who was going to be shuffling under the car and this girl wasn't going to soil one of her precious, homemade outfits for anyone. On her shoulder was a bag containing all that she believed she needed, having done her research and purchased the appropriate equipment. YouTube was so brilliant in this regard – when she had learnt not to be distracted by fashion shows from Milan, London and Paris. She already knew that she had a good eye and a steady hand – those fabulous creations of hers didn't tailor themselves.

For a moment, the pair, who looked conspicuous simply in their efforts not to (although fortunately nobody was up yet and watching), just stood there, unmoving. Were they *really* going to do this?

Although not a word was spoken, a decision was clearly being made. Fortunately, the ridiculous vehicle was pretty high off the ground, so someone as slight as Janie, despite the daily Fruit & Nuts, could slip quite easily underneath. Which she did, while Matt performed the equally perilous and daunting task, as he perceived it, of standing guard.

Occasionally he would remind Janie of his presence, and more importantly of her perilous visibility, by kicking her feet as they wriggled out beyond the frame of the car. This didn't thrill Janie. She could appreciate the necessity on a security level, yet still had the unnerving sense that he was doing it simply because she was taking her time, and he was growing cold and bored.

"Sun's starting to rise," he mentioned at one point.

"And here's me turned up without my camera," came the irritated retort from ground level.

"What's taking you so long?" he whispered a couple of minutes later.

"Oh sorry, have you got another murder to get to up the road, Dr Shipman?"

Suddenly Janie felt a kick to her feet so strong that it almost sent her head shooting right out of the other end of the car. She began to yelp.

"SSHHH!" came the stern admonition, followed by a cheery. "Oh, hi there, *Siobhan*."

Matt hoped that only he could hear the groan slowly emanating from beneath the car on which he was now so nonchalantly leaning, but at least the legs were tucked in.

"Couldn't stay away, eh?" said the young car-leaner, with a smile as casual as he was able. But Siobhan was just staring at him. "Oh sorry. It's me... Matt Brownridge? You probably didn't recognise me—"

"Without your naked butt hurtling towards me. Took me a while. What are you doing here?"

He already had a misty recollection from the bathtub debacle that the young estate agent who had come to assess the property was rather attractive, even allowing for the extreme shock and horror (both hers and his own). This early morning's dappled light served only to confirm it big time.

Matt loved the spiky, short hair with all its different shades of blonde and brown and how it contrasted so coolly with her simple navy-blue, all-business, pinstripe trouser suit. He hadn't noticed how green her eyes were first time round, nor how full her lips. She certainly hadn't smiled much as yet, but he just bet her teeth were sparkling too.

"What am I doing here? Just – you know."

"No," said the young woman, "but I suppose I should just be grateful you've got your clothes on."

"Ha. Yeah. Sorry about that. Siobhan, isn't it? Lovely name. Bit hard to spell."

"I manage."

Matt laughed, although he had a feeling that it came out a bit forced. Probably because he was leaning on the chassis of a smart car beneath which his younger sister was severing the brakes in order to effect a fatal accident on its owners.

"Hey, listen, Siobh – is that what people call you?"

"No."

"Hey, listen, Siobhan, I owe you an explanation. See, every year – round about my dad's birthday – I play him this practical joke. Last year it was a bomb scare. Yeah. Year before – Ebola. Families!"

"Uh huh," enthused the young estate agent.

"So – moving on. What are you doing here? So early."

Siobhan opened her handbag and removed a compact but clearly expensive camera.

"Nothing as fascinating as you. I like to take photos of our properties at sun up. For the website. Punters seem to go for it. And it covers a multitude of sins."

"Wicked. Don't suppose you'd like to go out with me some time?"

Matt Brownridge hoped that it was only him that picked up the little moan emanating from under the car. He also hoped that if Siobhan had to flinch as she did, it was only because of the boldness of his invitation.

"I'll keep my clothes on this time," he added, rakishly. "Well…"

"It's very sweet of you," responded Siobhan, stemming his flow. "But it's against the estate agents' code."

"Code?"

"You know – like doctor-patient, lawyer-client. I'd have to hand back my digital tape measure."

"I'm not the customer," corrected Matt.

"No. Okay. You got me." And then, to his surprise, Siobhan offered up her first proper smile, which was indeed toothy and radiant. "But hey, you just make sure your lovely mum and dad retain us as sole agents for the property and also find their new little flat through us, then we'll talk after completions. Deal?"

With this, she walked briskly away, skirting round the neatly trimmed hedge and into the front garden of the desirable Brownridge residence, looking purposefully through her camera as she went.

Still leaning on the car, Matt could only stare after her, taking in the slim, pinstriped legs above pristine trainers, glints of a radiant new sun on her lustrous hair and the air of insouciant competence that set all his juices flowing, despite the double assassination on which he and his tarmac-based accomplice were currently engaged.

Right now, this Siobhan appeared as fully detached as the house she was bent on selling, but he knew that things – especially women – could switch just like that. Didn't his own mother spurn her blunt airline passenger's initial advances until he somehow won her over, as she herself tells it, with a promise to buy her an engagement ring three times as big as the one she currently sported on her finger.

It was the tiny but insistent metallic knocking from somewhere nearby that brought Matt Brownridge back to reality and caused him to stand upright just a few inches away from the tampered car.

"Can I come out now?" whispered Janie.

"Yeah. Quickly."

Slipping out from under the machine, lethal tool bag zipped and gripped, Janie Brownridge hurried off down the street and round the nearest corner towards their own inferior but hopefully far safer vehicle in an awkward, Groucho Marx scuttle.

It was just seconds after Janie had vanished that Siobhan chanced to turn back for a moment towards the road. Perhaps this was because she could feel the weight of Matt's lustful gaze upon her or hear his heavy breathing.

She lowered her camera, although she soon wished that she hadn't.

Smiling uneasily, she just managed to glimpse, over the low front hedge, the powerful car of her newest (and potentially most lucrative) client as it slid very slowly and soundlessly forward of its own accord.

The young estate agent didn't have time to warn an admiring Matt, who was still standing in louche mode just inches away from the bonnet. The huge vehicle knocked him flat onto the ground and proceeded to run over him on its way down the suburban road. A road which, unfortunately, was on a rather steep incline, which perhaps the wannabe killers should have taken into account before allowing gravity to do what it does best.

Although it wasn't strictly within her remit, Siobhan decided that she had better do the honours this time and call the ambulance. She wondered briefly, as she strolled over to check on a flattened and moaning Matt, whether the same paramedics might come again – one of them had been rather cute.

*

"*Couldn't you have WAITED till I'd gotten out the way?*"

Janie could see her brother's face on this occasion as he lay strung-up on his back in the hospital bed, but it didn't make conversation any easier. For what had to be the very first time, she found herself feeling grateful that their parents had owned such a monster of a car, as the bulk of it had passed right over Matt, leaving only a multi-fractured leg, broken wrist and smashed-up Amazon delivery van in its wake.

"Oh, sorry," said Janie, "I must have missed that bit about time-release brake-cutting in *Homicide for Dummies.*"

They were all set for a major, hospital-friendly, stand-up row – although, of course, only one of the combatants could actually stand up – when the doors to the ward were flung open and Ray Brownridge stormed in.

He was followed, as ever, by his equally upset although perhaps not quite so uncontrollably incensed wife. For a moment, Janie was concerned that her irate father might simply hack through the forest of suspended limbs on his way to his accident-prone son.

"*Somebody cut all the bloody brake cables!*" he told the world, as Matt and Janie exchanged a swift but guilty glance.

"Well, don't look at me," said Matt.

"Why the hell would I look at you?" puzzled the older man.

"My money's on Murray's Minicabs. First they try to nick my drivers – now this. He never liked me, did he, Bobbi?"

"Hated your guts, my darling. Still does." She threw into the air a look that was intended to embrace them all in its efforts to appear sympathetic, supportive and appalled at the same time, but, sadly, the new and very expensive Botox injections – a recent gift from her spouse – weren't allowing her to do much more than make her seem like a chronic IBS sufferer. "Your father's got the police onto it. He's very shaken."

"It's like I got hit by a truck," added Ray, shaking his head. The irony of this was lost on him but not on his would-be assassins. "Anyway – BobRay Cars is on the market now, so they can try to kill the next bugger. Ha!" He shifted uneasily on the spot, as a slight shiver ran up his frame. "I hate hospitals. We're not stopping. Come on, sugar lump – Luigi's got us down for 8.00 this evening and you know how he goes all Italian when we're late."

With a curt nod to his children, Ray Brownridge steamed out. Bobbi clattered close behind on her brand-new Manolo Blahniks. At the door of the ward she suddenly stopped and turned awkwardly back. Retracing her steps towards the bed, she tried her darnedest to smile.

"Oh Janie, sweet. Nearly forgot," she said quietly. "The birthday cake…?"

Janie just nodded, as ever.

"Thanks for coming, guys!" Matt called out painfully to the skittering heels and the swinging door. Manoeuvring himself back to Janie, he just shook his head in despair. "See that? *See that!* They could hardly wait to get away. Their own son."

"I know." Janie sighed. "Mind you, we did just try to kill them."

"Only goes to prove we were right," said Matt Brownridge, broken but unbowed.

The secret of a successful hit is to know your mark. Intimately. Whether they're learning to scuba-dive in the local pool – not a pretty sight but needs must – or testing out a brand new Rolls Royce and using up the earth's precious resources. You have to be attuned to where they like to go, what they like to do. Within reason, of course. I'm a killer not a Peeping Tom. That's just disgusting.

DEATH BY CHOCOLATE

*W*hen Matt Brownridge could finally walk again, he and Janie decided that the whole sorry enterprise would benefit from some intensive and dedicated research, with Google leading the field as primary source and Wikipedia as back-up. *CSI* and its ilk had proved a dead loss.

But the more tech-savvy member of the Brownridge hit-squad had to point out that criminals these days were far more likely to be caught because of a cyber trail than anything else, other than possibly DNA, CCTV or the fact that it was so bloody obvious who did it.

So, one Saturday, they both arrived from opposite directions at a small internet café, in a town some distance from their own, an establishment they had, of course, discovered via the internet. Without acknowledging each other, they found unoccupied seats one machine apart and began their trawl.

After a few minutes, a nondescript man in his forties took the space between them and began his own search. It was clear that he knew exactly what he was looking for, whilst his fellow surfers were floundering amongst sites ranging from 'electric wiring' to 'lethal chemicals'.

At one point, Janie became rather excited when the words 'Polonium 210' popped up on her screen, but the initial elation dissipated when Matt caught a glimpse of the site and mouthed '*seriously?*' over the head of the middle man.

It must have been at least a half hour later when Matt, who was heavily into a really interesting article about asphyxiation by ligature, heard Janie utter a loud gasp. Her neighbour was too preoccupied even to blink, but Matt could see the words 'warfarin' and 'rat poison' as if they were flashing in electric red 64-point.

They stared at each other, over the head of their mutual neighbour. Neither one of them could believe their eyes. It seemed almost too good to be true.

Suddenly, a large shadow appeared to hover over both of them. They each leapt to cover their screens, as the smiling manager approached with two steaming ham and cheese paninis.

"Compliments of the house," he said. "For our new customers. And no need to hide your screens, loves. There's nothing I haven't seen before." He looked at the middle screen. The customer was watching a clutch of excited bonobos engaging in noisy group sex. "I tell a lie," said the manager.

*

Rumpleteazer was sufficiently grown-up to have put the painful events of that naked stair-slalom evening well behind him. This afternoon, he appeared to be watching his former assailant – and that kindly, albeit weirdly dressed, human who often gave him his injections – with genuine, unbegrudging interest. The old tabby was no expert, but the pair certainly seemed to know how to set a good table.

The young woman was back in the kitchen now – he could hear the blender, so there was a good prospect of some serious licking – but the curious limping man still in this room (the room with the big table to snuggle under and the well-stocked bar to climb upon) was clearly pondering some special finishing touch.

The one thing on which old Rumpy-Pumpy, as he was known to his loving if occasionally over-boisterous male owner, wasn't overly keen was the lingering smell of paint. There were paint-pots and brushes still in a corner of the room and the newly refreshed paintwork was stickily gleaming.

"*Janie?*" called her brother, into the expansive kitchen.

"What now?" she yelled back.

"What side do the wine glasses go on?"

"Same side they always bloody go on!"

"No need to be sniffy," he said in a loud mumble. "I'm only trying to get things right."

There was a loud clatter from the kitchen and the blender stopped mid-whisk. Janie stomped back into the dining room holding a pharmacy box of pills. The young woman in the Mona Lisa apron appeared to be losing it.

"I am in that sodding kitchen, trying to make a really nice dinner that'll kill off both our parents swiftly yet tastily, and you keep bothering me with your stupid bloody questions!"

"Sorry," said Matt Brownridge, contritely. "What side?"

"Left side," replied Janie, softening. "And align the napkins so the patterns are all facing the same way."

Even the cat could feel the sigh.

"Oh, does it matter!" muttered Matt.

"It's their last supper. Show a bit of respect."

Janie began to align them respectfully herself. Matt stopped her with one hand and snatched back the napkins with the other.

"I can *do* it!" insisted Matt, petulantly.

"It's quicker if I—" snapped Janie, making a grab for them. "FUCKING LEAVE IT!"

The inevitable sibling struggle ensued, the pushing and the shoving and the smacking, an unwieldy wrestling match with no holds barred. Fired-up, of course, in the intensely febrile atmosphere of this very special evening, the wok of emotions quite naturally over-stirred. Were somebody to have witnessed this altercation, however, from a safe distance, they might have been forgiven for assuming that the combatants were a couple and that the spat was composed in part of something distinctly sexual. Or, if not quite sexual, then somehow uncomfortably possessive.

Predictably, the tug-of-war napkins split in two. As Janie reeled backwards, away from her toppling and still unsteady brother, the box of pills in her other hand went flying. The contents immediately spilled out onto the carpet and some even rolled onto the only recently completed paintwork.

"Now look what you've made me do! *Idiot!*"

Janie crawled over the floor, making certain that she picked up or peeled off every single one of the scattered pills, some of them now with a vibrant pistachio tint. She seemed to be on the verge of tears.

"You know you're not meant to get pills dirty," she said, scrabbling around.

"I really don't think it's critical – in the circumstances," Matt reassured her, squatting uneasily down to help. "Will it be – y'know – painful?"

"Not if you don't watch."

They found each other under the table, reaching for the same pill. For a moment, they froze, eyes unblinkingly on each other, hands outstretched as they contemplated exactly what they were doing and, more portentously, what they were actually about to do.

The siblings might have stayed there, hunched on the carpet for days, but a third head suddenly arrived between them, lurching purposely towards the one overlooked oblong treat. Matt swatted the chubby cat away and grabbed the final tablet of warfarin. The cat glared at him, remembering the stair incident and vowing revenge.

"They'll be here soon," said Matt softly, as he eased himself upright.

"I told them 7.00 prompt. Said it was a surprise."

"That's for sure. Well, let's hope they're hungry."

He could sense Janie lightening up as she went back into the kitchen.

"When aren't they?" she said. "You know them – they can eat for Britain. Anyway, they like my cooking. About the only thing about me they do like." He heard a deep and rather sad sigh. "I'll go grind some more of Dad's warfarin. For safety."

She disappeared into the kitchen but then popped her head back round the door.

"Don't eat the cake," she advised.

*

They had expected their mum and dad to turn up in one of Ray's better and cleaner fleet cars. The unsuspecting couple arrived in a brand-new Belladonna Purple Rolls Royce Phantom.

The siblings watched from the front window as their parents disembarked. Ray and Bobbi were wearing identical designer tracksuits and sports bags, matching not only each other but also the car they rocked up in. Light from the recently illuminated lamp posts bounced off the bling that newly rattled on their wrists and dangled flashily around their necks.

"Classy as ever," muttered Matt, as he and his fellow hyped-up host for the evening shuffled anxiously away from the table of doom towards the hall and the front door. They could hear their parents talking as the house key turned in the lock.

"Well, I think it's really sweet of them," they heard Bobbi say.

"After screwing up my last birthday dinner, it's the least they can ruddy do," countered Ray, as he opened the door.

Janie suddenly remembered that she was still wearing an apron. She swiftly whisked it off to reveal a brand-new creation in chartreuse and puce. Meantime Matt became all smiles as he welcomed his 'guests' for the evening. He truly hoped that they couldn't detect the blind terror lurking behind his tightened face but reassured himself that they wouldn't sense his emotional journey if he had a noose around his neck and a suicide note pinned to his chest.

"Come in, come in, make yourself at home," he gushed.

"Welcome, birthday boy," smiled Janie.

Ray Brownridge just rolled his eyes and strolled into his own dining room. The siblings threw each other the same nervously encouraging look and quietly followed their parents.

The table was candlelit and looked beautiful. Bowls of assorted salads had been carefully spaced out, bottles of the couple's favourite wine sat right by their places and a choice of breads sent out their home-baked aromas from a wicker basket. On a heated hotplate nearby was a tempting lasagne.

"Did you see how we've repainted it?" asked Bobbi, switching the lights back on and killing the atmosphere at a stroke. She spread her jangly arms around in a gesture that wouldn't have looked out of place on a Boeing 747. "The guy just finished yesterday. Siobhan thought it might make for a quicker sale."

"She's good news, that one," endorsed Ray, plonking himself at the head of the table. "It's a bugger selling a luxury property these days. You kids are so lucky you're just renting."

"We're blessed," agreed Janie, switching the lights back off again. "Well, as you can see, dinner's all ready. Just you make yourselves comfortable. And take the weight off your – jewellery."

"Ooh, this all looks very nice, darling," said Bobbi, "but it's a bit of shame we can't enjoy the new paintwork now we've paid through the nose for it."

With a sigh, Janie flicked the lights back on. "Happy now?"

"Yes, that's much better," said Bobbi. "Is that one of your 'creations'?"

"Er – yeah."

"I'll say one thing for you, Janie Brownridge, you never give up."

"So," said Ray, already pouring out the wine. "What are we having? Is there a 'me 'n' u', eh?"

Janie pointed proudly to the hotplate. "There's lasagne or lasagne."

Her father almost choked on his Rioja. "*Lasagne!* Girl, are you trying to kill us?"

"NO – the lasagne's fine!"

"*Janie!*" warned Matt, stepping briskly in. "What do you mean, Dad?"

"We've just been with our personal trainers," explained Bobbi. "They've put us on the low GI diet. We mustn't go near anything refined."

"That shouldn't be too much of a stretch," said Matt. He glanced across to Janie, but she was almost in tears.

"I made it specially," she moaned. "You love my lasagne."

Bobbi just gave her daughter one of her smiles. Case closed.

"You two eat it, love," said Ray gently. "We'll have some of that salad. Salad's okay."

"Especially for randy bunnies, eh?" Bobbi chuckled.

"You'll never lettuce alone!" countered Ray. "Geddit?"

"Ha, Nice one, Dad. Well, it'll leave more room for the next course. Eh, Janie?"

Janie still looked pissed that her lasagne was rejected. She grabbed the steaming bowls off the hotplate and stomped back into the kitchen. With a shrug to their parents, her brother followed.

"Did you *see* that? DID you, Matt?"

Janie was almost in tears as she scraped the uneaten lasagne into the black plastic bin by the sink.

"It doesn't matter, Janie."

"Doesn't matter? DOESN'T MATTER! All that bloody

work – and she just throws my lovely lasagne back in my face. It was made with love, Matty."

Matt began to stick candles into the large, delicious-looking cake on the kitchen island.

"I know. But no harm done," he reassured her. "The rat poison's in the cake."

"I do know the rat poison is in the cake, Matthew. Because I put the sodding rat poison in the cake. That is not the… Well, I'm going to cut two particular rats a jolly nice BIG poisonous slice!"

By the time Matt returned to the dining-room, Bobbi was already clearing away hers and Ray's salad plates. The couple were deep in excited conversation and didn't notice their only son edging towards the wall.

"…And they've got this luxury lodge just outside the Serengeti in Tanzania – you can almost shake an elephant's—"

Suddenly the lights went off. The door slowly opened. Ray and Bobbi's heads swivelled to see Janie entering the darkened room with a magnificent chocolate cake, a forest of candles burning on it.

"*Happy sixty-eighth birthday – belatedly – to you,*" she sang, "*happy birthday, dear…*"

"Now this you have got to eat," enthused Matt. "Both of you. What with it being so good." He patted his tummy. "Wish I had some room left myself, after that lasagne I scarfed down in the kitchen."

"Me too," said Janie. "Yum!"

To his credit, Ray Brownridge succumbed with a smile as Bobbi gave a reassuring nod.

"Well," he conceded, "as it's a special occasion – and I'm worth it." With this, he blew out all the candles in one saliva-laden blast.

He was just reaching out a newly man-braceleted hand for the cake slice when the doorbell rang.

"*Who the hell's that?*" shrieked Janie over-loudly, a sign to anyone who knew her well – save, of course, her own parents – that her nerves were jangling like a tambourine player on Space Mountain.

"Answer it and you might find out," suggested her dad, his hand still hovering over the death cake.

Matt, staring at Janie in confusion, went out to open the front door.

Standing there – and looking, to his eyes, even more stunning than on previous sightings – was Siobhan. Matt attempted manfully to convert his initial projection of superhuman shock into one of instant delight and welcome.

"Oh. *Siobhan.* Hi!"

"Well, don't look so pleased," said the young woman, clearly still locked into first impressions. "What time's the ambulance booked for?"

Matt could only smile weakly as she brushed past him towards the dining room. Whatever scent she left in her wake took him to new heights of lust and more profound depths of panic.

"Everybody in here, are they?" she said, pushing open the door. Ignoring Janie, she beamed at Ray and Bobbi, who greeted her like an old friend. Ray actually stood up and hugged her, only narrowly avoiding ramming a cake slice into her ear.

"Hello, my darling," he said, "glad you could make it. You look good enough to eat – if I wasn't on a diet!"

Siobhan roared at this and gave him a playful smack.

"Janie, dear," said Bobbi to her daughter, who stood frozen in the doorway, staring at Matt. "Switch the lights on, would you?" While Janie did as bidden, Bobbi beamed at the new arrival. "So, sweetheart – what do you think?"

Siobhan looked around the room admiringly as Janie just looked daggers.

"Wicked," said the estate agent professionally. "He's done a lovely job. It'll be gone in no time now, Mr Brownridge."

"Ray," said Ray.

"Ray. And I've got my trusty camera." She tapped the leather bag on her shoulder.

His father turned to Matt, who clearly couldn't take his eyes off Siobhan. He didn't think he had ever encountered an estate agent more beautiful.

"So – got something to say, Mr Drool?" asked the homeowner.

"No – what d'you mean, Dad?"

"Your mouth's open," explained Janie, shaking her head in disdain.

"An apology, maybe?" suggested Ray. "For all the grief you've caused this beautiful young lady."

"Oh. Right. Siobhan… sorry if watching me get my leg and arm squashed by my dad's runaway car upset you."

"These things happen," said Siobhan, graciously. "Well, to you. Anyway, Mr – sorry, Ray – and Bobbi, if I take the photos now, we can have the website updated by morning and after that I'm sure—"

"Oh, but now you're here, lovey, you have got to stay and have some cake," insisted Bobbi. "It's our Janie's one skill."

"*Mu – um!*"

"Oh yes, indeed," added Ray. "That's why we invited you."

Janie and Matt exchanged a horrified look.

"Oh… well… it does look a bit scrumptious," said Siobhan, appraising the cake as she would a desirable property not yet on the market. "Maybe just a—"

"NO!" came the high-pitched scream from nearby. They all turned to stare at its source.

"*Matt!*" admonished Ray.

"Sorry, Siobhan," said Matt, lowering the register several notches and attempting to be cool, "but – but hey, you're sweet enough as it is."

The young woman smiled a bit oddly, while Janie looked like she could happily poison them both.

"Jesus wept!" she said.

Siobhan paid no attention, as she was bent on going for a slice. Ray had already done the honours and carved out some serious chunks. So the young woman was rather taken aback when Matt brusquely snatched the entire plate away from her.

"And, anyway, it's *our* cake," he explained, reasonably, walking with his precious gateau to a far corner of the room. "Janie made it especially. For Brownridges only. See, it's even got brown ridges on it," he added, with a weak laugh.

"Matthew Brownridge, don't be so ridiculous," admonished his mum. "That gateau could feed an entire bloody African village. Give the poor girl a slice this minute."

Siobhan could see that things might be getting ugly. She only wanted to take a couple of photos and be on her way. She could honestly live without cake.

"There's really no—"

"NO!" insisted a very irate and ruddy-faced house-vendor. "You take a nice big slice, love. It's *my* birthday and I sodding insist."

Ray demonstrated his adamancy by striding over to his errant son and lunging for the cake. Matt swiftly moved it even further out of his reach and when this looked futile, he tossed it to Janie, like a rather squidgy frisbee. Janie staggered backwards under the sudden weight but, to her credit, she caught it with only a few spent candles flying free.

Thinking on her slightly wobbly feet, she offered the bemused and by now rather scared visitor a kindly smile.

"Siobhan, I do know a thing or two about the fuller figure. My customers at the shop are all a bit like you. Thick ankles, tendency to spread. I'd keep away from cake. For a while at least."

"Eh?" said Siobhan, looking downwards. "What's wrong with my—"

"Siobhan," barked an outraged Ray Brownridge, "EAT THAT BLOODY CAKE!"

Seriously intimidated but never one to ignore a customer's instructions, Siobhan reached over once more for a slice of elusive but clearly very rich and incredibly fattening chocolate cake.

Matt caught his sister's look of sheer desperation and did the only thing he could do in the circumstances. He dove into the cake like an Olympic swimmer, hands outstretched, and stuffed slice after calorific slice into his mouth as fast as he possibly could. At one point, his eyes glanced up from the rapidly disappearing plate towards Janie in a plea for assistance that he was clearly never going to get. She just looked at his increasingly chocolate-smeared face in horrified disgust, as if observing an over-indulged child at his own birthday party, and signalled very firmly that she wasn't having any.

The others simply watched this bizarre gateau-gorge in mounting horror. Once you got over the initial repulsion, it was actually quite compelling.

To their credit the paramedics came remarkably swiftly this time.

*

It was most probably his serial vomiting, brought on by the unprecedented, world's fastest cakeathon, that saved Matt Brownridge from being warfarined to oblivion. He managed at least three upchucks on his parent's drive alone, including one on the new Rolls Royce, which even Matt, in extremis, managed to appreciate.

The elder Brownridges and their cake-deprived estate agent actually waved to the ambulance guys this time, as by now they seemed almost like family friends. None of them noticed old Rumpleteazer happily gobbling up the morsels of dessert that Matt hadn't quite managed to stuff down his throat.

It really was a very respectable cake.

In the ambulance, between regurgitations, Matt managed to whisper a few strained words to his shivering sister. Words that were about to change everything.

"I reckon we might need professional help."

"You think?" said Janie.

*

It is a curious thing.

A person would never think of performing Elgar's Cello Concerto in E minor *at the Royal Festival Hall, would they, if they'd never picked up a cello? They wouldn't expect a wee picture to be hanging in yon National Portrait Gallery if they hadn't ever stuck their brush in a palette.*

Or, worse still, if they were colour-blind.

Yet hundreds of people every year think they can quite merrily bump someone off, without even bothering themselves to acquire those basic homicidal skills.

The only place these folk will appear, my friends, is prison. Or, of course, the nearest hospital.

So, as they say, down these mean streets a man must walk, if he wants to walk like a man.

Or something.

MURDER IS MY BUSINESS
(VAT INCLUDED)

*M*att Brownridge would probably not admit it, especially not to his little sister, but he was really scared.

Lucky to be alive, of course, thanks to Janie grossly under-prescribing the warfarin (which was only pretty low-dose anyway) and the hospital assuming that the little pig in Accident & Emergency had simply OD'd on cake. But scared right now because they were suddenly entering the big league.

Naturally, they were apprehensive for other reasons too. It was late, they were in the seediest and least well-lit part of the city, and they had already been accosted twice by unshaven men for cigarettes, which they were convinced was only a preamble to full-scale assault.

"*You're sweet enough as you are, Siobhan.*"

"Give it a rest, Janie!" snapped Matt, just before he tripped over something, which turned out to be a person sleeping rough." Sorry, mate," he said, as the body groaned. "Sad, isn't it?" he added, as he gave the disturbed sleeper wide berth. "That could be us one day, if we don't—"

"How do we know there even *is* a pub here?" said Janie, who didn't want to get into the homeless conversation. Not again.

"We've tried every other dank and crappy street in Bristol. If it's another trendy gastropub, I'll buy a gun myself. Maybe we should just use the dark web."

"How do you get onto the dark web?"

"Well, you… no idea," said Matt, after giving it some consideration.

They reached an unlit doorway that looked worn-down, unsavoury and seedily promising. Matt turned to Janie, who just nodded. So they pushed open the door.

The corridor was narrow and dingy, paint peeling everywhere, sawdust on the floor and cracked mirrors hanging crookedly off the walls, Even in the dim light they could spot mould around the skirtings. The place ticked all the right boxes.

One more shabby, frosted-glass door and they were in. Matt and Janie gazed around the large room in the hazy light then looked at each other. The place was packed. Men in suits and ties with expense accounts were roaring with laughter at each other's jokes, while slick, glossy women imbibed Guinness, gin and gossip after work.

Matt and Janie just stared. Appalled.

Suddenly a tall, smartly dressed man in his early thirties, rather good-looking in a blond, public-school way, bumped into Matt, spilling the week's guest beer over the night's newest guest.

"Oops! Sorry! I am such an idiot. Sorry." He turned to Janie. "Got your boyfriend damp! Sorry!"

"Oh, that's okay. He's not my boyfriend! He's my brother. Really. See, same nose!" She gave the man her best smile. "I don't have a boyfriend. Currently."

"O-kay," said the tall guy. "Great here, isn't it? A real, honest-to-goodness working-class pub! Check out the loos – you can get dysentery just by walking past." And with this Pevsneresque observation, he was gone, leaving a disappointed Janie.

"We're never gonna find what we're looking for here." Matt sighed, as Janie followed the tall blond guy with her eyes. "It's full of people with Teslas! How the hell do you ever meet psychos and sociopaths and scumbags?"

"Match.com usually," said Janie, then noticed that Matt had moved on.

"*The barman!*" he suddenly exulted. "He's giving me the eye. And he looks dodgy. He's even got a scar. You always ask the barman! Come on."

They pushed their way through the raucous yuppie crowd to the bar. A youngish guy with slicked-back hair, pointy sideburns, worn Black Sabbath t-shirt and the welcome hint of an old facial wound was pouring drinks. He certainly fitted in here far better than his clientele.

"Matt – easy," warned Janie. "You know."

"I'm not a fucking idiot – '*Hello, mate, we're looking for someone to do in our parents – know anyone?*'."

"Just saying."

Matt leant over to the barman and spoke in his quietest yet most knowing voice. "S'cuse me, mate. Wonder if you can help me?"

"Depends what you need help with," said the man in the broadest of local accents, which Matt for one found reassuring.

"Well, it's kind of personal, but…" He paused to look around and take a breath. "I have this – problem, see. And I want to get in touch with someone who might be able to… y'know, get rid of my – problem. Once 'n' for all. Like permanently. Get my drift?"

The barman stared at him – hard. Then nodded slowly.

"So," continued Matt, his hopes rising, "you know anyone?"

The barman nodded again then leant forward. When he spoke, his tone was professionally confidential.

"See the guy in the corner with the beard?"

Matt just nodded.

"He's a Freudian. Great with problems of a sexual bent." Matt was shaking his head in puzzlement, but the barman was on a roll. "Emotional abuse? Big fella with the beard at the snooker table – Rogerian. Very person-centred. And that woman right there in the corner."

"With the beard?"

"Psychodynamic." Matt looked frustrated, especially when the barman nodded to an empty chair. "Gestalt. Ha! What am I like!"

"Right, Janie," said Matt, grabbing his sister. "We're leaving!"

Janie wrenched her arm away from him and leant across the bar towards the man. "We're looking for a – y'know – hitman," she said quietly.

"Oh! If you'd only bloody said," replied the barman solemnly. "Dave don't come in here no more. Not since it got all wanky and 'bohemian'. Try the wine bar down the street. Big black dude. He'll be in the corner with a glass and a newspaper. On his own. Can't miss him."

*

The wine bar down the street was more Matt and Janie's kind of place. No slumming yuppies supping in squalor, just freshly painted walls in pastel colours and French impressionist posters in frames on the wall. The sort of jazz where you could almost recognise the tune was playing softly from hidden speakers.

They spotted Dave straight away.

He was a hefty, slightly overweight African-Caribbean guy of around Matt's age with a thick beard and dreadlocks. Occupying the back corner as described, this large and vaguely threatening figure was indeed drinking from a bottle of cheap white wine and reading *MOJO*. Matt had hoped he would be poring over something like *Soldier of Fortune* or *Glock Monthly* but perhaps this would have been a bit too in-your-face. The man certainly looked like he could hurt someone – even the glance he was giving his periodical seemed threatening.

Quite tentatively, Matt and Janie approached the man's table, sensing that too sudden a movement might trigger a response they would all regret, but especially Matt and Janie.

The man known only as Dave took his time to acknowledge their presence, and when he did look slowly up, there was something about him, despite the unexpected softness in his eyes, that was distinctly unnerving.

"Hi. Dave?" ventured Matt.

The seated man nodded fractionally, so Matt pressed quietly on.

"Okay to talk…?"

Another brief nod.

"See, we have this – problem. A big problem. This – weight on our shoulders. Well, weights. Each shoulder. That we'd both like to – to be without. You understand? And we need to get in touch with someone who might just possibly – if he's available, that is – maybe, y'know, sort of help us to—"

"Lose your virginity."

"*No!*"

"What he's trying to say, Dave," explained Janie, once more, "is – are you the, y'know, hitman?"

Matt glared at her. Again. Surely this wasn't how it was done. Very deliberately, the man in question set down his glass and his magazine and stared at them.

"Think you'd better sit."

He had a voice that went down to his boots, which footwear Janie couldn't help noticing, with a not altogether unpleasant shudder, were vintage, mid-calf, embroidered leather. She dragged over a chair.

"Thanks," said Matt, who wasn't interested in footwear. "We've got the money." He sensed Janie's look but ignored it. "We'd want total anonymity. Obviously."

The man was staring intensely into Matt's determined face.

"R–ight. Okay. So…"

"Our names aren't important. Here's the address." He swiftly handed the man a piece of paper but could see that Dave was having some trouble deciphering it.

"69 Blythewood Avenue."

"NO! No, that's the Jacksons," said Matt. "They're lovely. Don't hit *them* for God's sake. It's number 49. Home to a Ray and Bobbi Brownridge."

The look the man gave the siblings was perturbing, even allowing for the fact that he was an assassin for hire, and they were soliciting his exceptionally specialised skills.

"Hang on. *Really?*" he said, shaking his head. "I used to go to Scouts with their son."

Now it was Matt's turn to stare. "...Dave Forrester?"

"*Matt Brownridge!*"

Janie rolled her eyes. So much for anonymity. "Might as well just put it on Instagram." She sighed.

The man now known as Dave Forrester gave a little laugh. "I knew I recognised you. How've you been, matey? I used to have such a crush on your little sister." With a start, he turned to Janie. "*Janie?*"

"Hi, Dave. You've - grown. Love the hair. And the boots. Can we get on with...? Please."

"You haven't changed," persisted the large man. "Well, you have, obviously - you were ten. You're still a looker!"

"Am I?" said Janie in surprise. Flattery and compliments were hardly her daily fare, either at home or at work. Or anywhere, really. So she wasn't quite certain how far one should take this. "Er - thanks. Now, about this job."

"Hey, I remember now!" said Matt, almost gleefully. "You ran that protection racket with the Cubs."

"And the junior Sea Cadets," added Dave, proudly. "We had this no-drowning option."

"You've moved on."

"Well, you have to."

"*For Christ's sake!*" said Janie, raising her voice then just as swiftly lowering it. "Can we make this quick, please? Someone will see us."

"It's okay," the suddenly amicable man reassured her, "they know me here. And by the way, I'm not married. Believe it or not!"

"Totally believe it, Dave," said Janie. "Now – money. For the – you know."

"I'm offering five grand," announced Matt. "For the pair."

"Er – Matt...?" said Janie.

Dave Forrester began to mull. "Five grand...?"

"Six – six grand," countered Matt. "My final offer. To do both of them. Simultaneously – at the same time."

"I know what simultaneously means."

"Sorry. It was that dyslexia thing you had—"

"*Matt*?" interrupted Janie.

"Both?" clarified Dave, who was clearly a stickler for details.

"Parents, yes," said Matt. "Ray and Bobbi. They come as a pair. Noisily and incessantly."

Dave Forrester rose up from the table, reminding Janie of some primordial creature emerging from the swamp. He was even larger than either of his customers had assumed.

"Let's talk outside," he said, nodding briefly to the lady behind the bar.

It was raining as they walked down the bleak alleyway together. They stuck close to the brickwork, avoiding the odd passer-by, most of whom did, at least to Matt and Janie, look pretty odd indeed.

"Right!" said the big man after some minutes, during which he had appeared lost in thought, which had to be a good thing. "Two numbers. We call them numbers. Not hits or marks or any of that Sopranos shit."

Matt nodded in interest. He didn't know this.

"Six grand?"

"Okay. Seven thousand five hundred. My final offer." Matt ignored with some difficulty his sister's pointy little elbow in his ribs.

"Uh huh," said Dave Forrester, agreeably.

"Half upfront. Half when the job's done. It's all we can afford."

"It's actually a helluva lot more than…" chimed Janie. "We're a bit strapped actually, Dave. That's kind of why we need to – y'know."

"You wouldn't be the first."

"Plus, of course, they're really awful," added Janie, in mitigation. "Racist, sexist, you name-ist. It's not just the money. We're not greedy people, Dave."

"*They fuck you up, your mum and dad,*" quoted Dave.

"See, Janie, even he's heard about them!" gushed Matt. "Take it or leave it, Dave."

"So – three thousand seven hundred and fifty quid upfront. In cash. Got it on you?"

"What?" said Matt, thrown. He hadn't computed this bit. "Er – no. *Here?* We'll meet tomorrow. Somewhere less public. Give you the money *and* the full details. Of the – numbers. Deal?"

"Wednesday morning. 1.30 in the morning. Just under Clifton Suspension Bridge. And the girl comes alone."

"*What?*" said Janie, looking up at the big guy who she really didn't remember from twenty years ago, although some quite disturbing things were slowly coming back. "Uh-uh! No way am I—"

"*Deal!*" said Matt and shook Dave's hand to clinch it. Even the man's grip was a killer. Matt didn't look at Janie, but he could still tell she was pissed off.

With this handshake and a slight nod, Dave Forrester faded into the darkness, leaving the siblings to gawp at each other. They knew that they were feeling uncomfortable but couldn't be completely certain whether it was because of the creepily dark streets or what they had only just arranged. It was probably both.

"Seems a nice enough bloke," said Matt, because the silence was just starting to chill his blood.

"He's a ruthless killer."

"Yeah – but that's just his, y'know, day job. It's not like he's a psychopath or anything. *Dave Forrester* – ha! And nobody thought he'd amount to anything. I remember at Cubs—"

"We've still got a problem," said Janie, interrupting the boyhood reminiscences. "Thanks to you – big mouth."

"What?"

"I've only got three thousand in my Building Society account. That was from our grannie. What possessed you to offer seven and a half grand?"

"I know the market. I'm in telesales." He turned to her, although he could barely see her in the darkness. "Janie – there's only one thing for it."

*

"*Four grand?*" said Ray Brownridge.

Matt and Janie had found Ray and Bobbi on their well-tended back lawn, doing tai chi. They didn't appear particularly limber, but they did look rather tranquil. It was clear from the way they reacted to Matt and Janie's arrival and subsequent request that they weren't going to allow anything to disturb this tranquillity. To their children, it was as if a movie of their long-standing awfulness was being played back to them at the wrong speed.

"Four grand?" repeated Ray Brownridge, with enviable calm.

"Actually, four and a half," said Matt. "No, I can probably find the five hundred. Yes, four. Please. Grand."

The tai chi sequence for which his father was aiming would have been cruelly tarnished by intervening sensations of astonishment or even surprise, so Ray compromised with mild curiosity.

"Why the hell do you need— have you got some girl into trouble?"

Bobbi froze at this, wondering for a moment how a grandchild might affect their upcoming holiday schedules.

"*No!*" exclaimed an outraged Matt. "Is that what you think of me?"

"You wouldn't have the balls," said Ray serenely, one hairy arm outstretched.

Janie could see that this had made her brother quite upset. "*Yes, he would!* He would have the – y'know. He might," she defended.

"Oh Matt," said Bobbi Brownridge calmly, "what *have* you done now? It's not fair, it really isn't. This is derailing our tai chi, you do realise that?"

"Sorry, Mum. Hey, you remember when I was a kid, and I used to love those fruit machines down Weston?"

Ray and Bobbi nodded but Matt wasn't certain that this didn't just form part of their meditative routine.

"Well – it's got a bit worse over the years. And these men – they—"

"They what?" said Bobbi. "You haven't bought a fruit machine from strangers?"

"No, of course I haven't bought a fruit machine. How could I lose money on my own fruit machine?"

"You could," said Ray. "You ought to calm down, son. Try tai chi."

"I don't want to try tai fucking chi! Sorry. Sorry, Mum. Well, okay then."

Matt tried gamely to mimic the potentially euphoric sequence of movements his parents were very slowly and inexpertly undertaking. Janie had a go too. But the siblings weren't really in the right place mentally, what with the fundraising and the imminent homicide. Each silently comforted themselves, however, by thinking that even a tai chi black belt or the like would be put off their stroke should they simultaneously to be begging their father and mother to assist in the financing of a contract on themselves.

"Dad – it's a bit hard to calm down," said Matt, giving his tai chi the elbow. "If I don't let these men have the money – they – well, they'll kill Janie."

"Eh?" said Janie.

"Or worse."

Nobody said anything. The silence grew deeper and deeper. Janie and Matt exchanged horrified looks.

"Dad?" said Janie, eventually.

"Four grand…?" mulled Ray. "That's a lot of money, son."

"*Seriously?*" said Janie.

"Just saying, love." Ray Brownridge had the grace, or lack of it, to pause his tai chi. He was clearly making some informed calculations, which of course was how he had got to where he was. "Okay. Here's the deal. You pay me back at base rate plus two per cent. And do night work on the cars – for free." With this, he went back to his tai chi.

"*He had to think it over!*" said Janie, as they walked back into the house.

"Base rate plus two per cent?! His own kids! They don't bloody deserve to live."

Behind them, the tai chi-ers continued blissfully with what was left of their lives.

FOLLOW THE MONEY

*J*anie wasn't in the best of moods at work the next day.

It could have been because of the impending 'money drop' (or whatever it was called in the trade). Or it might have been, at least partly, because one of her regular customers, currently in the extra-large changing room, was still refusing to believe that there could be any connection between what she was trying to force over her ever-expanding body and what she regularly chucked down her ever-open gullet.

"How are we doing, Mrs Randall?"

The woman eventually emerged in a black-and-white striped dress about three continents too small for her. Janie thought she looked like a zebra about to have quins.

"Well?" challenged the lady, a bit breathlessly.

"Er, love that pattern on you," enthused Janie professionally. She was usually quite gracious with her customers, the majority of whom were 'outsize' through no particular fault or weakness of their own and were often quite distressed about it. "*Love* it! Do you think it might be just a wee bit too... tight around the shoulders?"

"Mm, possibly," conceded the lady, breathlessly. "Don't you do it any bigger then?"

"Hard to believe but I'm sure we do."

"Then go and GET one! Now, girl. Shoo! Quick, before I pass out."

Janie slumped off to the storeroom but not before glimpsing her customer having a forage in her handbag and pulling out a half-eaten cheeseburger.

As she began to sift through the oversize dresses, losing herself in the acres of costly material, Janie's mobile rang. She answered it through a mouthful of polyester.

"Tents 'R' Us."

"I'm calling on behalf of Fenton Financial," came the voice. "Are you completely satisfied with your home protection?"

"Sod off, Matt. I'm working."

"You're not satisfied? Well, let me tell you about our package."

She could tell he was in earshot of his boss, but she really wasn't in the mood.

"Tell that jumped-up little estate agent about your package. Oh no – too late for that. She's seen it and passed."

"You never can tell with insurances. Sometimes you're paying out more than you think."

"Eh?" said Janie, before finally understanding. "Oh great! So now I'm completely broke. The most talented, visionary designer of my generation. I bet Nicole flaming Farhi could afford to have her parents killed ten times over."

"Well, at least now you can relax. All the details will be handled for you. Smoothly and expertly. So, Janie – if I can call you Janie – are you alright with all this? Janie…?"

For a few seconds, Janie couldn't speak. Reality was making her momentarily numb.

"Yeah… I'm alright. I suppose. Bit nervous. See you later."

She hung up and realised that she had begun to shake and was apparently powerless to stop it.

"Was that a personal call?" said Mrs Edwards, glaring into the storeroom.

"No, it was Bristol WeightWatchers asking if they could count on your support."

"Excuse me?"

Janie yanked out a dress from the rack and barged past her boss.

"Ah! That looks just the job!" said the zebra lady. "And they do say vertical stripes are slimming."

"Know what else they've discovered is slimming? Not scarfing Huge Macs out your handbag. C'mon, Orca."

With this, she began to herd Mrs Randall back into the dressing room.

"She hasn't had her Fruit & Nut today," explained the proprietor.

"*And you, Janie. Have a nice day,*" said a concerned Matt Brownridge, some miles away, into a totally dead line.

*

Aside from the occasional hooting of an owl and the odd suicide, the world famous Clifton Suspension Bridge tends to be relatively quiet at 1.30 on a weekday morning.

So, when Janie Brownridge began walking towards the halfway point of Isambard Kingdom Brunel's masterwork, holding a medium-sized aluminium suitcase, she could reasonably assume that the large, dark figure ambling towards her was the person whom she had driven rather tentatively out here to meet. If he wasn't the aforementioned person, she feared that she could be in real trouble. Even if it were to be him, she reckoned that tonight would be no picnic.

In this, she was almost totally mistaken.

"Dave?"

The looming figure almost smiled. In fact, she was pretty sure that he did smile, which took his far smaller and infinitely more vulnerable client completely by surprise.

"Janie! Nice to see you. Good drive?"

"Mmm. Not a lot of traffic. What with it being half-past silly o'clock."

"Great. Have you eaten?"

"I'm sorry?" she said.

The man just beckoned her to follow him.

*

The iconic bridge loomed large in the background. Occasionally a vehicle would move across it like an errant glow worm. Random people going God knows where at 1.30 in the morning, oblivious to the drama taking place way below on the dewy grass of Clifton Down, where Dave Forrester was escorting Janie Brownridge to a small picnic area he had lovingly created.

Perched on this damp green carpet was a foldable IKEA table, with two equally foldable canvas chairs. A large, perfumed candle, set directly in the middle of the table, flickered in the very early morning breeze, casting its delicate light on a small wicker hamper. Beckoning his guest to pull up a chair, Dave opened the hamper with a restaurateur's flourish to reveal an impressive selection of finger sandwiches, accompanied by fresh fruits of the season and a choice of wines.

"Red or white?" said Dave. "The white should hopefully still be chilled."

For a moment, Janie simply stared at the offerings. She couldn't look at the man himself.

"This is... do you always do this?"

"Gotta do something these days to stay competitive. So – what's your poison?"

"*Excuse me?* Oh, sorry. Er, the red. Please."

The host uncorked the bottle with some dexterity. She couldn't help wondering if the pointy corkscrew thing had recently been at somebody's throat – or at least the hands that wielded it so adroitly.

"Ah – ooh – not too much. Driving."

"So, are you married, Janie?"

Where did that come from?

"Yes, Dave."

The big man, squashed precariously into the small canvas chair, seemed strangely disappointed.

"To my work. Fashion is a demanding husband!"

Now Dave just looked bemused. Janie swiftly realised the poor guy had no idea what she was talking about. *And why should he?* she thought sadly, suddenly wishing that she had worn one of her home-grown, more picnicky outfits. But truly, how was she to know?

"We should probably take care of business, before…" said Janie, then wondered what exactly was 'the after'. Sandwiches and some fresh fruit, she supposed; what else?

"Oh. Yes. Sure." Dave set down his wine glass, out of respect. "Okay."

Janie dumped the metal case on the table. "This is the – fee. It's all in there."

She clicked the catches on the briefcase and gently opened the lid. Inside was a small envelope and a lot of space. Janie shrugged apologetically to the about-to-be-hired killer.

"Matt kind of overdid it with the luggage. It's all in fifties. I realise that some shops don't accept them these days – I know Mrs Edwards doesn't, 'cos of forgeries – but I hope it's okay." She removed the envelope and handed it to him. "You'd better count it."

Dave shook his head. "I trust you. And if it was short, I'd just have to kill you too."

Janie smiled at this, a tad uneasily. To her intense relief, Dave smiled gently back. Convinced now that he wouldn't really kill her, at least probably not for the odd fifty pounds or so, she found herself smiling at the man for real. Which did take her a bit by surprise.

"The details are in there too," she added, pointing at the envelope. "Mum and Dad's address. Which you know anyway, from when you used to... We can't give you house keys, I'm afraid, 'cos they made us give them back. After the last – attempt."

Dave stared quizzically at her.

"Long story... Anyway, you've got the day they do their weekly shop up at Harrods and Fortnums and, well, most of Bond Street actually. Also Mum's trendy hairdresser. Dad's golf club. Their new posh country club. Etcetera. It's all there. In sort of a spreadsheet."

"I wish all my clients were so thorough, Janie. I reckon it's the welfare state – takes away any sense of responsibility."

"Absolutely, Dave. Couldn't agree more. Kills the initiative – to, er, kill. Ooh and remember, you've really got to make it look like an accident."

Dave's rather warm brown eyes looked suddenly steely. Janie recoiled as she glimpsed the unbridled danger within.

"You're not talking to an amateur, you know."

"Sorry, Dave."

The man stared a moment longer then gave a slight nod. All forgiven.

"And I don't want them hurt," insisted Janie. "The – 'numbers'. Deceased is quite sufficient. Thank you. Dave."

Another, graver nod from Dave.

"So... if we need to contact you, what do we do?"

"You don't," said Dave, which, for a moment, caused Janie some confusion. "I'll contact you."

At this point, and as if part of a pre-written script, Dave Forrester withdrew a small, moleskin notepad from an inside pocket of his leather jacket and handed it to her along with a silver pencil.

"I'll need your phone number. Email address. Date of birth." He noticed the slight flicker of surprise in the more violent flicker of candlelight. "I do horoscopes in my spare time," he explained, with another slight smile.

"I'm a Pisces," said Janie.

"I KNEW you were a Pisces. I'm Aquarius!"

"No way!"

They gazed at each other for a few heady seconds, saying nothing, just taking in the moment. The post-drop picnic moment between a hired assassin and a young wannabe fashion-designer. That sort of moment.

"More wine?" said the hitman, already filling her glass.

"I suppose it wouldn't kill me," said Janie Brownridge.

*

She found her brother pacing up and down the tiny living room when she returned to the flat sometime after dawn. Her first thought, surprisingly, was that she didn't realise people actually paced. She thought that was only in soapy films and tacky novels.

Janie only caught on that she was humming happily to herself when Matt began to speak, and she understood that she should perhaps stop so that she could hear what he had to say. Although, she had a pretty good idea already.

"*What the hell time d'you call this?*" he said. A bit shoutily, in Janie's opinion.

"Absolutely no idea. Didn't you go to bed?"

"Go to bed? Go to fucking bed! How could I go to bed when you were out there in the dark, arranging to have our parents whacked? I thought he'd killed YOU. *And* stolen the money. I nearly called the police!"

She looked alarmed.

"I didn't. Obviously. But I was frantic! Couldn't you at least have sent me a text?"

"I… didn't want to wake you," she said, lamely. "Anyway, I hadn't realised it was so late. Early. Whatever. Sorry." She began to smile a bit zanily, even by her own standards, as she felt a glow beginning to rise on her face, which could have been the alcohol, but perhaps wasn't. "It was a lovely evening."

"It was a money drop! To a hitman!"

This was just like her brother. He always wanted to put a damper on everything.

"With gourmet sandwiches," she explained, in mitigation. "And a choice of wines. Apparently that's what—"

"*He came on to you!* Our killer! I don't bloody believe it."

The pacing resumed, but at an even more frantic pace. Because of the size of the room and the unruly furniture, he had to do it in awkward circles around her, which made her think of Red Indians around a campfire – or Native Americans, as she should probably call them now.

"That has got to be against some sort of professional code," he persisted. A horrible image – in fact, quite a few horrible images – suddenly flooded his brain. "Oh shit – you didn't…?"

"NO!" the lady protested, after some thought. "And since when did you become my – my moral high ground?"

The excessive pacing was beginning to make her dizzy – or dizzier. At least, far too dizzy to stand. She flopped onto the lumpy sofa, barely feeling the loose spring as it punctured her backside.

"Matt – it's *over!* This whole… thing is now in the capable and surprisingly well-groomed hands of an expert, who'll do it quickly – humanely – and without a trace. We can stop worrying."

Although his face was a bit of a blur, she could feel her brother's mood lightening.

"You're right! Oh my God, Janie, we can get on with our lives. Well, properly start our lives – our new lives. Light at the end of the tunnel. Light and a decent bloody inheritance. For the first time ever, I have prospects."

"Without people doing us down all the time," muttered Janie, almost to herself, wondering if her words were coming out in any way intelligibly. "Rubbishing absolutely anything and everything we do or say or even think. Totally destroying our self-esteem. Killing us softly with their crap." She began to giggle. "That's a song isn't it?"

"*Exactly!*" exulted Matt, who had clearly picked up the gist. "You can do your dresses without worrying that no one would be seen dead in them. Especially not our mum. And I can find a better job and finally sort out my personal life. Even make up with Siobhan."

"*Siobhan!*" Janie gasped in horror. "Are you sure you want to, you know, go out with an estate agent?"

"You've just had a hot date with a professional assassin!"

"Yeah. But… an estate agent?" She felt her eyes closing. "Anyway, Dave will call us after the job is done."

"So – we couldn't stop it, even if we wanted to."

Janie could hear the uneasiness in his voice. "No."

"No… right."

"Uh huh."

She managed to force her eyes open, to find his own looking down at her. Neither of them were able to hold the gaze for long but instead retreated back into their own private, not altogether tranquil, thoughts.

They remained there for some time.

THE BEST LAID PLANS

*A*s he checked out his reflection in the window of Roland & Tibbett, Award-Winning Estate Agents, his glassy image tucked between computer-enhanced photos of overpriced houses, Matt Brownridge was disappointed. For once, this was not related to the way he looked. In fact, he reckoned that he currently presented as pretty shit-hot. The slight deflation was due entirely to the fact that he couldn't spot Siobhan at any of the desks.

"She's booked out all day, I'm afraid," explained her oleaginous colleague, when Matt eventually ventured inside and explained his urgent need to contact Ms Siobhan Davies in person. "But I can tell you where she'll be for the next hour, if you want."

"Yes! Yes, thanks, I do. Want."

"I have to ask. Why do you need to see her exactly?"

Matt hadn't foreseen the question but felt he parried back a hastily invented answer with considerable aplomb.

"Er… I need… the spare keys to my parents' house. Yes. I left my… my iPad mini there. And my parents are away, and I don't have keys anymore – it's a whole big thing. Parents, eh?

"Yeah. Can't live with 'em. Can't kill 'em!"

With this, the young agent, who Matt noticed was more slickly dressed than his hardly managerial position might surely warrant, headed off to a computer at an empty desk to source the relevant information.

Meanwhile, a familiar figure walked out of a rear office and past Matt on his way to the exit.

"*Gourlay?*"

Gourlay – for it was, indeed, the enviable man himself – paused and turned with one of his gleaming smiles.

"Bloody hell, Matt. We don't see each other for fourteen years…! You alright? When we last bumped, y'know, at that Thai place – hardly *authentic* Thai food, by the way – you seemed sorta emotional."

Matt tried to recall the occasion, as he had been sorta emotional a fair few times over the past weeks and months. Ah, yes.

"I *was* emotional, Gourlay. You're right. Uncle Clive had just died, I'd had a stupid argument with my dad, and… I've got some very major business deals coming up. Seriously mega. You moving house?"

"Not exactly. Roland & Tibbett manage my property portfolio – have done for years – including the apartments in New York and Rio. And if you ever fancy a short let overlooking Sydney harbour, you should talk to Siobhan Davies."

"Oh – right." Matt nodded. "I believe she's handling my parents' house. She – seems nice."

Gourlay offered his old schoolmate a smile that was more knowing than Matt might have wished. Matt wondered what was happening on his own face to elicit this.

"She is." Gourlay laughed. "Hey… like me to put in a good word for you?"

"Well, I don't really think…" He noticed on Gourlay a grin that went right up to his eyebrows but ploughed on anyway. "Could you? *Wow!* That would be – thanks, Gourlay. I'd really appreciate that."

"Matey. I knot your woggle, you knot mine."

Matt had little time to ponder on how he could possibly improve on this person's woggle, or, indeed, any other part of the man's charmed life, but his attention was soon diverted to the shiny, pointed shoes of the estate agent as he returned with the vital information.

With this now clutched in his hand and a realisation that the object of both his mission and his desire was only a few unaffordable suburban streets away, he left to find her, feeling more confident than in their previous encounters. Which, when he thought about it, probably wasn't saying very much. Indeed, if the meeting passed without the paramedics turning up, he considered that he would be ahead of the game.

After only a few minutes, and with some assistance from Google Maps, Matt spotted Siobhan Davies escorting a young, wealthy-looking couple out of a well-preserved Edwardian three-storey terrace. Even though the words she employed were themselves relatively formulaic, she seemed to invest them with a sincerity and expertise he found both stimulating and more than a little intimidating.

"…The vendor REALLY wants a quick sale and – between you and me – I reckon he could very well take a sensible lower offer. So I'd think fast if, I were you. Or I might just buy it myself! *Joking!*"

The young couple were laughing happily as they hopped back into their Audi and drove off with a grateful wave. Siobhan's friendly smile only disappeared when she glimpsed Ray and Bobbi Brownridge's elder child loitering across the road.

"You do realise there's a very thin line between 'vendor's offspring' and 'stalker'?"

"I need to get into the house." Matt immediately perceived the confusion, as he crossed the leafy road towards her. "My parents' house. Not this one."

"That's a relief. For a second, I was afraid you were branching out."

"It's just round the corner. You've got the keys, apparently. I left my iPad mini in there and it has all my business forecasts and projections and – stuff. Any chance – please – Siobhan?"

"Oh alright." The young woman sighed. "But you do understand that I'll have to come with you?"

As this was the entire object of the exercise, Matt proved himself to be a perfect model of understanding.

"*Really?* Oh, well… if it's not putting you out. I love what you're wearing, by the way."

"Considering you were either wearing sweet bugger-all, massive alloy wheels or a face full of chocolate, I'm not sure that was much of an endorsement."

"Like it!" said Matt, feeling that if they could josh like this, the morning was going splendidly.

*

The house appeared to be empty, as Matt had assumed that it would be. Unless his parents had already amended their only recently devised schedule, Wednesday morning was champagne brunch at their new, exclusive (but patently not *that* exclusive) country club.

"*Hello?* MR AND MRS BROWNRIDGE?" yelled Siobhan, just to be on the safe side. Although, the way she was currently thinking, the right side of safety would surely be in numbers. "Nope. Probably out spending your inheritance, eh?"

Matt forced out a deceptively sincere laugh, as they strolled into the living room.

"Hah! Nice one. Well, good luck to them, I say. They earned it." And now that she had been cunningly put off the scent… "Siobhan?"

"You look for your little iPad," said the estate agent, not desperate to hear what else Matt had to say. "I might as well check some measurements in the kitchen while I'm here. I think I could finally have a cash buyer in the wings. With no chain. Holy Grail!"

Matt suddenly looked upset. He wasn't certain whether this was because of a potentially disappointing brush-off or the shuddering reality that this precious home, the one in which he and his sister had grown up, albeit not that happily, was about to be in the hands of a total stranger (whilst that same stranger's magical, soon-to-be-transferred cash would inevitably be squandered in a manner so flagrantly disgusting that it brought tears unbidden to his eyes).

"...Just a couple of things he needs to know," continued the oblivious agent, "and it saves me making them up out of my head!"

"If you need anyone to hold your tape—"

Siobhan stopped him with a flaunt of the curious gizmo newly arrived in her hand.

"It's a laser," she explained. "With Lightsaber attachment, if you get too frisky."

With a swift, demonstrative flash, she left Matt in the recently pistachioed front reception room, searching desultorily for an iPad mini that was never there in the first place. But he wasn't giving up without a fight.

"Look, about the other day," he called out towards the kitchen. "I wanted to apologise. It's been a weird few weeks and – I really like chocolate!"

"Yes, I got that," came the reply. She didn't appear too inclined to continue what, for Matt, might have been a stimulating conversation.

He wandered into the other reception room, still chatting. "So – what made you want to become an estate agent?"

"Greed, primarily. And it gets me out of the house."

Matt noticed a load of cardboard boxes on a table. Most were open, some had been fully unpacked. Amongst the shiny and clearly expensive electronic items – including, ironically, a brand-new iPad mini that wasn't his – was a state-of-the-art video camera and a small, flat-screen TV. Shaking his head at the almost obscene excess, which he would dearly love to emulate some time, he picked up the camera.

"So… what qualifications do you need?" he shouted.

"Very few, actually. And they don't include small talk."

"Oh, I'm sure they – ah – okay."

Realising that this once promising seam had now been fully exhausted, Matt idly pressed a button on the camera. To his surprise, the television screen soon glowed into life and an image of his father appeared. He was seated at the head of the dining table, staring into the lens, with Bobbi snuggled very close beside him, looking less like a dinner companion than a conjoined twin. They both appeared to be giggling. This was confirmed when their only son tentatively switched up the sound.

"Stop it! *Ray!* I'm not letting you do that on camera!"

"Oh, you'll get used to it. I think pensioner porn could be a big growth area."

"I know one big growth area!"

"Jesus Christ!" muttered Matt and immediately smacked a button to stop, and hopefully even erase, the vile spectacle of his parents enjoying their unsavoury and wholly excessive love for one another, courtesy of costly technology and his inheritance. Unfortunately, the action only served to fast-forward this home-grown masterpiece, so he hit another button. The picture returned to normal speed.

This time, it was Ray alone on screen, addressing the camera. He wasn't giggling any more.

"…Video will and testament. We decided to do it like this so that you don't just get to hear what we've done but to understand *why* we've done it. So, Matt, Janie, pin your little ears back and listen up for once."

Matt Brownridge's normal repulsion instantly transformed itself into wary fascination, as he sat down a few feet from the screen.

"Your mum and I decided a couple of years ago that we could leave both you kids a whole lot of money and property when we died—"

"DAMN RIGHT!" Matt heard himself screaming. As did the estate agent in the next room.

"What?" said Siobhan, popping her head round the door.

"Nothing," said Matt, finding the correct stop button this time. "Keep measuring."

The moment she left, he was at the video again. He realised that he wasn't breathing but hopefully could make up for it later.

"…But just recently, as you know, we thought, 'what would be the bloody point of that?'. It would just make you even softer and more useless. Reliant on money you hadn't worked for. We know you two and we think that would be a disaster."

"For who?" argued Matt. "FOR WHOM?"

"For you, tosspot. For both of you. Now, as we've already told you, and as even you have probably noticed by now, your mummy and me, we're going to bloody well fritter away most of our hard-earned assets just as fast and happily as we can, before we shuffle off this morbid coil, eh Bobsy?"

Matt could sense the jolly nod of concurrence offscreen.

"But if, by any chance, we *don't* manage to get through it all, we really didn't want to ruin you kids and cut off all your ambitions with a substantial inheritance."

"Eh? No! Cut them off. Cut them *all* off!" cried Matt, almost in tears. "I fucking deserve it! BLOODY RUIN ME!"

This time, Siobhan made a full-bodied re-entry. Matt stopped the video once again.

"Are you sure you're alright?"

"Fine. Yeah, fine, Siobhan. Flaming iPad! Grrr!"

Casting him a final suspicious look, Siobhan left him to his own devices. Or lack of them.

"…So suffice to say," continued his onscreen dad happily, "plans are in place."

As his father suddenly paused to look off-screen, Matt could hear Bobbi's voice, but it was too indistinct to decipher. His father, however, was acknowledging the interruption, even if he wasn't best pleased.

"...Yes, love, I know you still have your doubts, but Big Daddy knows best. Matt, Janie – we love you. Really. Despite – well, everything. All the failures, the disappointments, the total cock-ups. But we've made a brand-new will and we're leaving all our unspent money, however little that is – *hopefully!* – to the Feline Groovy Home For Neglected Cats."

The ensuing silence was almost painful. At least at one end.

"NO FUCKING WAY!" yelled Matt finally, shaking his head as if he'd just been attacked by a swarm of drunken bees.

"They are, of course, delighted with the whole idea," continued Ray, obliviously. "The owners, not the cats. Well, the cats too, probably. Brilliant creatures. As you know, the home gave us our lovely Rumpleteazer – wherever the hell he is these days, dirty stop-out – and before him, Jellyorum, and before him, old Mr Macavity. And, of course, there was Eric... well, we hadn't seen the musical then."

"BASTARD! You never had any sodding intention of—"

Siobhan was back in again. "The soundproofing in this house is shocking! What are you ranting about now? Oh, that's your dad, isn't it – on the telly?"

"Yeah," said Matt, his eyes still fixed firmly on the frozen screen. "And know what, Siobhan – he's leaving all the money they don't manage to piss away before they die to some manky bloody cats' home!"

"Ahhhh. Bless!"

"Even if he dropped dead today – I mean, heaven forbid – me and Janie wouldn't get anything! Not a bloody sausage."

"Oh well," commiserated Siobhan, clearly not giving a toss.

"It would all be for nothing! NOTHING!"

With this, he hurled the matt-black, barely used camera into the equally recent flat-panel TV screen, doing serious, brand-new damage to both.

"You're taking it well," said Siobhan.

As he turned to her for the first time, the young estate agent was able to watch Matt Brownridge's slightly pasty face convert from pure undiluted anger through blank realisation to equally unadulterated panic, as if some casting director in the sky was attempting to gauge his range. It was quite fascinating for her, actually.

"*Shit! DAVE!* I've gotta stop Dave! Get our money back. Janie will know where he is! I've got to find Janie! SHITTING HELL!"

He swiftly pulled out his mobile phone and ran, wild-eyed and frantic, towards the front door. But then, just as instantly, he stopped, as he sensed that Siobhan was, perhaps unsurprisingly, staring at him. Matt turned to her with a self-deprecatingly apologetic smile.

"Um, you've caught me on a really bad day."

"So, you do have the other sort then?"

For a moment, it seemed to both Siobhan and Matt that the man could actually be about to explain the whole thing to her, but he soon realised that this might not be the best or most prudent use of resources.

"Next time – I promise. You'll see the real me, Siobhan. I'm actually usually very calm."

This welcome shaft of self-perception was slightly undermined by his pelting out of the front door, kicking over a new stone lion on the recently scrubbed step and screaming an enormous 'FU-UUUUCKKKK!' into the leafy suburban air.

HIT AND MISS

The newly installed and constantly moving Swiss T-bar ski lift was about to hoist two expensively over-equipped English Brownridges into the clear blue sky. Their personal instructor was waiting for them at the top of the finest dry ski slope in the rarely snowy south-west. Having met them briefly down at the bottom, he could happily wait for them all day.

"This is the life, eh Bobsy?" said Ray Brownridge to his wife, clomping around in his skis. "I bet Janie wishes she was here skiing with us." He turned to his right. "I said, 'I bet you wish you were here doing this with us'."

Janie, who was standing right beside them at the T-bars, holding their bags, extra skis, a choice of footwear and après-ski refreshments, simply nodded as she watched her parents once again admire each other's outfits, in anticipation of the slow and, to her, rather precarious upwards journey.

"Make sure you're strapped in when you get on those things," she advised. "We don't want any accidents."

The centre was rather busy. It was local schools' half term and there were quite a few excited children there with their parents. She assumed that most of these visitors were, like her own parents, in training – or at least on damage-limitation exercises – for a forthcoming proper ski trip somewhere expensive, with snowy mountains and foreigners and ambulances.

For a moment, she wondered if Dave Forrester might be here, lurking amongst the crowds. But she would probably have seen him, as a guy like that would stand out anywhere and this would hardly be the optimum venue for a clandestine and meticulous kill. Of course, she was thinking like an amateur. What did she really know?

What she did really know was that, if she had the time and the money, she could do something amazing with ski apparel, which to her was a bit bland and predictable. Something perhaps utilising the wintry footprints of snow-dwelling animals? Or a reindeer-antler motif? Maybe soon, when she has her own fashion house.

"What are *you* looking so grumpy about?" asked Bobbi, who wouldn't recognise a creative brainstorm if it smacked her in the face.

"This was meant to be my day off," muttered an obligingly grumpy Janie.

Bobbi turned back from mounting the T-bar. "You should be happy to spend a few precious hours with your parents. We're not going to be here forever, you know."

Janie looked suddenly guilty.

"No, we've booked two ski trips already, on two different continents," announced Ray, a bit loudly. "AND a luxury Caribbean cruise! And that's only in the next three months! *'Sing Viva – British Virgin Islands'.*"

"Ooh, nice!" said Janie, genuinely, knowing that they'd never get there.

Ray began to mount the T-bar. "Gangway! Here I go – off to get piste! Geddit, love?"

Bobbi, just inches behind him, roared with laughter.

"Watch me ski. S – K – I," he spelled out loudly to anyone in earshot, as the lift sailed upwards. "*Spending Kids' Inheritance…!*"

The jolly Brownridges were halfway up the slope, wobbling

a lot more than everyone else because they were turning to each other to conduct a banal après-ski-related conversation, when the first shot rang out.

It coincided with Janie's phone ringing, but she was too busy ducking, like everyone else in the place, to answer it. Especially when further shots followed, and people began to scream.

The cable holding up Ray's lift was soon dangling by a metallic thread. A later shot skimmed Bobbi's head and severed the other cable. They both hung there for a moment then dropped to the ground, which fortunately wasn't a mighty fall, and they had plenty of body fat to cushion them.

"*What was THAT?*" exclaimed Bobbi, understandably. She found herself hiding behind the dangling T-bar and a rather large child who had tumbled off the one behind her. There were skiers of all levels of expertise falling and scurrying and inexpertly panicking everywhere.

"*This was meant to look like a bloody accident, Dave!*" grumbled Janie, but she shut up when a Chinese family, hiding with her behind a wooden snack table, kept staring.

As the shots continued, Janie joined the mass exodus of people running towards their cars. She thought she could hear police sirens in the distance, but she was certainly not going to hang around to find out. Nor was anyone else, although Janie would have loved to have reassured them that they weren't the ones in the line of fire. After Dave's near misses, however, she wouldn't actually be prepared to swear to it.

When they all finally met up outside at Ray Brownridge's brand-new Rolls Royce, each of them as pale as the snow that at least two of them were expecting to be to toppling into any time soon, the vehicle's proud owner flung open the door and practically pushed his trembling wife inside. Janie found her own route into the back seat, which was really rather comfortable, in an excessively sybaritic sort of way.

"*What the hell is going on?*" said Ray, shaking his head so hard that he could barely see to start the car. "Somebody in there was trying to kill us! Again!"

"NO!" protested Janie. "Why would anyone— they probably just built a rifle range way too close to the ski slope." Even she could hear how pathetic this sounded. "Or – or maybe they were aiming at someone just ahead of you on those lift thingies."

"Don't give me that. He was aiming at us," yelled Ray, his body still shaking. "I bet it was one of Matt's one-armed ruddy bandits! What did he do with that four bloody grand I loaned him? Probably gambled it away again, the silly sod." Ray was still struggling with the ignition as he ranted.

"No. No, Dad! We paid them back! They – they sent a receipt," she elaborated. "And a really nice thank you note."

"Oh. Okay. Well, whoever the buggers are, at least they didn't hit the Roller," he said, because he was basically a glass-half-full person.

As if on cue, a passing people-carrier, fleeing the scene at ferocious speed, sideswiped the pristine Rolls Royce with a force that left it shuddering.

"*Bastards!*" shouted Ray Brownridge, as his wife began to cry.

Janie looked at her phone and realised that she had sixty-five unanswered calls from Matt. As if she didn't have enough to think about. Well, she wasn't going to pick them up now. It's not like he would have heard from Dave.

She checked her phone again and realised with some surprise that she was quite disappointed she hadn't heard from him either.

HIT ME BABY TWO MORE TIMES!

The wine bar had proved less than useless. They informed Matt that they hadn't seen Dave Forrester for a couple of days and had absolutely no idea where he might be.

To compound this, Janie was continuing to act equally unreachable and most probably was not even checking her phone. Matt, naturally, hadn't wanted to leave any incriminating messages on her voicemail or text but could now see no alternative. Not if he seriously wished to prevent the worst from happening.

Perhaps there was still time to disabuse his misguided parents of the notion that stray cats were more important than one's own loyal and un-straying offspring. The fact that he could see no irony in this was testament to the panic in his bones, a dread that was growing with every unresolved second that passed.

"Janie, if you get this – you have *got* to find Dave and hold him off! At least until Mum and Dad change their sodding will back. Okay, long story. You got any idea where he lives? You know him better than I do. Call me!"

He stopped by his hurriedly and rather dramatically parked car, ignoring the traffic warden whose disapproving head was almost shaking too much to write him his ticket. Matt wished he had remained in touch with some of his childhood friends, but most of them had moved on and away. Or at least away from him. And anyway, they had probably been too scared of Dave Forrester to maintain any sort of connection.

There was only one person he knew who might possibly put him on the right track.

*

When he opened the door of his penthouse apartment to a clearly frantic Matt Brownridge, Gourlay was wearing embroidered sandals and an ornate Chinese dressing gown. For a scary moment, Matt wondered if his sister had had a rare commission but then told himself that this was most probably a cool item of clothing, just one totally outside his frame of reference.

"Hello, mate?" said a surprised Gourlay. "Short time no see. Excuse the appearance. Bit of jet lag." He noticed his old school friend staring. "Shantung silk. Handmade. I know a guy – if you're interested."

"Oh right. Well, of course I am. Very. Gourlay, do you remember Dave Forrester? From way back?"

"Dave Forrester... Dave Forrester...? Didn't he run a protection racket for the Cubs?"

"And the Sea Cadets. Yeah. You don't have his address by any chance, do you? I can't think of anyone else who might."

"Why?"

"Why? Good question. Well, I'm – organising a reunion. Yeah. A tribute to Uncle Clive."

"Great thought. Sorry, mate, these days I don't exactly hang out with the Dave Forresters of this world. Present company excepted. Hey, how are things with – what was her name – Siobhan?"

"Oh, slowly but surely, y'know. I'm a grower. Watch this space."

"Good man," said Gourlay, patting Matt on the back. "Well,

I did put in a word. Bigged you up. And I think you might just be in luck."

Despite everything, Matt was genuinely thrilled. "*Yeah?* Thanks, Gourlay! Appreciate it. What did you actually – no, gotta run."

Disappointed, yet not altogether despondent, Matt rushed back towards the lift.

"Who was that, babe?" came a voice from the bedroom, as the front door closed.

"No one you know," he called back to the off-duty estate agent. "Prepare to be royally gazumped!"

MOMENTS OF TRUTH

*B*obbi and Ray, still very shaken, were gulping down several stiff brandies in their brutally cleaned and 'beautifully appointed' kitchen-diner, while Janie made them some equally comforting and very sugary tea. Sod the weight-watching for now, the poor couple were surely suffering. As, indeed, was Janie, although she would be pushed to define the exact quality of that suffering, as there were so many elements to choose from.

"*The world's gone bloody mad!*" moaned Ray Brownridge, looking heavenwards for endorsement. "If you're not safe on your own local dry ski slope, what's it gonna be like up an Alp?"

Janie felt like reassuring her clearly alarmed father that people are rarely shot at in Alps, but she wasn't entirely certain of this and didn't really feel it would greatly aid the current conversation.

"We've never done anyone any harm," protested Bobbi. "Why would someone want to kill us?"

Janie just stared at her but, of course, this counted for nothing. And anyway, her mother's face was suddenly being pushed hard into her husband's ski-suited chest, as he held her tight enough to smother her.

"I'm sure it wasn't personal, love," reassured Ray. "Must have been some homicidal maniac or – or a bloody asylum seeker."

Ray Brownridge didn't spot the look on his daughter's face nor hear her appalled gasp. When did he ever? This time, perhaps fired-up by his near-death experience, he seemed to be on a mighty roll.

"Yup. I bet you any money it was one of them buggers. They happily sail into this country in their little floaty boats, breaking all laws known to man, grab every bloody handout that's going, use up our hospital beds, take our jobs, marry our women, eat weird food in our cinemas, get our subsidised prescriptions."

"Or free, gratis and for nothing if they're over sixty-five," added Bobbi, from almost inside her husband.

"Exactly!" endorsed Ray. "Then they shoot the whole bloody place up, without even a by-your-leave or a beg-your-pardon! Fucker probably couldn't even spell shotgun."

For some reason, it was this monstrous impugning of any poor foreigner's intellect and education, regardless of who they were or the traumatic hardships they may have suffered in life, that really made Janie Brownridge see red. It not only stoked her anger up beyond broiling point but also seriously clouded her judgment, as she now said something to her parents that, with every subsequent breath, she wished she could instantly take back.

"That is SO unfair! And – and so bigoted. And bloody typical, if you don't mind my saying so."

She could, of course, have stopped there and just watched Ray and Bobbi as they shook their heads condescendingly at their woke little girl, the words 'Janie, oh Janie' echoing through her sweet liberal brain. But she didn't. She ploughed remorselessly onwards.

"If you must know, dear parents, it wasn't a poor, innocent asylum seeker!" she practically yelled. "It was a nice respectable little home-grown local lad. An ex-Scout, in fact, from your old buddy Clive's Scout troop! *See?* What do you think of that?"

"WHAAAT?" said Ray, incredulity splashing his face like a cup of sweet tea.

Janie realised immediately that perhaps she had gone a wee bit too far. So she grabbed the half-drunk brandy bottle and took a hearty swig.

"Nothing," she said, before belching fire.

Ray and Bobbi Brownridge, still joined at the zip, just stared at their daughter in horror.

By this time, and to her credit, Janie realised that she couldn't just pack up the latest revelation and stuff it into one of her voluminous bags like an oversized evening kaftan. This baby wasn't going to go back into the womb anytime soon.

"Mum... Dad," she said, shakily, "I think we need a little chat."

*

At the same time that his little sister was about to let the homicidal cat out of the bag, Matt Brownridge was cursing every manner of cat he set eyes on. And there did appear to be quite a few on the streets of Bristol (some maybe even escapees from the Feline Groovy Home) as he traipsed the busy city centre in search of – well, he wasn't actually quite sure, as he imagined professional assassins tended to keep in the shadows, especially when they were executing their... executions.

He decided to hit the phone again.

"Janie! *Switch your bloody phone on!* I've scoured the entire city – everywhere Mum and Dad might be – and there's still no sign of Dave the Hitman!"

He would always remember the ensuing moment, as it made him briefly think there might indeed be a God. Albeit one with a vicious sense of humour. At the exact second that he put his phone back in his pocket, a dusty white van drove slowly past him. On the side of the van, in big black letters, were the words 'DAVE THE HITMAN'.

It took another second for this to register and a couple more before he decided to leg it up the road in some consternation after the vehicle in question. He thought that he knew sufficient about the world of commerce to be aware that it did often pay to advertise. But surely not if you were a practitioner of one of the darkest arts of all.

Dave Forrester was totally unaware of the demented figure pelting up the busy road behind him. Nor did he hear the hoots of angry motorists as they tried not to kill some idiot running into the road, frantically waving both his arms at a slow-moving white van. The obliviously contented van-driver was far too busy enjoying, at maximum volume, a recently discovered early track recorded by the person who was to become known as The Artist Known As Prince, when the artist was simply known as Prince. Carried away by this magical find, he was only just able to stop at some traffic lights and avoid being smacked by a bus.

What the big man couldn't avoid, stationary as he was now obliged to be, was some apparently total stranger almost ripping away his front passenger door. For once it was the client who appeared distinctly homicidal. Especially when he could make out, through the grime, the small print on the side of the van.

"*I want a word with you!*" Matt panted.

Without waiting for an acknowledgement and summoning a strength he hadn't known he possessed, he yanked a mortified Dave Forrester straight out of his musty van.

As disgruntled motorists manoeuvred around the stationery vehicle, Matt yelled into the van-driver's newly hangdog face.

"*A mobile DJ? A sodding mobile DJ!*"

Dave simply nodded but couldn't resist offering his assailant a clutch of business cards he kept in his pocket for such occasions.

"Well, if I was an actual killer for hire," he reasoned, "would I really write it on the side of my fucking van?"

Matt took a begrudging second to concede this. *"You took £3750 from us!"*

"See? Crime doesn't pay," explained Dave Forrester, with a touch of nostalgia. "I found that out when I did that protection racket in the Cubs."

"What happened?"

"Those Cubs travel in packs! It bloody hurt."

"But taking money from two harmless, decent people," moaned the erstwhile client. "That is SO dishonest!"

"Hey, I was in serious hock to some very nasty dudes. The Bristol DJ Wars of 2024? Huh? *HUH?!* I needed money fast – and, suddenly, there you were offering me decent dosh for some wanky crackpot scheme. What was I gonna do – say no? It's not like you'd go to the police." He could feel Matt's angry breath on him. "Anyway – I'm really fond of your sister."

"You keep your filthy, record-spinning hands off my sister! She's just an innocent young woman."

"She gave me money under a bridge at night to kill her parents! But I still like her. By the way, you're not going ahead with that, are you?"

"…None of your business."

"You should really have gone onto the dark web," advised Dave Forrester.

"I know. How do you…?"

"How should I know? I'm a mobile DJ."

Matt's phone began to ring. Dave nodded to him that he should answer it, although Matt didn't really need permission.

"Yeah?" answered Matt. *"Janie! Finally!"*

Dave kept mouthing 'tell her I said hi!' to Matt, but he was pointedly ignored. Matt was too busy looking even more gobsmacked than when he first discovered the hitman's true calling.

"What are you doing at Mum and Dad's?" he yelped. "I thought we agreed. Oh, okay, I'll be right there." He put his

phone back and returned to Dave. "Something's going down. Something mega. She couldn't say what. See you – hopefully never. And I want that money back!"

"Yeah, that'll happen," said Dave Forrester, but only to himself. His old boyhood acquaintance and erstwhile client Matt Brownridge was already running at some speed towards his by now multi-ticketed car.

A VIEWING TO A KILL

*W*hen he finally arrived at the family home, in a state of some considerable agitation, Matt Brownridge felt like smashing his rusty old Micra right into his dad's brand-new Rolls Royce. He managed to assuage his wrath, however, by admiring for some glorious seconds the newly acquired and clearly excruciating set of dents on this flashy vehicle's once gleaming flank.

Jumping out without even locking the car – who's going to steal a heap of junk parked next to a Roller? – he rushed up the path to the freshly painted front door. A few seconds after ringing the bell, he heard various bolts and locks being drawn back and released. This struck him as odd in the circumstances.

The door opened just a fraction. Janie was standing there, looking unusually solemn. He stared at her while she peeked around either side of him, as if checking whether the road was clear.

"Come in," said Janie, unnecessarily. His bafflement still on max, Matt followed her into the kitchen.

He could tell at once that his parents weren't happy. The contrast was probably even more marked than in normal families, because his mother and father were rarely less than mutually ecstatic. He also noticed that the blinds were drawn in every window, which was kind of peculiar. It took only a moment for the penny to drop. Which it did with a mighty clang. He turned to Janie in horror.

"*You didn't?*" he accused.

Before she could even nod, Ray was in there, snarling.

"What the hell were you bloody thinking? Hiring a hitman to kill your own poor, innocent parents! With *my* sodding money!"

Matt just laughed at this, which probably wouldn't even have fooled someone who had never seen him laugh before.

"Tsk, Dad! What's she been telling you? Janie, you silly sausage. Yes, he's *called* Dave the Hitman. But he's a mobile DJ! It was for a – a surprise party for you, Dad. He's got all the oldies."

He reached into his pocket, causing his parents to flinch for just a moment. But all he withdrew were a few of Dave's business cards, which he jovially handed around. Ideally, he felt that Janie should have gone along with this charade a dash more enthusiastically and joined in the obvious joke, but she didn't.

"A… a DJ?" she murmured, gazing down at the glossy card.

"You have got to start living in the real world, Janie," chided her brother, shaking his head theatrically. "It's her artistic temperament."

"*He shot at us, Matt!*" protested Janie, almost in tears. "Dave, your 'DJ', shot at us! On the dry ski slope."

"He bloody near killed me," chimed an outraged Ray Brownridge. "*And* your poor mother. I don't think the Roller will ever be the same again either."

"Or my Balenciaga ski pants," added Bobbi, pointing downwards to a jagged tear where the almost lethal bullet had left its mark.

Matt felt he had entered a madhouse or an alternate universe.

"But it couldn't have been Dave. I keep *telling* you – that's not his M.O! He plays records. Rubbish, mostly, from what I could—"

"Then who the hell was it, Mr Smartypants?" challenged his trembling mother.

"*That would be me*," came a voice they had never heard before.

A tall, excessively slim, somewhat androgynous figure, with dyed blond hair and a smart but slightly crinkled linen suit, stepped out from a cupboard under the stairs, brushing himself down whilst brandishing a rather serious-looking and efficiently silenced gun.

"Good afternoon," said the visitor, in a high-pitched but not unmusical Glasgow accent.

I bet you'd forgotten all about me. That's my M.O. Well, you know what they say in our business – 'bad things come to those who wait'.

"Who the flying fuck are you?" asked Matt, although, if he hadn't, someone else surely would have done.

"Er, Matt – excuse me?" said Ray. "Still my kitchen. Yeah, who the fuck are you? And excuse my son's language."

"My name's Struan," introduced the tall creature.

"Sorry – doesn't tell us much," said Janie. "Nice name though. I'm guessing Scottish. So, what are you doing here?"

"Do you want me to do the mime?" He pointed his gun towards Ray and Bobbi's heads and made shooting noises with his mouth. They were rather accurate. As was the fake falling backwards with an exploding skull.

"*You're a killer! A hitman!*" cried Matt, as if he was on some sort of game show.

"Give that man a cuddly toy."

"Well, like the girl said, what are you doing here?" enquired Ray Brownridge, quite reasonably. "We're not some rival bloody gang members."

"You must have the wrong address, dear," added Bobbi, rather gently, considering the circumstances. "We don't have any enemies."

For some reason, the thin man looked at Janie, who surprised herself by nodding her head in total agreement.

"What about Murray's Motors?" suggested Matt, recalling his father's previous accusations. But he could tell that Ray wasn't listening. He was focussed on the willow-like and rather fey but nonetheless threatening Scotsman with the gun.

"Hey, matey," said the puzzled homeowner, "are you sure it's not that Albanian couple you want – the ones with all the bloody kids just moved in to number 43? They seem a bit dodgy to me."

This was the point at which Janie totally lost it. But it had been a trying day.

"*There you bloody go again!* With the stereotyping. Oh, of course, they're foreign, they're Eastern European, they must have done something that warrants being popped off by a Scottish psychopath. Sorry, Struan – don't mean all Scots are psychopaths. I've met some lovely Scottish people. Not you, obviously. Anyway, the family at number 43 are Romanian."

"Janie, your father was only saying—" defended Bobbi.

At this point, Struan felt that it behoved him to interrupt. "Excuse me. EXCUSE ME! I haven't got the wrong address, petal. My people don't give me the wrong address. I get a very clear briefing. Very thorough. In a lovely binder. With nice black and white photographs. *And* some useful links."

"Briefing?" said Matt. "Who from?"

"Well, from people who want your mum and dad dead. Obviously." It was like wading through treacle with these people.

"*Who would want them dead?*" persisted a curiously outraged Matt. "All they've ever done is try to get by, provide a good home, raise their two kids so they could make their own way in the world… who could possibly want them dead?" He could feel everyone in the by now pretty crowded room staring at him. "Yes, alright. But aside from us – who would wish them any harm?"

"Ever hear of the Feline Groovy Cats Home?" asked Struan, quietly.

No one said anything. They just stared. This seemed to come out of left-field.

"Why the hell would the bloody cats' home want us dead?" asked Ray Brownridge.

"We've always been very good to their cats," protested an outraged Bobbi. "If Rumpleteazer was here, he'd tell you so himself."

"Yes, where is old Rumpy?" asked Ray, looking around.

"*You're pissing all their money up the wall!*" explained Struan.

This was actually a new experience for him. The majority of his victims didn't engage with him in prior conversation. Or, if they did, it was usually a plea for mercy rather than a request for clarification.

"On fancy cars," elaborated the softly spoken hitman, using his slim fingers for added emphasis. "And costly holidays, tasteless baubles and useless knick-knacks. Money that, by rights, should be going in extremely large quantities to those poor wee moggies when you pop off. Money for feeding and attending to forlorn felines. Some of the wee fellas have cat dementia! Going through other pets' cat flaps, chasing chocolate mice…"

"Do you get a lot of work from charities then?" asked Matt, interestedly.

"I tell you, pal, my diary is bursting. It's a huge growth area. You'll find us all on the dark web."

Janie turned to Matt. "See, I told you! Actually, Struan, for future reference, how do you get onto—"

Suddenly, Ray Brownridge began to laugh. It wasn't a pretty sight, as it made his huge face go all red and his rather beady eyes become quite watery. Also, it seemed rather inappropriate. But the man had precious little sense of occasion, so the laughter just built and grew until it became practically hysterical. They all looked at him as if he had suddenly gone insane or the completely understandable fear had taken over in a really big way.

"*Ray?*" asked Bobbi in some concern. "Ray, lovey?"

"Did I say something funny?" asked Struan. "I'm not normally known for my gallows humour. Or my bon mots. That being said, I do occasionally crack out a wee gem."

"Ray, my precious, calm down," insisted Bobbi, practically in tears. "Your heart!"

"Yeah, don't peg out now, Dad," advised his son. "There's no need."

Eventually, Ray calmed down, although it was a struggle.

"I was laughing because we – we changed the will."

"Yeah, we know that." Matt sighed.

Ray began laughing all over again. "Not sure how you know that but no, we changed it again. Didn't we, Bobsleigh?"

"But I saw the video!" said Matt.

Bobbi looked extremely concerned. "You didn't see the bit where we…?"

"Don't go there, Mum."

Ray shook his head. "I changed it again *after* the video! We went right round to our solicitors – you know, Andy McGrath, from the golf club? The Feline Groovy Cats' Home now only gets 3.5 per cent."

Bobbi turned to her children. "Seeing the video – you know, all spoken out loud – well, it made your dad and me think it was a bit mean not to leave you and Janie anything."

"Your mum reminded me of the meal you made for us – for my birthday," said Ray. "And the lovely cake – that you gobbled up in front of poor Siobhan." Ray turned to Struan, who was looking a bit baffled. "You should have seen him. Like a flaming Dyson he was."

"Well, good for you, Dad," said Janie, with genuine affection.

"You're a star, Father," agreed Matt, in some relief.

As they stared at the older man's face, a light seemed to go on.

"…It was *poisoned*, wasn't it? You little fuckers!"

"I don't remember," said Matt, a bit weakly, in his sister's opinion.

"Anyway, we're still going to spend spend spend to the not-very-bitter end, aren't we, Bobs?" He glared at his son. "So bad luck, Dr Crippen."

A loud sigh from the only non-member of the Brownridge family caused them to look back in Struan's direction. He was rather grumpily disassembling his gun and putting it back into the purpose-built pocket of his deceptively well-cut jacket.

"Well, have a nice day," said the thwarted assassin.

"Eh? Where you going?" said Matt, his mind racing.

"Home. Or maybe I'll catch a matinee in town, if there is one. I'm not going to terminate anyone for 3.5 per cent. It wouldn't even cover my fee. There's a Donkey Sanctuary job in the Cotswolds up for grabs. I'm very partial to the Cotsw—"

"*WAIT!*" cried Matt. "Not so fast. Struan, is it? I'll cover your fee! You know – from the proceeds."

"*What?*" exclaimed Ray and Bobbi, in unison as ever.

Matt moved closer to the well-dressed killer. "How do you like to be paid?"

"Er, Matt," said Janie, but Struan had already begun to reassemble his weapon.

"Well, I'm not into suitcases on Clifton Bridge at God knows what unearthly hour," explained the killer for hire, managing to throw an epicene but nonetheless pointed leer at Janie. "Even allowing for the perks that go with it."

"You were watching?" Janie gasped.

"Professional interest. I'm surprised you didn't catch your death." He turns back to an appalled Matt. "I've a nice wee bank account in the British Virgin—"

"Hang on a sodding second," butted in an appalled Ray Brownridge.

"Sorry, pal," apologised Struan, "I'm afraid you're a non-voting member."

"*I'll double it!*" cried Ray, a tad desperately.

"Not following, pal."

"To let us go. Double bubble. If you've got to top someone, top Matt here instead. You can spare the girl without any reduction."

"Thanks, Dad," said Janie. "But I do have a name, you know."

"Eh? *Dad!*" shrieked Matt, at a high pitch even for him.

But his father wasn't listening. In fact, he was holding up a podgy finger in order to emphasise just how little he was listening.

"Come on, sunshine." Ray smiled nervously. "Make me an offer. Hey, I'm a businessman. You're a Jock – you lot are very astute. I'm sure we can come to some sort of mutually beneficial arrangement."

"Base rate plus two per cent?" suggested Matt. To which Ray only nodded, like it was a fair starting point. "I'm your bloody son!"

"*You were going to kill me!*"

Matt just shook his head. There was still no reasoning with the bastard.

"I'm afraid it's non-negotiable," said Struan. "Not if I want to get out of here by Christmas. It's your names on the print-out. 'Ray 'n' Bobbi'. The paperwork's a killer."

The hitman cocked his gun and pointed it towards the older couple, who could see their dreams of a hedonistic, self-serving and incredibly enjoyable retirement going right down the toilet.

They heard a sharp sound, and everyone closed their eyes. But it wasn't a gunshot. It sounded more like a doorbell.

"Expecting anyone?" asked Struan, because, of course, he needed to know this more than anyone.

"Yeah, the police," ventured Ray, but Struan just glared dangerously. "No – no one."

The armed Scotsman thought fast. It was what had kept him alive and out of gaol for so many years, despite some quite recent setbacks.

"Well, I suggest you get on and answer it. The 'Jock' will be right behind the lot of you – with his trusty weapon cocked. And ever so many of the wee bullety things. So don't try anything that reeks of bravado or stupidity."

Ray simply walked at half-speed towards the door. Behind him, in a line, were Bobbi, Matt and Janie. Bringing up the rear was Struan, complete with gun. It was like a conga dance in a Trappist monastery.

When Ray eventually opened the door, they saw his favourite estate agent Siobhan Davies on the front step. Behind her, a middle-aged Asian couple were hovering politely.

"Hi, Ray," said the young woman brightly, her professional smile full on. "I had thought you'd still be out dry skiing. Then I saw your car. Someone's put a very nasty dent in it." They could almost see the sudden alarming thought as it shot through her estate agent head. "Couldn't have been anyone from this area though! Absolutely no way! So – these are the Sharmas. I told them they just *had* to see your lovely home."

Ray appeared distinctly unenthusiastic, which Siobhan found odd. Yet perhaps not quite so odd as the line of people directly behind him; although, of course, the weird son was there, which probably explained everything.

"Oh. Right," said the potential vendor, adding in a listless monotone, "I suppose you might as well come in then."

He stood aside as best he could so that a slightly bemused Siobhan could usher her hopeful couple into the hallway, which by now was standing room only. She managed to flash Ray and Bobbi a beaming, full-toothed smile as she squeezed past them, in a clear attempt to encourage reciprocal and frankly prudent good cheer.

"As you can see, it's a very spacious hallway," said the young woman, who could make a virtue out of anything. "Ideal for family gatherings."

As if to demonstrate this and make room for the unexpected

visitors, the gang managed to shuffle aside and back themselves up against the wall of the hallway, remaining as one relatively solid, long, snakelike lump.

The Brownridge family appeared uncertain as to whether these three new arrivals represented potential salvation or imminent collateral damage. The phrase 'caveat emptor' had never felt more appropriate.

"Ooh, the whole family's here," enthused Siobhan, gamely. "And – someone else." She turned to the Sharmas, thinking on her feet. "It really is very much a family home, Mr and Mrs Sharma. Even the kids can't bear to leave."

"Hi, Siobhan!" said Matt, attempting a semi-normal smile. "Looking good."

"Oh please," snorted Janie, although more to herself.

"You should talk!" retaliated Matt, only slightly louder.

"*Shall we see the living room!*" suggested Siobhan, with far more enthusiasm than any room, living or dead, should engender. She flung open the door and practically shoved her potential buyers inside.

The Sharmas stepped into this main reception area a bit uncertainly, standing just on the threshold before venturing further inside. Siobhan, directly behind them, threw the others a look that was an interesting mix of professional elan and intense WTF.

As she moved further in, she could sense the rest of them shuffling behind her, still in some sort of straggly line, like a unisex chain gang. She suspected that the weird-looking one – although none of them were exactly *Hello Magazine* centrefolds – was bringing up the rear.

"Ray, would you like to talk us through?" suggested Siobhan, hopefully. "After all, it is your beautifully appointed, fully detached, highly desirable family dream home." She turned to the Sharmas. "It's killing him having to sell it."

She was quite surprised, as she turned round to look at him, that her client appeared unusually nervous. The large man was actually sweating, which, to be honest, she found a bit repellent.

"*Eh?*" said Ray, as if he had just been asked to reel off the periodic table backwards. "Er, yeah, well – as you can see, it's all been very recently redecorated in – in the very best of taste." He heard a snort from Struan and turned round to glare at him.

"*Chacun a son gout,*" mumbled the hitman, which Ray could only assume was Glasgow underworld slang.

"There's... well, there's... fitted cupboards – see?" continued Ray, pointing manically all around the room.

He could sense Bobbi behind him gesturing too, with both arms. Once a flight attendant...

"And... and there's double-glazing throughout. Very warm. And cool! Depending. This dividing wall here's just plasterboard – I know how you people like your through-rooms..."

He ignored Janie's sigh, although it was really loud and extended.

"And – and look, gas-fired central heating. Because sometimes the winters round here can be – well, they can be *MURDER!*"

Ray paused as his eyes widened and his head nodded slightly backwards to emphasise this last word and all that it entailed, but he just ended up looking a bit deranged and thyroidal. Yet he appeared undaunted or, at least, only slight daunted.

"...And we're all set up for satellite TV."

"Get on with it," said Struan, who really wanted to have this all wrapped up and sorted so that he could make it to the Cotswolds by supper time.

"You can have the dish," said Ray. "We're – we're leaving the diamanté curtains. And – and you can even take over our cleaning lady, Fernanda. Alright, she's Portuguese but she's terrific if you need – *HELP!*"

This heartfelt plea, which came out more like a scream, achieved nothing other than total mystification. But Ray was so concentrated on his task – and the others so invested in whether his ostensibly cunning wordplay would strike the slightest chord – that they totally failed to spot Janie Brownridge dipping gracefully down just a fraction, with bended knees, as she simultaneously leant over towards a nearby occasional table. On it was a tall vase of such ugliness it could have formed the inspiration for one of her own more elaborate designs.

"It's been a h-happy home," sighed Ray, with a catch in his voice that was hardly out of place in the circumstances. "The kids were both born here – Matt and Janie. We – we were hoping to have grandkids, but it looks like maybe that's not going to happen. Well, not in my lifetime."

Bobbi reached out from behind to hold her husband's hand tightly, as Siobhan just looked confused.

Meantime, Janie leant even further across.

"Anyway, there's a nice school down the road – and the usual shops – and a good garage. It's Shell, I think. No – no, it's – it's ESSO – S! Yes, *S.O.S!*"

"O-kay," whispered Struan, finally, "enough with the Bletchley Park. Just let them look round your lovely kitsch home, then we can—"

At this point, Janie's hand came up, vase now firmly gripped, and smashed the ceramic atrocity swiftly down on the erstwhile assassin's dyed-blond head. The man sank immediately onto the floor.

The family group inevitably parted at this point, like a link chain when one of its links is unexpectedly severed. And mayhem ensued.

First, Bobbi turned round and stamped down hard with her designer trainers on the prone Struan's gun hand. She immediately followed this up with a swift grab of the released weapon from the floor, easily avoiding a thoroughly dazed hitman's feeble attempts to retrieve it.

306

Meantime, her husband had the grace, or perhaps shrewdness, to apologise to the somewhat stunned visitors.

"Excuse me, guys. Sorry about all this. Won't be a sec."

He proceeded to raise his still ski-booted foot and kick the prone Scotsman several times very hard in the crotch, as the Sharmas watched, transfixed.

"*You fucking sadistic mercenary gay Glaswegian bastard!*"

"There he goes again!" said Janie to the world.

"What the hell have you done?" said Matt to Janie.

"Something I should have done years ago. Acted on my own!"

The Sharmas couldn't help but notice that the prevailing genre had suddenly switched from gritty suburban noir to cutting-edge domestic drama, both of which were equally disconcerting. They were also the first to observe a reinvigorated, though possibly neutered, Struan making a last desperate lunge for his gun. Janie, however, was there before him. She deftly snatched the weapon away from a totally shell-shocked Bobbi.

As the youngest Brownridge waved the firearm up in the air – and everyone instinctively ducked – the gun went silently off. Plaster immediately fell from the ceiling.

"*It doesn't usually do that!*" said Siobhan swiftly. "These 1950s villas were extremely solidly built."

But everyone could see that her heart really wasn't in it anymore and her face had gone as white as the falling plaster. She stared at Matt with a horrified look on her face.

Not before time, Mr Sharma grabbed his traumatised wife firmly by the trembling hand and yanked her towards the front door. When he spoke, it was rather fast but still very courteous.

"The living room does feel a little bit cramped. Even if we knocked through. It's a very nice house but I think maybe we'll leave it for the time being. Thank you very much. Have a lovely day."

And with that they were gone.

Showing amazing powers of recovery, Siobhan equally swiftly yelled after them, "*DON'T YOU WANT TO SEE THE FUCKING DINING ROOM?*"

It was apparent to all that the Sharmas did not. The frustrated and more than slightly mortified estate agent turned back to her clients and their patently disturbed hangers-on. She was clearly losing it.

"What IS it with this family? You're mental. You're all sodding mental!" She turned to Matt. "Gourlay told me you were a total loser!"

Even in her agitated state, Siobhan could tell they weren't paying her their full attention. The entire Brownridge family was now sitting atop a struggling Struan. Two members on his long, slim body, one on each skinny arm. Janie was still waving the gun.

Matt turned to Siobhan. Carefully raising one hand away from his captive, he made the phone sign with his fingers.

"I'll call you," he said, for absolute clarity.

Siobhan threw him a look as lethal as the weird guy's recently snatched gun and left the room, the house and hopefully this entire godforsaken family, slamming any door she could find on her way out.

Matt looked gutted. "Should I go after her?"

Ray, Bobbi and Janie were unanimous in their opinion on this idea. Yet they now remained in a slightly directionless and indecisive silence, until Struan the killer, talking through his obvious discomfort, broke the ice.

"Hey, listen, kids. I'm doing a special autumn offer. Two parents for the price of one. £15,000. With dinner. Three courses."

"Fifteen thousand!" spluttered an outraged Janie. "Dave Forrester was charging us half that!"

"Dave Forrester was a mobile DJ," said Matt.

"Even so," said Janie.

They could all feel Ray swivelling heavily around on the prone and flagging hitman in order to face his daughter.

"Janie, give me that gun right now. I'm your father."

"Janie," urged Matt, "stop pissing around. Fifteen thou's not bad – considering all we're going to get when it's done."

"Janie, dear," said Bobbi, "it hurts me to say it but you're never going to get any sort of man with all this aggression inside of you."

"I concur with that wholeheartedly," said Struan, although nobody could see that it was any of his business, what with him not being family. And they weren't quite certain what 'concur' meant. "Janie, petal, just hand me back my wee shooter, would you, please? I can do the rest from here."

To their astonishment, Janie stood up and immediately began to yell. All this with the gun still waving dangerously in her hand.

"WILL YOU SHUT THE FUCK UP ALL OF YOU WITH THE 'JANIES'!"

She started to walk around the recently spruced-up living room, waving the gun. "All of my life, somebody's been telling me to do something. Bake me a cake, Janie; inject my cat, Janie; eat your Fruit & Nut, Janie; help me murder our parents, Janie. And good old Janie, she just nods her silly little head like one of those wanky wobbly dogs in the back of a car."

As if on cue, they heard the loud screech of a vehicle outside.

"Well, I'm sorry," she continued, ignoring the noise, "I'm finished with all that. I want out of this family. I want a life of my own."

"A life of your own?" sneered Bobbi. "Ha! What sort of a life?"

Suddenly, the door was flung open and, like the hero in a trashy movie, Dave Forrester was there, in all his magnitude, bathed in sunlight from the window. He took in the scene, which wasn't exactly what he was expecting.

"The front door was on the latch," he explained.

"A life with him!" concluded Janie. "Hi, Dave."

"Thank God I'm not too late," said the relieved man. "Hi, Mr and Mrs Brownridge. Looking good. Considering." He turned to Janie. "I thought you were going to do something silly."

"Quite the reverse, dear," said Janie, poetically.

"*Dave Forrester!*" said Ray scornfully, shaking his huge jowly head. "A life with Dave Forrester? He's just a mobile bloody DJ."

"Did you know that already?" asked Matt, out of curiosity.

"Everybody knows that. And you paid him my four thousand quid! Dickhead."

"He was always a bad sort, that one," opined Bobbi.

"Just see you wipe your prints off that gun when you're finished, love," advised bad-sort Dave.

Janie just shook her head. "Nah. Know something, babe? They're not bloody worth it."

She moved over to the big DJ and put her gun arm around him. "Come on, Mr Hitman. I don't care about the money anymore. I've found something far more important than money."

"A mobile DJ," said Ray Brownridge, disparagingly.

"Da-ad, like shut uuuuup! Honestly!" whined his thirty-year-old teenage daughter as she dragged her new partner off.

The remaining family watched her go. As did Struan, although his view was slightly restricted.

"Not trained to kill with your bare hands, are you?" asked Matt.

"Not from this position, heart. If you get up, I could probably swing it."

"Just sit where you bloody are," said Ray, although the man was actually more lying down than sitting.

That was when they heard the police sirens.

"Oh crap." Struan sighed, somewhat resignedly.

"Good old Siobhan," enthused a rather relieved Ray. "Thank heavens for mobiles, eh, Bobbi? Reminds me, I must get that brand new Apple jobby everyone's raving about."

"We're very disappointed in you, Matthew Brownridge," said his mum.

Matt just sighed. Same old, same old.

"You can't even kill your own parents properly," grumbled Ray. "Easiest thing in the bloody world, I'd've thought."

Matt sprung up from sitting on the Scotsman, which was getting pretty uncomfortable anyway.

"*NOT WHEN YOU'VE GOT PARENTS LIKE MINE!*" he explained loudly, channelling his departed sibling. "Not when you've got parents who do you down all the time. Parents who crap on your confidence at every turn and make you feel like you can't do anything right. Until you're almost too screwed up to do a bloody thing. Well, sodding watch this."

Matt instinctively ran into the hallway and towards the front door, but fairly swiftly decided that this might not be the most advantageous route. Not with the police outside, probably armed to the teeth. So, he immediately swivelled on his Oxfam trainers, ran into the kitchen and out of the back door.

He could already smell the intoxicating air of liberty as he cut across the garden towards the shrubbery by the back fence and the hopeful promise of a new life.

Unfortunately, his dreams were crushed only seconds later when he tripped over what he thought was a branch and knocked himself out on a concrete fencepost beside the newly stained garden shed.

He was later to discover that what had, in fact, caused his downfall was the decaying corpse of a deceased cat, whose early demise had been effected by an overindulgence in chocolate cake, one concocted ironically to finish off a couple of rats.

Meanwhile, back in the house, a team of heavily armed policemen were listening to three extremely stressed people telling stories so preposterous that they just wanted to shoot the lot of them.

SCROLL FORWARD

*O*kay – here's what you've been waiting for. My unique *perspective on death. You ready?*

Death's not very nice. If you get the chance – avoid it.

Ray and Bobbi did.

And all because my wee bullets went a millimetre shy of their target at that stupid ski-run – something I'm deeply ashamed of but knew had to happen someday. Arthritis sets in. And a bit of a wee tremor. Nobody kills forever. C'est la vie. Or le mort.

Ray and Bobbi Brownridge, my last marks (we do call them 'marks' in the trade, by the way) are enjoying their twilight years to the tasteless, hedonistic full. Most of them on a big tacky yacht on the Med called BOBBI 2. Without trauma, without regrets. People don't change, you know. At least not the live ones.

Well, good luck to them, I say. I don't bear a grudge. And as for their poor, grown-up, screwed-up, mixed-up children...

Picture a small village hall in the south-west of England. Some pre-pubescents are having a disco. They're bopping wildly to not-very-funky music, played by not-overly funky mobile DJ Dave Forrester and his bizarrely dressed but deliriously happy bride, Janie.

And, in a travel cot beside them, sleeping blissfully through it all, a tiny baby in a glaring, patently homemade Babygro, designed in shades and semblance of vomit. Which is surprisingly practical in its own way.

The baby's name is Clifton.

And my man, Matt?

Well, he's scored himself a bit of security at last. And a proper job. Typing the frank and totally unexpurgated memoirs of yours truly, the 'charity assassin', in our prison library. A book which he assures me will make us both our fortunes.

The wee man seems quite content, in his own sad but not wholly unappealing way.

It should be out for Christmas. Kill for a copy.

HELMUTT

A few weeks after the third miscarriage, he brought home a dog.

It was a curious-looking animal, an unplanned meld of German schnauzer and something the schnauzer had happened to meet in the park. Or so he assumed. He found it odd that, unlike other species that come to mind, dogs seem happy to mate with anything. But then he looked at his wife and himself and realised that humans were probably not so different.

He had always thought, until now, that the attraction of opposites was what made them such a team. But now, he was at a total loss. He wanted so deeply to say or do something that would diminish her pain, yet the stoicism, the silences, the just-getting-on-with-things were so agonising that he could hardly bear to be in her presence. He thought it would be so much easier if she just broke down and went to pieces or punched him or screamed at the God in whom she had never believed for a moment and was hardly likely to turn to now.

Whenever they went for a walk these days – and they had always enjoyed walking, because open spaces and greenery appeared to make the trickiest conversations far easier and any problem that much more solvable – they would encounter children. Swarms of them, legions, multitudes. In pushchairs or wellies, running, climbing, sloshing, screaming. It was as if some government agency had alerted the local public that their town was about to be bombed to oblivion, so anyone under the age of ten must be evacuated forthwith to the nearest nature reserve.

He knew that a dog, even one as cute and cuddly as this, with its shuffling gait and hairy face like a dour old Victorian schoolmaster, couldn't replace a baby. He wasn't that stupid.

He also knew that, so far as he was aware, she wasn't really a dog person.

Yet he needed so desperately to do something for her, if only as a gesture, an acknowledgement, and this was all he could come up with.

Naturally, he couldn't parcel up the creature and watch her face as she undid the string and removed the festive wrapping. But he did observe her, as she slowly opened their front door to his unexpected knock.

He was taken especially by her large grey eyes (schnauzer-grey, now he thought about it), as they followed his own eyes downwards. These had always been his favourite of her features, along with her soft, full lips, now gently parting to say, "Get that fucking *thing* out of my house this instant."

He had been expecting a tricky conversation after this, but the ensuing silence threw him.

In his head, he had genuinely pictured her initial and quite natural reluctance to entertain the new arrival transforming in time to at least some appreciation for the misguided kindness that had prompted the purchase. And a sort of tentative yet inevitable bonding thereafter. The finality of 'one week – either *it's* outta here or I am' had rather taken him by surprise. Although, in retrospect, it probably shouldn't have.

Perhaps he might also have worked out that, whilst he went out to his office every day, she could do her job from home. But he promised faithfully that until a new and more appropriate family could be secured for Helmutt (the dog's whimsical given name, the refuge insisting that a rechristening would be one change too many), he would walk, feed and do all the socialising with their temporary guest.

He was as good as his word. For five days, morning and evening, he tramped the streets of the quiet suburb in which they had lived since they first got together, talking to Helmutt about life, love and everything in between.

318

He could honestly say that these were the most convivial conversations he was having at this time – Helmutt was an excellent listener, despite the language barrier. Talk at home, when it occurred, was mostly about bills, elderly parents and household chores. It certainly didn't touch on anything emotional. Or canine.

On the sixth day, Helmutt went missing.

Or had 'gone walkies', as his new mistress chose unhelpfully to call it. This apparently had occurred just minutes before the husband came home that evening. A door, improperly closed, had blown open and man's best friend, quite ungratefully and with a speed rarely associated with his lineage, unless greyhound was somewhere in the mix, had scooted off.

The man was thankful that his wife had agreed to accompany him on the search, although he suspected that this could be attributed more readily to a small but nonetheless appreciated measure of guilt than a genuine concern for Helmutt's welfare. He had a feeling, however, that the quest – whatever its outcome – might not prove totally unproductive.

As it was dark by this time, he carried a large torch. They tried to ignore the looks they were receiving from passers-by as they called out the errant animal's name into the crisp night air. It made him think for a moment that these people, commuters and strollers, might possibly assume that they had lost a child, which, of course, came close to the truth, but the pair would have been more careful and wouldn't have named him Helmutt.

It was well over an hour later that they hoarsely abandoned their search of possible new haunts and intriguing hiding places. They returned in some frustration to their small, empty, terraced house.

Sitting on the doorstep, looking genuinely hangdog, was the escapee.

The tears and sobbing could probably have been heard from there to the local shopping centre and beyond. Anguish and pain, so long contained, seemed to bounce off the walls of the sleepy little homes like gunfire.

"Finally," came the gentle voice.

He turned to look at her in surprise as the tears continued to stream down his anguished face.

It was some days before he asked her, half-jokingly, as all three of them walked together in the sunshine, whether it was she who had let the dog out.